PRAISE FOR *LAST SEEN*

"Author J. L. Doucette gi[...]g winters, three-dimensional [...]riting. An enthusiastic welcome [...]

—**LINDA BA**[...] [...]rd-winning author of the *Carlotta Carlyle* mystery series

"There's a detective named Antelope, at least two registered sex offenders, a scoundrel in pricey ski gear, his lying mistress, and tellingly, his missing wife. At the middle of this many-sided mess is Dr. Pepper Hunt, psychologist—clear-eyed, intelligent, beautiful, brave. You'll fall in love with Pepper and with J. L. Doucette's subtle, immersive, beguiling tale."

—**BRYAN GRULEY**, Anthony, Barry and Strand Award-winning author of the *Starvation Lake* mystery series

"With clear, crackling prose, at times breathtaking, and characters so real that I felt flesh and bone back on that wild western landscape, mingling with the people and inhabiting their world. Combine Doucette's voice and prose with a story that haunts and intrigues again and again, and we know we are in the hands of a very talented writer. I loved these characters. I loved the terrain. I never wanted to leave. This is the kind of writing that stays with me long after the novel is finished."

—**DIANE LES BECQUETS**, author of *Breaking Wild*

"*Last Seen* is a tantalizing psychological thriller in which J. L. Doucette masterfully weaves a chilling plot around a cast of complex, well-drawn characters led by psychologist, Dr. Pepper Hunt, a woman running from her own nightmare past. As the tiny Wyoming town searches its frigid horizons for a missing local woman, Dr. Hunt and Detective Antelope spark some warmth in an investigation all their own. A suspenseful ride that will keep you turning pages to the very end!"

—**MICHELLE COX**, award-winning author of *A Girl Like You* and *A Ring of Truth*, from the A Henrietta and Detective Howard series

LAST SEEN

LAST
SEEN

A DR. PEPPER HUNT MYSTERY

J.L. DOUCETTE

SHE WRITES PRESS

Published 2017
Printed in the United States of America
ISBN: 978-1-63152-202-4 pbk
ISBN: 978-1-63152-203-1 ebk
Library of Congress Control Number: 2017930640

Cover design © Julie Metz, Ltd./metzdesign.com
Interior design by Tabitha Lahr

For information, address:
She Writes Press
1563 Solano Ave #546
Berkeley, CA 94707

She Writes Press is a division of SparkPoint Studio, LLC.

To my parents, Joseph and Louise,
for stories read and stories told.

In my solitude, you haunt me
With reveries of days gone by
In my solitude you taunt me
With memories that will not die

I sit in my chair, filled with despair
No one can be so sad
With gloom everywhere, I sit and stare
I know that I'll soon go mad

In my solitude, I'm praying
Dear Lord above, send back my love
Dear Lord above, send back my love

—Duke Ellington, Eddie DeLange, Irving Mills

MONDAY
DECEMBER 20

CHAPTER 1

It was the Monday before Christmas, and I was in my office at the Hilltop Medical Center, waiting for the next crisis to happen. I'm one of three psychologists in Sweetwater County, a land area the size of Connecticut where antelope outnumber humans three to one. It was my turn to take calls for psychiatric emergencies at the county facilities: hospital, jail, and courthouse. The pager was silent at my waist. Outside, the high desert sparkled under fresh snow.

Last year, on the run from the wreckage of my life, driving through a blizzard in southwest Wyoming, my Jeep spun out on the interstate. I never meant to stay here. But when the storm cleared, the contours of the stark desert revealed the spinning planet. Every afternoon the wind came up and swept my mind as clean as the bare earth. The emptiness worked for me. There was nothing familiar to remind me of all I'd lost. It took two weeks to repair my Jeep; by the end of that time, I knew I wasn't leaving.

From my office window I had a view of White Mountain at the western boundary of Rock Springs. I was taking a quiet moment, watching the sagebrush rustle as the wind passed through like a swarm of invisible snakes, when I saw the Chevy Tahoe pull into the parking lot. It was the last peaceful time I would know for a while.

Sheriff Carlton Scruggs stepped out of the Tahoe and slammed the door. I knew him; he was married to my secretary. I took my Beretta Nano from its carry holster and slipped it into its hiding place.

A minute later, Marla was at my door. "The sheriff is here, Doctor."

She always referred to her husband as "Sheriff" and addressed me as "Doctor" in the office, though we'd become friends in the year she'd worked for me. Marla still looked like a beauty queen: platinum blond spiral curls, five foot two inches tall. She was Miss Lander, Wyoming in 1985, the year she graduated from high school. Cheerful, efficient, and organized, she scheduled patients, managed the office, and handled the billing so I could do the fun part of my job.

The sheriff came in with his jaw clenched, a man on a mission with no smile for me. Being sheriff was serious work, and he did it justice. For him it was an honor to serve and protect. In Wyoming, the sheriff's office is an elected position. He'd held the position for ten years and showed no signs of quitting.

His black Stetson hat grazed the ceiling and his presence filled the room. A big man, tall and broad-shouldered, he used his size to impress and intimidate. From what Marla told me, he had a softer side, but I'd yet to see it. They were transplants also, from another county in Wyoming, and understood what it was like to start over in Rock Springs, where many jobs came with a sign-on bonus—also known as "combat pay"—as incentive to relocate to what some people see as the least charming town in the state. For those of us who loved it here, the bad press was a good thing, because it kept the population down.

"I'm here about one of your patients," Sheriff Scruggs said. "Kimi Benally. She was reported missing this morning. She hasn't been at work since Thursday."

I'd seen Kimi on Friday for her weekly session, but I couldn't tell the sheriff that. Kimi had a habit of disappearing, so I wasn't surprised that four days had gone by before anyone even noticed she was gone. During the session, she'd been paranoid and skittish, not in good shape. Now she was missing.

"I'm sorry you made the trip," I said. "I can't talk to you about a patient unless you have a signed release. But I don't have to tell you that."

Marla smiled to smooth the awkward moment.

"Give us a minute alone," the sheriff said and looked at Marla.

If she minded being sent away, she didn't let it show. She quietly closed the door behind her.

There were ethical land mines hidden at the place where the mental health and legal justice systems intersected. I waited for the sheriff to ask me a question I wouldn't be able to answer.

"This is serious business. We've been told she's in treatment with you. Can you at least answer that?"

"All I can say is I can neither confirm nor deny it."

"That's all you can do for me? She's been gone for days, and with the weather, I hate to think what might have happened."

He folded his arms and held his ground. I understood his concern, and the urgency. He showed no signs of leaving. I couldn't tell him anything, but I could hear him out, and maybe that would help us both. He wasn't used to hearing no. But there was something else. It mattered to him that Kimi was missing.

"Why don't you tell me what you know?"

"She hasn't been at work since Thursday. The person who made the report claims she had an appointment with you Friday night. We're on the same side on this one. She might have said something that could help us find her."

HIPAA confidentiality laws allowed cooperation with law enforcement when a crime has been committed, but only with proper court orders. The fact that someone had filed a police report did not mean a crime had been committed. No crime, no disclosure.

"I'm following the law and the ethical guidelines of my profession," I said, my voice firm.

"You were the last person to see her. Are you sure you can't help me out here, Doc?"

"I'll need either a court order or a release of information signed by the patient. That's the only way I can talk to you."

"If that's what it takes. I'll be back."

He stood up and without saying another word, he was gone. A few minutes later, Marla came back.

"I hope he didn't get too pushy. You know him, he's trying to do his best all the time, and sometimes it takes a toll on his manners."

"No worries. I'm used to working with law enforcement. He's one of the best."

"He was itching to ask me, but he didn't. He understands I'm sworn to secrecy about the patients. It's kind of creepy, though. We could be the last ones to have seen her. Oh, I almost forgot— the jail wants you for a psych consult. They have a woman in custody with a prior suicide attempt. They took precautions and put her on suicide watch. And guess who it is? Kimi's mother, Estella Benally. The clerk said she's talking crazy."

I checked the pager, thinking I might have missed it. "Why didn't they page me?"

"They know I work here. It's just as easy to call me. I know all those guys."

"Next time that happens, tell whoever it is to page me. You shouldn't have to be in the middle, that's why I have this thing."

I was almost out the door when Marla said, "I bet it was Cedric Yee who reported her missing. He knew she was seeing you. He came with her one time and sat in the waiting room the whole time she was in with you."

"Really? I didn't notice."

"That's why you need me. I notice everything." She smiled and patted her shoulder, proud of her detection skills. Her long silver nails had holly berries painted on the tips.

"I probably won't get back this afternoon," I said. "You can take off early if you want."

Her face lit up. "If you need me, I'll be at the mall. I haven't bought a thing for the sheriff yet, and he always goes overboard for me at Christmas. Only five shopping days left."

In the car, on the way to the county jail, I thought about Kimi and the things she'd said in our Friday session, the things I couldn't disclose to the sheriff.

Kimi was my first patient when I opened my psychology practice here. She walked into the office without an appointment, and I knew before she said a word that she needed help. Her dark eyes scanned the room for hidden dangers before she opened her mouth; it was only after she was satisfied she was safe that she looked straight at me with haunted eyes and said, "I think I'm losing my mind."

On Friday, as on that first day she came into my office, she'd just come out of a dissociative episode, and it had scared the life out of her. The last thing she remembered was picking up the arrest log at the County Court in Green River that morning—she was a reporter for the local paper, and needed it for a story. By the time she got to my office, the sun was setting over White Mountain. This wasn't the first time she'd dissociated. But on Friday she'd somehow lost a whole day out of her life.

Dissociating is a symptom common to victims of trauma, a way of escaping intolerable emotions. Trauma treatment is a long-term endeavor that involves intense emotions and crisis calls in the middle of the night. I knew it from both sides. Just two years before Kimi stepped into my office, my husband had been murdered. I was still on the mend from my own trauma.

"I woke up at a truck stop halfway to Utah," Kimi said. "I don't know how I got there. All the way back I couldn't shake the feeling I was being followed."

While I sat with her, snow spun in angry circles at the window. Marla had already gone home. When the session was over, I locked up, and Kimi and I left the office together. A cold wind blew hard off the desert. Sheets of snow rose from the ground and swirled around us like dancing ghosts, ice crystals stinging our faces.

Kimi held out her arms and twirled on tiptoe, her red boots turning easily in the new snow. She laughed and said, "Snow devils! It's a winter whirlwind! So magical! The snow devils came for me."

She danced for a few minutes in slow, graceful turns, the snow lifting and blowing around her. Finally, she stopped and said, "I'll be all right. You drive slow, now, get home safe. You're not used to this weather."

I didn't know what to think of the shift; minutes before she'd been afraid to leave the office, but now, at the sight of snow devils, she was fearless and free. I waited in my car as she drove away; at the end of the road, her taillights winked, then disappeared. I was alone in the eerie darkness, the moon and stars held captive by storm clouds. An hour later, the blizzard raged and the wind blew at eighty-five miles per hour at the airport weather station. Sometime during the night, all the roads out of town were closed. And in the heart of the storm, Kimi vanished, all traces of her leaving obscured by time and snow.

CHAPTER 2

When Cedric Yee said he wanted to report a woman missing, Sheriff Scruggs didn't know if he could do it again. *Missing woman.* The words hit with the force of a blow.

As he drove away from the psychologist's office, he recalled his first meeting with Kimi. He'd just worked a double shift and was too keyed up to go home. He was driving north on Highway 191, out past the fairgrounds and away from the lights of town. It was late October, the weather was already turning mean. A hard winter would follow. A big orange moon poured down on the desert and revealed the ancient Native carvings on the tall sandstone cliffs in the distance.

On a lonely stretch of road near the county cemetery, he spotted a black car on the shoulder, invisible except for the glint of moonlight on the rear window. He pulled over and flashed his high beams: a figure with long, dark hair sat in the driver's seat. As he approached the vehicle, cold air crawled up from the ground, and he shivered. Mist hung over the desert like forgotten spirits escaped from the nearby graves. The woman inside the car stared straight ahead, still as a corpse.

He got the door open fast and stood ready to catch her if she fell. The chill of the night and the wind blowing in broke the spell. She shivered and turned to him, seemed to register what was in his face, the fear and confusion. He watched as she came back to herself in pieces, saw recognition settle in her eyes.

She rubbed at her slender arms to keep warm. She was barefoot and wearing a white tank top and thin cotton pajamas—not dressed to travel the night alone.

"Fugue state," she said and shook her head, gave him an unexpected, coy smile. "Sometimes I space out. It must be that moon up there tonight. We call it the 'Moon of Falling Leaves.' A gorgeous thing, isn't it? Looks like a peach, the biggest and brightest of all the moons."

So, she's Arapaho, he thought. Of course, he should have known. That ebony hair like silk.

"On your way over to the reservation tonight, miss?"

"I have no idea where I'm going. That's the thing. Some part of me must have wanted to be there. I'd better take the rest of me back home to bed. Don't mistake me for crazy. I'm as sane as you."

He asked for her license and registration. She opened the glove box and handed them over, along with her press pass. "You don't know me, but I know you, Sheriff. I'm Kimi Benally. I work at the *Rocket Miner*. I cover the crime desk. Sooner or later, we'll run into each other at a crime scene, and you'll remember me."

He lectured her on all the things that could happen to a woman alone in the world at night, the things he'd seen with his own eyes, dark things he'd never forget.

She'd held up a hand and said, "I don't need this tonight."

"I'll follow you, make sure you get home safe." Then he worried he'd gone too far. Maybe she wasn't headed straight home, and what business was it of his?

But she said, "Sure, if you need to protect and serve tonight."

On the slow drive back to town, he became aware of a tentative yearning coming back to him, like a half-remembered melody. She lived at the edge of the desert in the end unit in a row of townhouses. When she was safely inside, he stayed there for a while, in no hurry to leave, strangely content to be keeping watch. A light came on in an upstairs window, and a pale hand waved, then disappeared, behind curtains closed against the night.

He met her again a few months later when, as she had predicted, a crime brought them together. It was New Year's Day, a quiet shift of minor problems, stolen credit cards, DUIs, and too many domestic violence calls—many from high-end neighborhoods where supposedly these things didn't happen. The rest were from the trailer parks, but that was no surprise.

The day had been easy, sliding into boredom, nothing he couldn't handle with his eyes closed and his hands tied behind his back. That could have been a sign, if he was looking for one.

He was on dinner break and headed to the recreation center, making good on his resolution to work out every day. It was dusk, and the sky was glowing nuclear orange, January showing off her only claim to fame: spectacular sunsets. The minute the sun dropped behind White Mountain, the sky went dark and the temperature fell ten degrees.

KRKK was playing his favorite Supremes song, "Some Day We'll Be Together," and he was reaching for his gym bag when the radio dispatcher announced that a rape victim was being transported to Sweetwater County Hospital.

He was five minutes away from the emergency room. His workout could wait.

In Sweetwater County, violent crimes of a sexual nature made up 2 percent of the overall crime rate. As sheriff, he kept his eye on these things. He needed to know the extent of the threat.

Kimi Benally waited outside the victim's cubicle, holding a spiral notebook, a yellow number two pencil tucked behind her ear. She looked like a schoolgirl, or somebody's fantasy of a schoolgirl. He recalled a white blouse, a navy blue skirt. She looked clean and untouched. It made him want to touch her.

He checked that impulse when he looked in her eyes. In that moment, they shared a spark of intimacy that, in his experience, came only from a dangerous mix of sex and violence. Did Kimi notice, and was she frightened by how much she resembled the battered victim? Something ethereal in both of them, delicate features, long black hair.

They left the hospital together. It was impossible not to feel protective after what they'd seen and heard. The woman had been abducted at knifepoint, punched and cut with the knife, raped and sodomized, her life threatened if she told. He'd felt anger and tender sympathy when he took her statement. She couldn't look at him as she answered his questions, and trembled as she told him what had been done to her.

Outside the hospital, the wind blew hard out of the desert, a force against their backs, as he walked Kimi to her car. By then the moon was on the rise, a silver disc low on the horizon. The night before, when the rapist took the woman to the mountain, storm clouds had covered the moon.

He remembered the moon that first night and what Kimi had said. "What's your name for this moon?"

She smiled and looked up. Her face, washed with moonlight, was radiant and innocent. "The Moon When the Snow Blows like Spirits in the Wind."

"That's kind of beautiful," he said. "I'll remember it when my head's wrecked with the world's evil, like what we heard in there."

CHAPTER 3

In the time it took to break winter camp and ski down to the Elkhart Trailhead, Kevin Cahill's world shifted from normal and manageable to bizarre and totally out of his control. Like a sudden collapse of snow in the slide of an avalanche as it takes your life down, gone and buried in minutes.

It was a perfect morning, classic Wyoming winter: a robin's-egg blue bowl of sky above endless trails of new powder sparkling like crushed diamonds. There was no better way to describe the pristine scene. He was carrying a fifty-pound pack of winter camping gear on his back, but he hardly noticed the weight. He'd never felt stronger. After three days of skiing and winter camping in the backcountry, he felt like Superman—no, he *was* Superman.

Then a sheriff from down in Pinedale was on the radio. He didn't give a reason, only said that Wyoming Backcountry Sports wanted Kevin to bring his crew down off the mountain. What the hell was going on? He was supposed to have a week to scout the route he'd be using for all the upcoming winter tours. It had to be some surprise shift in the weather forecast.

He wanted to punch something but knew he had to keep it together. His crew looked up to him for his mental strength under pressure. If he lost it over something like this, he'd wreck his image and his reputation as a guide. Guiding put money in his pocket and food on the table. His endurance and skill in the wilderness made him who he was. This sucked, though. If he could, he'd stay in the mountains forever. Especially now, with what had gone down with Kimi the other night, he wasn't ready to go back. He didn't want to face what was waiting for him. But his luck had run out.

He began breaking camp and packing up, working slowly and methodically, maintaining order and composure with every move. In his head, he searched for something positive to push out the disappointment he felt at having to go back. He beat back thoughts that threatened to break through and turn his mood blacker.

He could tell from the way Tracy was looking at him she was happy with the way things had gone down. It hadn't been sympathy sex the other night; he was sure of it. Sleeping with her hadn't been in his plan, but after what happened with Kimi, what did he have to lose? Tracy stayed close behind him as they skied down to the trailhead, the two of them leading the others.

He spotted the deputies as he came out of the trees. The Sweetwater County cruiser blocked the Suburban that was waiting to take him and the crew back to town. Two deputies stood with arms crossed, watching, as he came out of the trail. From a distance they looked like matched pieces in a set of plastic toys, stiff and solid. He knew they'd come for him.

He crossed the snow-covered parking lot, came to a quick stop right in front of them, kicking up snow with his edges. Deputies Collins and Garcia of the Sweetwater County Sheriff's Department introduced themselves.

"Are you Kevin Cahill?" Garcia asked.

All of a sudden, he wanted to run. A brief swirl of vertigo; he swayed, planted his poles, and was steady again on the skis. The taste of bile at the back of his throat, sweat and chills, as if hypothermia was setting in.

"The one and only," he said. Why was he joking?

He stepped out of his skis and dusted the powder off the bottom. Exhaustion made him ache to drop his pack right there in the snow, but he didn't want them to see his weakness. After the exertion of skiing, he was sweating and felt chilled to the bone.

The deputies didn't seem to notice his distress. They stood

on either side of him, their large bodies crowding him, isolating him, making a kind of privacy screen.

Then Tracy was right beside him, asking, "What's wrong? What is it, officers?"

It should have been him doing the asking, but he didn't know what to say. He felt like a kid in trouble, afraid to say anything, afraid to make things worse for himself.

"This is a police matter, miss," Garcia said. "We need to speak to Mr. Cahill in private."

Tracy didn't move. That was why he liked the girl. She wasn't easily intimidated.

The officer stared her down, gave her a minute, and then, when she didn't move, he told her, "I'm going to need you to join the others, miss. This doesn't concern you."

Tracy stayed put, didn't move a muscle. She stood right by Kevin's side, the weight of her pack pulling her shoulders back and pushing her breasts forward. Even in her down jacket, she was voluptuous, her amazing tits right there in his face. It was surreal how he could see her body that way, in this situation, with the deputies standing right there and taking it all in.

"Kevin?" she asked, taking her time saying his name. Her southern drawl and all her southern ways could make him homesick at times.

"It's okay. I'll catch up with you later."

"Yeah, it's okay," the other officer, Collins, mimicked.

"Move along, miss," Garcia said. He waved his hand at her as if directing traffic and motioned for her to leave them, shooting a look at Collins that signaled he was in charge.

Tracy stood there for a moment longer; she was a confident young woman, not used to being told what to do. Kevin saw her face register that something big was happening. She pouted and shook her hair out from her ski hat. Then she skied away, her blond curls bouncing on her back, to join the rest of the crew. They were all working in silence, packing the Suburban, doing a good job of ignoring what was happening with Kevin and the deputies.

It was Garcia who again took the lead. "Sorry to tell you this, Mr. Cahill. Your wife's been reported missing."

Kevin sighed. "How long has she been gone this time?" *Too many times*, he thought.

Garcia looked straight at him. "She was reported missing this morning. It could be three days since she's been seen."

"Have you seen her since Friday?" Collins added.

"Wait a minute, wait a minute. Hold on here. My wife's been gone for three days?"

"Kimi Benally, the reporter at the *Rocket Miner*?" Collins confirmed. "A coworker says she didn't show for work today. She hasn't been in the office since late last week."

Kevin let the pack drop off his back. He felt light-headed again and took a deep breath to get some blood to his head.

Across the parking lot, the crew was finished packing up.

"We're ready to take off," Tracy called. "Are you coming?"

He made a move to reach for his pack.

"You're riding with us," Collins informed him.

"We're keeping this quiet for the moment," Garcia said. "We'd appreciate your cooperation."

Kevin looked down at his skis. "Hold on while I get rid of this gear." He hoisted the pack on his back and skied over to Tracy, who took his things from him and handed him his boots. She gave him a long look before getting into the driver's side of the Suburban, taking the lead because he couldn't. The door slammed with a final, angry sound. Kevin watched as she eased the vehicle slowly out of the parking lot and everything familiar rolled away.

The deputies put him in the backseat. A wire safety screen separated him from where they sat in the front. Both of them were clean-shaven, with buzzed hair and pink scalps under wide-brimmed sheriff's hats. To him, they looked like kids in costume: overdressed and ridiculous, playing at cops and robbers, with him as the bad guy. The whole thing felt like make-believe.

Better make some calls, he thought—they'd expect him to. But when he looked at his phone, it showed no service. He'd call Kimi's brother when he picked up a signal.

Twenty minutes later, with the mountains behind them, they passed through winter desert, sagebrush and snow fences. He searched the horizon for wandering mule deer, whose home they were disturbing. The sun was still with them, but it didn't matter now. He'd missed out on a great day on the mountain. He was being carted back to civilization. The truth was, he didn't like cities, especially grubby little cities like Rock Springs. People annoyed and confined him. He wondered, not for the first time, why he'd ever bothered to get married in the first place.

He spotted a herd of antelope in the distance, antlers held high, and a sense of rootless longing rose in him. Beyond the tinted windows, the bare, sculpted planet rushed by.

CHAPTER 4

Soft light coming in, filling up the room. Diego opened his eyes and immediately shut them again. It was either early in the morning or late in the afternoon. Cold air seeped in through the torn plastic bag he'd taped over the window—winterization trailer park style. Blankets on the floor, bare feet exposed and stiff as frozen meat.

He was still on probation and wasn't supposed to drink, but he was hungover anyway. He had three days until his monthly parole check-in, and by then his blood test would be clean.

Most of the time he drank alone. Last night there had been a woman. He'd made himself stay beside her longer than he wanted to, until his head was clear to drive. A simple public intoxication charge could have him on the express bus back to Riverton Honor Farm in the snap of a finger.

One thing he'd never done was drive under the influence. Though he'd done a lot of other dumb stuff, he'd avoided the family legacy. He'd pass on the chance to get plastic flowers and his own white cross planted beside the highway. Vehicles were lethal weapons. He thanked his father for that lesson. Big James hadn't left him anything else.

He'd been dreaming of bees. The pillow buzzed under his head, and he suddenly understood why. He grabbed the vibrating phone. His brother-in-law's name flashed in his hand; it had to be something with his sister. He pressed the answer key.

"Hey, Diego, I got a situation," Kevin said.

He considered hanging up, but coughed and thought, *What the hell?*

"Have you seen my wife?"

"What the hell?" Diego said. He coughed again and spit into his hand.

"Is she with you?"

"Hold on."

Diego sat up and found his shoes. On her wedding day, Diego had promised his sister he'd be nice to her husband, but some promises were meant to be broken.

Outside the wind wailed, and the trailer shook on its foundation. He banged open every door, found no one in the cold, empty rooms. "She's not here," he said. "Where are you?"

"On my way back to town with a couple of deputies."

"Are you being serious here? Because I'm on my way over there with a knife if this is your idea of funny."

"Truth, man. She's gone. I swear. Someone from work reported her missing."

At the sound of those words, he felt a chill. His bed was a memory he was willing to forget. His sister was missing. He wouldn't sleep until he found her.

"Since when?" he asked. "She's gone how long?"

"They're saying maybe Friday."

"It's Monday. Why are you just calling me now?" He headed to the bathroom and let go a urine stream heady with rum and tequila. Swaying slightly, he rested his head against the bathroom wall. Was it the booze or the fear that threatened to take him out of consciousness? He sat on the floor and put his head between his knees. He put the phone on speaker, and Kevin's voice bounced off the cold tile.

"I've been working up in the Winds. I didn't know until the deputies pulled me off the mountain."

"Who called the law?"

"Someone from the paper, when she didn't show for work this morning. When did you see her last?"

Diego wasn't one to keep track of days and times. Kimi was in and out of their place all the time, checking on their mother, finding a minute to play with her nephew.

"Last weekend sometime . . . Sunday."

"Ask your mother."

His mother had gone out without turning off the radio. From the living room the familiar sound of a talk show, her favorite diversion, gave him comfort. He ran the water cold and stuck his head under the shuddering faucet, came panting awake. His face in the mirror was Jesus himself on the cross, lanky hair draped over sorrow. Diego took a moment, closed his eyes, prayed Kimi had left town with a secret lover and this asshole on the phone would never find her.

"I figured if anyone would know it'd be you, little brother," Kevin said.

Asshole had that right.

Diego couldn't believe the guy. He pictured his pretty-boy face flattening under his fist—straight nose turned twisted and ugly. He'd love a chance to expose the bone and soul of his sister's scumbag husband.

Back in the bedroom, he pulled Converse high-tops over his bare feet, left the laces undone and dragging. He was still wearing the same sour T-shirt and sweatpants he'd slept in.

"Can you ask her?" Kevin asked into the silence.

"What?" He was having trouble following the conversation.

"Has your mother seen Kimi recently?"

"She's not here."

"There's nothing else to do right now. If Kimi shows up or you hear from her, let me know. I doubt it. She'd come home to me first."

"As far as she knows, you're up in the Winds."

"But I'm here now. She'll come back."

Diego knew Kevin was speaking this way for the benefit of the deputies listening to his conversation. He was working at making a good impression.

"Not if she left you, man."

The ghost of his father lingered in the quiet rooms. He had to get moving, do something, find his sister. He tossed blankets, flipped the mattress in search of his keys; the clatter of metal on vinyl signaled his success.

"No way did she leave me."

Diego had forgotten he was still on the phone. Why was he bothering to talk to him anyway?

"You sure?"

"It's one of her disappearing things. No big deal. Sorry I bothered you."

"My sister's missing, asshole. It's a big deal."

It was good his mother wasn't there. He didn't relish telling her this news. She existed at the edge of reality on a good day; the slightest breeze of stress could push her off. It was better to wait as long as he could. And Little James was with Charlene this week, so he didn't have to stress the kid out, either.

He pulled the metal door hard behind him to keep it closed against the wind. Out in the biting air, the smell of alcohol rose from his pores. He licked his left hand and tasted salt and booze: he was a human margarita. He yanked the car door open and tossed his phone into the passenger seat.

He had to focus. He cranked the GTO's engine and shifted into reverse and out of the narrow drive beside the trailer. He had no plan, but that wasn't unusual. Unable to summon rational thought, he surrendered to instinct. He would find his sister. He had been her protector ever since their mother lost her mind, and he hadn't failed her yet.

A short stop at the McDonald's drive-through on Elk Street set him up for the night. His fingers found the warm bag of greasy burgers. The rich aroma of broiled meat shot into his brain like an arrow, bringing memories of campfires on the reservation. Suddenly, he was back with his lost sister and mother in the crazy nation they both inhabited, experiencing the grace of escape for a fleeting moment.

The food cleared his head, and he settled on a plan. He would drive every road in Sweetwater County, paved and unpaved, until he found her. He couldn't leave the county without permission, however, and that reality—which sucked on a good day—tasted sour enough today to make him want to spit in the face of the law.

In three days, he was scheduled to meet with Cassandra McKnight, his parole officer. He would plead his case, give it his best shot. Like his sister, Cassandra was a smart girl who'd gotten herself an education, a paper ticket to the white world. But Diego knew better. He'd cut the cord, left the reservation, but his blood would always flow Native. If he ever tried to forget, fool himself he fit in, someone always reminded him of the truth.

Cassandra was his sister's best friend. Her mother had raised her to look down on anyone who didn't strive to get out, and she was one obedient Native girl. That first day reporting to her, he'd come in like a whipped dog, and humiliation had filled the room they sat in like toxic fumes. But after a while, it got better. She wasn't the bitch he'd expected her to be. She'd returned to a place she'd intended to leave forever; he knew she had her own stories.

She was a tough one, however. Under the hard shell, stiff sprayed hair, and fake nails that would do a good job on some-body's back in the right situation, he sensed there was a gentle heart she worked hard to hide. And in the end, blood was blood. He was betting she'd take pity because Kimi was missing. Cassandra would know he couldn't trust anyone else to find her.

As night fell, a sinister snow came down. Diego resisted the idea of clues and what clues implied. But he was certain the snow would cover things and make it harder to trace her. It was time for a more precise plan. At the intersection of Elk Street and Dewar Drive, he decided to do the city in quadrants. He took the overpass into Old Rock Springs. The newspaper where Kimi worked was in this part of town.

His love for his sister was ruthless, its claim on him truer than any rule or sacrament. It had always been just the two of them. Their mother had always been a chronic hot mess of crazy and drunk. Estella existed in a time capsule, buried in 1980 with their reckless, dead father, who'd instantly ended what might have been an ordinary life for all of them when he crashed on that sharp curve. She was a lean shadow in the corner of Diego's days. Ever since he was a kid, he'd been prepared to lose her.

Kimi was married, but he knew that had an expiration date. For one thing, she'd married an asshole, and she would figure that out one of these days. The bond the two of them had forged as kids, when there was no one else, was invisible but real. It·resided in the hidden sinews of his heart, embedded in muscle behind a cage of bones where it lived deep and safe. Neither of them would ever have as strong a bond with anyone else. Marriages come and marriages go. Diego was sure this one was on its way out.

He knew his sister—knew that if she was happy with Kevin, she wouldn't be missing. Unless, of course, she'd chosen that way to tell him she wasn't happy.

CHAPTER 5

The historic building that housed the offices of the *Rocket Miner* was one block over from the sheriff's department headquarters, but Antelope wanted to check out Kimi's residence before meeting with the reporter.

Traffic was busier than usual in the streets of her neighborhood a few blocks north of White Mountain Mall. As he crawled along, he called his Aunt Estella at home. There was no answer, and the landline didn't have an answering machine. He'd have to try again later; Estella was old-fashioned and didn't carry a cell phone. He also tried Diego but didn't leave a message when his cousin didn't answer. He knew Diego would never listen to a message from him and might not recognize the number. It might be better to take a drive over there when he finished meeting with the reporter.

He parked across from the row of townhouses. Kimi's was the end unit facing the main thoroughfare, Foothill Drive. The weekend's storm had rendered sidewalks and streets treacherous with a skin of black ice. He walked slowly, watching the steam of his breath disappear in the wind off the desert.

At Kimi's house, neither the driveway nor the front walk had been cleared. The small patch of front lawn was buried in snow. His footsteps made a crunching sound as he broke the shiny crust of ice. At the front door he knocked and waited. He tried the door and it opened.

He stepped into the open room that contained living and dining areas and a narrow galley kitchen. Everything looked neat and in order. It was freezing cold inside the house. "Kimi?" he called out. A noise from upstairs—the sound of someone falling, something heavy rolling. He was halfway up the dark staircase, running, when a large animal lunged at his chest, pushed him down, and licked his face. He didn't know Kimi had a dog. Fortunately, she hadn't trained the fluffy black-and-white animal to be an attack dog. She licked his face and wagged her tail. When he continued up the stairs, she followed at his heels.

Kimi wasn't in the bedroom. The bedspread was pushed to one side, and there was a depression in one of the pillows. No signs of disturbance in the bathroom. In the second bedroom he found the first sign of trouble. Drawers in the desk and filing cabinets had been emptied. It looked like all the contents of the closet and shelves had been thrown to the floor. The dog stayed close by him until he went downstairs, at which point she disappeared through a flap in the back door. It was then he noticed the door was open an inch, the reason for the frigid temperature. The kitchen floor was wet from snow melt. If Kimi had left the door unlocked, the wind could have blown it open. There were no signs of an attempted break-in.

He picked up a red leash from the kitchen counter, and when the dog came through the door, he hitched it to her collar. He put in a call for crime scene technicians. The ransacked room upstairs was enough to warrant a visit from them. He'd take the dog to the station and hand her over to Kimi's husband to take home when he was done with him.

■ ■ ■

He left the dog with the clerk in the evidence room with a promise that it wouldn't be for too long. The day was cold but sunny, and he decided to walk to the *Rocket Miner* office.

Within ten minutes he was standing outside the three-story brownstone. The building had recently undergone a low-budget renovation and, in the process, lost the carved oak moldings and

banisters that had given the old building a touch of vintage character. New drywall painted the color of wheat left him cold. A thin
gray industrial carpet, straight off the bolt, released chemical tox-
ins into the windowless space. The first floor housed the administrative offices of the paper; he wanted the second floor.

He walked up the wide winding staircase and stopped before
a sign on the double glass door at the top of the staircase that read
Newsroom. When he opened the door, a short Asian man walked
quickly toward him. He had a round face and wore wire-rimmed
glasses. He wiped his hand on his jacket before offering it to Antelope to shake. It was cold and clammy.

"I'm Cedric Yee, the one who called. Come this way, we can
talk in private."

It was eerily quiet as they walked past the other reporters
at work in their cubicles, a soft chorus of tapping computer keys.
They entered the conference room through a wall of frosted green
glass. An oily citrus scent lingered in the air, traces of a weekend
cleaning crew. Antelope felt a headache coming on.

"Please, sit." Cedric pointed to one of a dozen red leather
swivel chairs set around a large oak table and collapsed into one
of them himself. He gripped the chair's chrome arms.

Antelope took a seat and studied the reporter: He had small
hands, white knuckles, manicured nails. He disappeared into the
drab colors of the room in elastic-waist beige slacks, a white polo
shirt, light brown soft-soled loafers, and white socks. Antelope's
philosophy as a detective was "Everything is relevant." Cedric
Yee was transmitting a desire to blend in but not quite making it.
Antelope knew from reading the blurb on the back of the Yees'
restaurant menu that the family came to Rock Springs at the time
the railroad was laid in the mid-1800s. He also knew that Cedric
was the first and only member of the family to work outside the
Yee restaurant since its opening.

Antelope was familiar with assimilation. Living and working
in Rock Springs, he was only fifty miles from the reservation where
he'd grown up, but the two places couldn't be more different.

Every spring, Antelope made the four-hour trip to Casper to

have his suits fitted by an aging Italian tailor who shared his love for opera. No one in either of his worlds, the reservation or the sheriff's department, was privy to his shopping or music preferences. Not belonging had its benefits.

"I'm here to take a statement and get some information regarding Kimi Benally," he began. "You became concerned when she didn't show up for work this morning, is that right?"

"Yes. She wasn't here when I got here. That was the first thing I noticed. She always gets in before me. I tease her about it. She's punctual and conscientious." Yee leaned forward, pulled a handkerchief from a back pocket, and shook it out. After wiping his brow, he carefully folded it and placed it on the conference table.

"So she's late for work. Things happen—flat tire, family emergency—to make someone late. Did you consider the possibility that she was delayed?"

"I did. That's what I first thought. Something came up. I told myself to give it a while," Yee answered. He was rocking back and forth, fingertips pushing on the table. "I called her cell. No answer, straight to voice mail. It's not like Kimi at all. Her cell is always on, and it's always with her."

"Except this time she didn't answer."

"That got me worried. Her phone is her lifeline. She's got a sick mother and her husband travels. He's away now. Lots of reasons she keeps her phone with her always." He picked up the handkerchief and ran it over his face again.

"Didn't show on time, didn't answer her phone. You became concerned. You seem to keep pretty close tabs on her."

Antelope was pushing the reporter for a reason. Yee's nervous energy said he was holding something back.

"We work in teams at the paper. Kimi and I are a team. You get to know someone's habits. It's her habit to be here early. So I called her, and when I couldn't reach her, I called the sheriff's department. I thought it was best. If something has happened to her, the sooner you know the better. Isn't that right?"

Yee was sweating. He needed the handkerchief again. Antelope looked at it sitting there on the conference table between them. Yee picked it up again, wiped the sweat from his face, and this time held on to it.

"You've worked together how long?"

"We are colleagues. For two years now." Yee took another swipe at his wet face.

"Is something wrong?"

"I'm worried this is my fault."

"How could it be your fault?"

"For a while now, Kimi has been the main reporter for all the coverage of the serial rapist. It's her byline he sees on every story. Maybe it drew his attention."

"Still not seeing how that's your fault."

"I'm the senior crime reporter. Originally, it was my story. I was the one who suggested Kimi take over. I thought it would be good experience for her, and she wanted it. I never thought it would put her in danger."

"You believe Kimi was kidnapped by the rapist?"

"That's where my mind went when she didn't show up to work." He cleared his throat. "How is the investigation going, Detective? So far you have nothing to go on, no clues as to who it might be, am I correct?"

"There hasn't been a rape reported since April. If we're lucky, he's moved out of the area."

The rapes of the four women in the previous winter had followed a pattern. The rapist had abducted each one from the parking lots of local stores at closing time, forced them to drive to isolated locations on White Mountain, and let them go after sexually assaulting them. Kimi hadn't been seen for four days. Yee's theory didn't hold up.

He needed something specific to help him find Kimi. He had to refocus on Yee. He shook his head and said, "You said Kimi wasn't at work on Friday either. When was the last time you saw her?"

"Thursday. I didn't expect to see her in the office Friday morning—I knew she had interviews scheduled—but we had plans to meet for lunch. It's a regular thing—we always have lunch together on Friday. That was the last thing she said to me when she left here,

'See you at lunch tomorrow.' But that didn't happen. I called. I waited. I called again. Left messages both times. After a while I ordered my lunch and returned to the office. I hoped I might find her there. I figured she was tied up in an interview that went long and couldn't answer my calls . . . But she wasn't at the office."

"Where had you planned to meet?"

"Every week we have lunch at the Wonderful House—my family's restaurant. Always my treat."

How did Yee ever get a story? Antelope had to spoon-feed him questions. "You know her habits. When she wasn't in the office Friday afternoon, did you worry?"

"I hope I haven't given the impression I'm keeping tabs on her like some office stalker. As I said, I figured an interview went long and, being Friday, she went home early. She'd mentioned her husband was working out of town. I thought maybe she'd made plans for herself for the weekend. We're not so close she would tell me something like that."

"Yet she told you she was in therapy. Most people consider that private information. It suggests she felt close to you."

"I'm not sure she would have, but as I told the sheriff, I've been worried about her lately. She's been distracted a lot. A few times I found her crying. One of those times, she must have seen my concern—that's when she told me not to worry, she was meeting with a psychologist."

"Let's go back to Thursday. How did she seem to you? Was that one of the days she broke down?"

"No tears on Thursday. But she seemed stressed—she kept more to herself than usual. Kimi is a chatty person. She usually shares her thoughts throughout the day. For the last while now—I know you're going to ask me, I'd say the last month or so—she hasn't been herself."

"The Friday morning interviews, what more can you tell me about those? Did she tell you who it was she planned to interview?"

"She didn't. That's not unusual. She was working on a few things. She didn't always tell me what she was doing. It wasn't like she works *for* me. We work together, as colleagues. Even though

I'm senior to her, she doesn't report to me. One of the things she has coming up is a retrospective piece on the serial rapist stories." Yee folded his handkerchief into a tiny square and put it in his breast pocket. He looked quickly at the door and leaned toward Antelope. "She's working toward a master's degree in journalism at the University of Wyoming. Sometimes she does research for her thesis, fits it in during a slow time. She keeps a low profile. Technically, she shouldn't be working on other things when she's on the clock."

"Would she have kept notes on her computer here?" Antelope asked.

"I only ever see her use her own laptop." Yee opened the handkerchief and held it over his face. "Forgive me. An image of her came into my mind. Please find her."

CHAPTER 6

It was two o'clock when Antelope left the *Rocket Miner*. It would be at least an hour before the deputies got back from the Wind River campground with Kimi's husband. He hadn't had lunch, and he might be tied up for a long time with interviews, so he headed to The Broadway Burger Station, one of his favorite haunts, just two blocks away.

The small diner was empty after the noon rush of office workers. Antelope ordered a double cheeseburger and took a seat at the low counter facing the street.

Christmas traffic clogged the narrow street, which was lined with antique shops and arts and crafts stores attempting to lure in crowds of shoppers by extolling the virtues of buying local. Across the street, the windows of the Department of Probation and Parole sported silver ribbons. He would have to tell Cass. He should tell her now, man up and walk over there. But he knew he wouldn't. Not yet, anyway. Kimi could be coming out of one of her spells right that moment and on her way home. Besides, Cass would take it hard. He didn't want to deal with her getting emotional.

He paid the check and walked out into the snapping cold and bright sun of Bridger Avenue. The storefronts and lamp posts were decorated with cheerful wreaths and red bows, but he knew in his bones that this wasn't going to be a happy holiday season.

He loved Rock Springs, ugly bumps and spots and all. Native American residents made up less than 1 percent of the population, roughly two hundred people total, and he knew most of them.

He thought of Cass again. She might know something useful; though he dreaded it, he had to call her. He pulled out his cell phone and punched in the number for Probation and Parole.

Cass's secretary got a bit of attitude in her voice when he gave her his name. She told him Cass wasn't expected in the office until tomorrow. She'd taken a three-day weekend.

He felt a wave of relief come over him: Cass and Kimi had gone off on a girls' weekend. He hesitated before calling Cass's cell phone, but reminded himself it was official police business. The phone went immediately to voice mail. The mailbox was full, so he couldn't leave a message to let her know the reason for his call. The sense of relief he felt at avoiding the conversation slipped away when he realized this meant there was no way to confirm Kimi was with her.

He thought of the worst-case scenario. If Kimi didn't show up soon, he'd have to deal with Cass. When a woman went missing, the first line of inquiry involved the local sex offenders—and they comprised most of Cass's caseload. He wasn't looking forward to it. He and Cass had a past, and he wanted to keep it that way—in the past. The woman was wrapped up tight, but she could unravel, and he didn't want to see that happen again.

■ ■ ■

When Garcia radioed that they'd picked up Kevin Cahill, Antelope had made it clear he wanted the first crack at the guy—no questions, no answers, just get the hell back with him as fast as possible. The man was just live cargo to them; that's how he wanted them to play it. This wasn't a case his deputies could cut their teeth on. This was *his* case. He knew it. He didn't know how he would make it happen, but he would. He was going to be the one to lead the investigation.

In a missing person investigation, the early hours were crucial. If Kevin Cahill had information regarding his wife's disappearance, Antelope had to get it out of him fast. He wanted the man uncomfortable and uncertain, in that vulnerable state of mind where he could talk too much, get confused, and eventually confess. That's what was needed here, not some cocky bastard who thought he'd gotten away with it.

He arrived at headquarters and stood outside for a few minutes, breathing in the bracing air in the last of the afternoon sun. Once he walked inside to question Kevin Cahill, he would become immersed in the case and carried along a trajectory he couldn't direct or control. He felt the thrill of jumping from a high place into deep water, letting go and giving in to natural forces. It was always this way with a new case. What was different this time was the resistance he felt. He knew he should surrender to the process and follow the facts, but he couldn't. He realized he was already caught in it. The arc of the story began before his cousin went missing.

A slither of dread moved through his muscles when he thought of Kimi being gone four days. It was too long a time to be one of the episodes he remembered her having as a kid. But what did he know of her life now? It had been years since they'd been close. Would Kimi go away for a weekend without letting someone know? From what he remembered of his cousin she was responsible to a fault. And working the crime beat for the newspaper, she would know what kind of hassle it created when someone went missing.

He walked into headquarters and climbed the stairs to the back window overlooking the parking lot. He wanted to get a look at Cahill as they brought him in. He'd met him when Kimi married him two years earlier, but he wouldn't recognize the man if he passed him on the street. What he remembered of their wedding day was fighting with Cass, champagne thrown in his face, the two of them falling into the river, and not much else.

The county cruiser pulled into the lot, and Collins opened the back door, freeing Cahill, who looked slight and short. Before taking a step, he stretched his arms, arched his back, and put on his ski hat. Under the circumstances, he was taking his damn sweet time—was acting so casual it might be calculated.

Cops can't stop being cops, Antelope thought as he watched the officers close in behind Cahill in a tight two-step formation, crowding him and taking charge. Cahill clearly wasn't happy, but should he be? He wasn't under arrest yet, but that could change.

CHAPTER 7

Kevin was prepared to shield his face like the criminals he'd seen on TV, but there was no need. It looked like any normal work day on D Street when they pulled into the parking lot behind the Sweetwater Sheriff's Department. The parking lot was empty. No sign of a camera crew from local television, no reporters from Kimi's paper. The losers who worked at that rag couldn't find a story happening right in front of them. But at least one of them had to know. The deputy told him a coworker had reported her missing. It had to be that pervert Cedric Yee, always keeping tabs on her. Let her try to deny it now. Kimi didn't like it when he accused her of letting Yee get too close.

The deputies flanked him as they entered the gray stone building. They walked too close to him, like he was a criminal they had to control, and it irritated him. He was a private citizen whose wife was missing. They should show him a little compassion, for Christ's sake, and a little respect to go with it. And he was starving. They had better get him something to eat and drink fast or he'd puke all over them.

Inside the station, the heat was stunning. *Who pays for this?* he thought. The county was supposed to be hurting for money. He had to get out of his ski gear, ditch the layers that protected him to twenty below.

They brought him to a room without windows. On the ceiling, long fluorescent tubes blinked and buzzed. "Have a seat." Garcia pointed to an orange plastic chair. "I'll let them know we're back."

"Time to pee and hydrate, and I'm hungry." He'd made a mistake giving his pack to Tracy to haul back. He carried enough provisions in it to survive for two days.

"You couldn't mention that before I got you settled in here?" Garcia said. But he led him down the hall to the public restrooms.

In the privacy of the one-room bathroom, Kevin took a deep breath and stripped down to his thermals. He stepped to the sink, splashed cold water on his face and wrists, closed his eyes, and hallucinated a mountain stream.

"Hey," Garcia said, opening the door without knocking. He pointed a thumb in the direction of the interview room. "Let's go."

A dark-skinned man sat at the table in the center of the interview room with a notebook and cassette recorder in front of him. His index finger rested on the play button. Kevin scanned the whole room: video camera in the right corner, a mirrored wall— the real deal, like on the crime shows.

"I'm Detective Antelope," the man said. "I'll be recording our conversation. Sit down, please."

The detective looked more like an attorney in his charcoal suit, blue shirt, and silk patterned tie. After being with Kimi for a year, Kevin recognized the Native American features. If they'd given him the case because Kimi was Native, would that help or hurt him?

The detective saw him looking at the video camera. "Don't be concerned. It's standard procedure in these matters."

Kevin shot a look at the window, the closed vinyl blinds, and knew he was being watched. A deputy came in and placed a bottle of water and a steaming cup of black coffee on the table.

"Can I get cream and sugar?"

"Take it or leave it," the deputy said.

Kevin picked up the cup and waved the man away.

The detective pressed the button and stated the date and time of the interview, and his name: Kevin Kyle Cahill. How did the guy know his middle name? The next words the detective said sent a shiver up his spine: "In the matter of Kimi Benally, missing person."

"How are you doing?" the detective asked. "My deputies didn't bring you the best news today."

Kevin sipped the coffee and immediately spat it out. He pushed the cup away from him.

"I appreciate you coming in to talk with me."

Inwardly, Kevin rolled his eyes. Did he have any fucking choice? The guy was too smooth, and Kevin had had enough. Rage, his old, dark pal, rose up and gave him strength. "What happened?" he demanded. "I'm doing my thing up in the mountains and all of a sudden my wife is gone and I'm here."

"A coworker reported your wife missing this morning when she didn't show up for work at her usual time. What can you tell me?"

"My wife is missing. That's all I know. The deputies wouldn't tell me any more than you did. They acted like I was a suspect or something. But I'm clueless, totally out of the loop, out of town for three days. You tell me. Where's my wife?"

Kevin concentrated on staying in the chair. His hands and feet were poised to punch and jump, his stashed boxer's training ready when he needed it. A wisp of memory came to him. "What's your name again?"

"Detective Beauregard Antelope."

Kevin snapped his fingers and pointed at Antelope. "I know you. I thought you looked familiar. You're Kimi's cousin, Beau. Am I right?"

"That's right."

"And Kimi said I never took an interest in her family and friends. I met you at my wedding—you had your arms around Cass. She's a hot one. Don't tell Kimi. My wife has been known to be jealous."

"Let's move on." The detective tapped his silver pen on the notebook.

"Is that a problem, you being related to her? They're going to let you do this . . . wouldn't that be some kind of conflict of interest or something?"

"Trust me, I'll use what I know of Kimi to the advantage of the case."

"I guess. Whatever."

"Every minute counts in cases like this, and we've already lost a lot of time."

Kevin looked in the direction of the video camera and at the mirrored wall and relaxed into the uncomfortable chair, letting his arms and hands hang loose at his side.

"What do you want to know?"

"Kimi was reported missing this morning. We haven't yet been able to establish how long she's been missing. The coworker stated Kimi was last seen in her office at the *Rocket Miner* last Thursday, December 16. When was the last time you saw your wife?"

"Before I left for the mountains."

"When did you leave?" Antelope asked.

"I was on the road by five in the morning on Friday."

"You left your house at 5:00 A.M.?"

"No, earlier. We took off from the Outdoor Leadership office at five."

"So you last saw your wife on Friday morning?"

Antelope looked up from his notes. Kevin knew he was taking too long, and maybe he'd already blown it by hesitating. He might as well come clean now. It was bound to come out anyway.

"Real early Friday morning was the last time I saw her. It was maybe still Thursday night. I'm not sure."

"What time on Thursday?" Antelope pressed.

"Not sure."

"Best guess," he said and tapped the pen again.

The action irritated Kevin. He felt like he was in school again, in trouble for not paying attention. He wanted to be back on the mountain. Better answer and get this over with. He wanted a shower. He wanted to meet up with the crew for a drink. He had to talk to Tracy.

"Sometime after dinner. We fought, nothing physical. Kimi gets tense before I go away. She says it's like I'm abandoning her or some bullshit like that. So what does she do? She leaves me.

How does that make any sense? I waited awhile and then left. I was tired of the game, and she knew I had an early morning, not that she cared."

"What time would this be, when you left the house?" Antelope asked.

"Man, I don't know—late but not too late, sometime around eleven, maybe. I'm not into time."

"Except for 5:00 A.M."

"You got it. Always on time when it's ski time." Kevin relaxed into the chair again.

"You leave your house at approximately eleven Thursday night. Your wife isn't home, and you don't know where she is. Where did you spend the night?"

Kevin had been slouched in the chair, but with this question he sat up straight. He did another scan of the video camera and the mirror and answered, "In my truck."

Antelope eyed him for a moment before asking, "You slept in your truck?"

"That's what I said. Is there a problem?" His left knee was bouncing against the table leg. He grabbed hold of it to stop it.

"It's December. Cold weather for sleeping in a truck."

"I've slept in colder places. I always have my winter gear with me."

"Was there a reason you slept in your truck?"

"Same old story. We argued. She took off. I got tired of waiting, met up with some friends at a bar, had a few drinks, decided it was better to stay put than try to drive home. Is that a good enough reason?"

"What bar and what friends?"

"We party at the Astro Lounge. My whole crew was there. Check with the bartender. Casey knows me—he'll tell you I closed the place like always."

Antelope gave him a blank stare, and Kevin felt the accusation in the silence between them.

"Are these questions bothering you?" the detective asked. "Because the whole point is that your wife is missing."

"Where did my wife go Thursday night? That's my question, detective. Do you know the answer?"

"Did you try reaching her when she didn't come home?"

"I was done for the night. If she wasn't coming home, I wasn't chasing after her. I don't do that."

"You left town for a week without knowing where your wife was?"

"Look, I assumed she'd come home at some point. I know it looks bad. But it's not the first time she's taken off."

"Did you worry?"

"About Kimi? No, I definitely did not worry about Kimi. She knows how to take care of herself. And like I said, she's been taking off a lot recently."

"What do you mean?"

"Hours at a time, and she can't remember where she's been. At least, that's what she tells me. She's seeing a shrink. It's some kind of a psychological problem. I don't know if I believe her, but the shrink does."

"Let me get this straight. Your wife has a problem that involves getting lost and you leave town for a week without knowing she's home safe?"

"When you put it like that . . . this has been going on for a long time, and nothing's ever happened. She said it happened when she was a kid, too. You're her cousin, don't you know this?"

Antelope said nothing, gave him the blank Native stare Kevin had come to know from living with Kimi. You saw that look, you knew you lost the battle.

"She'll be back. Kimi always comes back."

Antelope closed his notebook and laid the fancy silver pen on top of it. He folded his hands in front of him and shot Kevin one of those "if looks could kill" faces before saying, "Is that why you're not taking this interview seriously?"

Kevin definitely wanted to hit this guy. "This *is* me serious. I can't imagine life without her, all right? She'll be back."

"I need to talk to everyone she's close to—anyone she could have gone to or who might know where she'd go if she intended to run away."

"Wait a minute. You're saying she left me intentionally? No way Kimi would ever do that, man. Never."

"You'd be surprised how often it happens."

Kevin shook his head back and forth in protest. "I know my wife. She didn't leave me."

"Who do I need to talk to? I need names."

"Her brother, Diego, and her mother, but I wouldn't count on much from Estella. She'll be drunk or on another planet. But I'm not telling you anything you don't know there. Cass, always Cass. You still with her, by the way?"

"That's not for this discussion."

"Touchy subject? Sorry. I'm a little off my game. My wife is missing."

"Did Kimi have plans to go away with Cass?"

"That's it, man. Of course. That's got to be it . . . Cass!"

"Any idea where they might go?"

"Some place they can shop . . . Salt Lake, Casper, city places. I'm away a lot, so it works. Keeps her out of trouble."

"Anyone else? Who's she been spending time with recently?"

"Cedric Yee reported her missing, right?"

"Yes. Cedric's a friend?"

"I'm not sure what's going on there."

"Does Kimi consider him a close friend?"

"Too close. Him to her, I mean."

"Is that a problem for you?"

Kevin pushed the chair back and stood up. They couldn't keep him from standing up, could they? Antelope said nothing but watched him like a hawk as he paced from one side of the small room to the other. He made a point of looking at the camera and the mirror. He'd show them all. He had nothing to hide.

He came back to the table and sat down. He pulled down the sleeves of his jersey and made himself go slack in the chair. He looked straight at Antelope and said, "I stopped caring."

"She's your wife and you don't care?"

"Not about her—the endless fucking fights. Or whether Yee was putting the moves on her or not."

"What moves?"

"He tossed her the biggest story that rag ever covered. If that isn't workplace seduction, I don't know what is. She's been at the paper less than a year, and he turns over the serial rapist story to her . . . who does that? Someone who's looking to hook up, that's who. She disagreed, of course."

"Anyone else?"

"Kimi wasn't social. Any of them might tell you more. That's all I know."

Kevin was losing patience, felt restless in the cramped space. He'd handled himself pretty well. Tired and hungry, eyes burning from the glare of the light. He thought it was over, but Antelope started up again.

"Can anyone verify that your truck was parked at the Astro Lounge on Thursday night?"

"Can I ask what difference this makes? Aren't you wasting precious time you could be using to find her?" Kevin scratched under his right arm.

"I asked you a question. Can anyone verify? It's wasting time when I have to ask you again."

"Does anyone need to?"

Kevin could tell his answer bothered Antelope. The detective put down the notebook and pen and stared at him again. For a minute he thought the guy was going to go off on him. He wanted it to happen. Kevin fought to maintain eye contact, not wanting to lose at this classic test of dominance. Antelope held steady until Kevin blinked.

"I want a list of everyone you talked to at the bar on Thursday night."

He tore a page out of the notebook and handed him a pen— not the silver one, a blue plastic pen he pulled from a pocket inside his suit jacket. *This asshole thinks I'm the type to walk off with his pen,* Kevin thought.

"After you make your list, you're free to go. I'll be in touch."

"So we're done here?" Kevin asked.

"Don't leave town. I need to be able to find you."

"I'm headed home. Totally wiped."

"Things might be a little out of order. I noted signs of a break-in and ordered a search of the residence. I've got your dog downstairs, out of the team's way."

"Domino. She's Kimi's dog. She must be freaking out with Kimi gone so long." Kevin shook his head. "So what happens now?"

"I look for your wife."

CHAPTER 8

The Sweetwater County Jail was south of town. The strong smell of charcoal-broiled meat from fast-food places on both sides of Foothill Drive came in through the Jeep's heater vent. I was ravenous, but didn't have time to stop for a hot meal. Estella Benally was waiting for me in the county jail, and I was eager to evaluate her. I grabbed a protein bar from the emergency kit I carried for driving in Wyoming winter weather.

The traffic was heavy going west on Interstate 80—mostly big rigs, eighteen-wheelers hauling freight. At the second exit I turned onto Purple Sage Road.

Built in the oil boom of the 1980s, the Sweetwater County Jail was a tan brick structure sunk in a wide lap of desert, situated south of town. Several white mobile units, added in leaner financial times, supplemented the original structure. The mobile units swayed and shifted on their foundations in the strong southwesterly wind as I approached. *Not such a secure choice for inmates*, I thought. *More like a house of straw waiting for the wolf to huff and puff and blow it all down.*

I was used to conducting psychological examinations in the ancient, moldy basement jails in Massachusetts where I'd worked as a court clinician until a year ago. This facility, with its shining tile floors, was an upgrade. Despite the difference in the buildings, there was one thing consistent to all places of incarceration:

the strong scent of cleaning products and the smells they couldn't quite erase.

The cleaning crew at Sweetwater—young men with shaved heads, prison tattoos on forearms and necks, dressed in orange coveralls—work around the clock there, making it perhaps the cleanest building in the county.

I swiped my county visitor pass at the entrance to the jail, and a detention clerk gave a bored nod before pressing a button that opened the heavy steel door to the secure area of the cell block. I shivered at the sound of the electronic click as the door locked; my primitive brain registered being trapped.

The clerk pointed to the last cell. I looked through the small mesh window when I reached the steel door and saw a woman lying on the floor in the far right corner, curled into a fetal position. Long gray hair was splayed out around her head. Kimi's mother. My patient had spoken of a sad ghost lost to alcohol and shifting personalities. Kimi had been left to care for her little brother at an early age.

Estella had been arrested and charged with public intoxication when a school bus driver found her scaring kids at the stop in the Elk Street Trailer Park. Estella had fought hard when a police officer tried to get her in the car to take her home; his partner had called for backup, and it had taken four of them to restrain her and cuff her for transport to the jail.

The jail had mandated suicide checks, a standard procedure for all inmates. Estella was a frequent guest of the county, and because she had a documented psychiatric history, a higher level of caution was exercised whenever she was detained. The mental status examination I was about to conduct would result in a transfer to Sweetwater Memorial Hospital and a supervised room.

"Ms. Benally?" I called through the mesh. "Estella?"

No sound or movement came from the shape in the corner.

"I'm Doctor Hunt, a psychologist. I'd like to speak with you."

A hoarse male voice answered from another cell.

"Hey, Miss Doctor, I could use a doctor. Why don't you come over here and talk to me?"

"Estella. I'm Dr. Hunt. I need to talk with you. Can you look at me?"

"Let her sleep it off. I'm the one who needs your help."

Luckily, there was only one vocal prisoner today. Sometimes there was a whole chorus of profanity.

Estella dropped the blanket and showed black eyes under swollen lids. Looking at her was like looking at a corpse; she had the lost look of a haunted patient, the void of the psychotic patient.

She let out a brokenhearted banshee cry, scrambled up off the floor, and rushed at the door, spitting.

Two officers arrived at the door, keys jangling, ready to enter and restrain her.

"Quiet in there. Quiet down."

At the sight and sound of them, the bulk and muscle, Estella went silent and calm. She was no stranger to police power. But I knew better than to trust that her sudden change in demeanor would last. In a psychiatric patient, such stillness meant the same as the eye of a hurricane: it was a dangerously deceptive illusion.

"Have her transported to the hospital," I told the guards. "She needs to be sedated. I'll evaluate her there tomorrow."

At the hospital, Estella would be placed in four-point leather restraints and given antipsychotic medication to calm her and allow her to rest. It might be twenty-four hours before she would be lucid enough to engage in the kind of evaluation the law required.

"You got it, Doc," one of the officers said.

As I waited for the steel door to open, I heard Estella singing in a lilting Native rhythm, atonal and ancient, over and over, every time the same three words: "Whirlwind took Kimi."

． ． ．

Back on the highway, traffic was stalled. The dashboard thermometer read minus two degrees Fahrenheit. Vehicles slid on black ice. Somewhere ahead an accident blocked the road. It might take hours to travel the twelve miles back to Rock Springs. I was sandwiched between two eighteen-wheelers going fifteen miles per hour, my concentration split between the road and the session.

I wanted to be home wrapped in Zeke's Hudson Bay blanket, sipping an Irish coffee, going over the details of Kimi's last session. But the car would have to do for now. I grabbed a bottle of water and another protein bar from the survival kit.

■ ■ ■

At our Friday session, Kimi dropped her backpack and laptop bag on either side of her and fell back into the cushions of the couch with a sigh. She looked tired and thin in a black sweater, long black skirt, and red boots.

"I'm exhausted," she said. "It happened again."

"You had another episode?"

She described the process of resurfacing from dissociation, the return of sensation. "What's happening to me?" she asked. "Maybe Kevin's right and I'm as crazy as my mother. Is that what I have to look forward to, life in a mental hospital?"

Kimi had come out of the dissociation at the Little America Travel Plaza on Interstate 80, forty miles west of Rock Springs. She'd had no reason to be on that road and couldn't remember leaving Rock Springs.

She pointed to the red boots on her feet.

"Check out these boots, Dr. Hunt. I found them in my car. I have no idea how they got there. I haven't been on a horse in two years. Some part of me must want to be that girl again. Either that or the pervert who's following me wanted to give me a sexy upgrade."

"Someone's following you?"

This was new information.

"Sounds crazy, right? Sounds like something my mother would say."

"What have you noticed?"

"It's a sense I have of not being alone."

"You haven't seen anyone?"

"More evidence I'm crazy, right?" Kimi said. A tentative smile softened her face.

Even in the safety of my office, Kimi was unable to shake the fear. She kept checking the windows, where she couldn't possibly see anything more than the reflection of her own haunted face.

. . .

Traffic began to move. I thought of the sheriff going out of his way to come to my office. Why bother? He knew I wouldn't give him any confidential information. And he left as soon as I told him I'd need a court order. A missing person's report had been filed, but that wasn't enough to breach confidentiality. There was still no evidence a crime had been committed. The sheriff knew the law. So why had he come?

Was I really the last person to see Kimi before she went missing? Anyone watching from outside would have seen through the corner window the silhouette of two women, talking. An unwelcome memory came—the light from another office, late one night—but I pushed it away.

I hadn't written any notes that night. I'd left when Kimi did to get away from the eerie sense of being watched and followed that lingered in the empty room.

The line of vehicles ahead came to a stop again. Outside the window I saw grazing mule deer on a distant rise, velvet silhouettes in the glowing copper dusk. It was four o'clock on a December afternoon, and soon it would be dark. Miles ahead, radio towers rose from the desert, their blinking lights a beacon at the city limits.

It had been clear to me that Kimi was falling apart. The affair had taken a toll. The secrecy, guilt, and fear of discovery had grown into paranoia. For the first time, I wondered if her fear of being mentally ill like her mother could have pushed her to suicide. The thought that I might never see Kimi again brought a deep sadness that stayed with me all the way home.

CHAPTER 9

Yellow tape bordered the driveway, one loose end lashed at the mailbox like a deranged Christmas decoration. When he spotted the truck from local TV Channel 7 idling in front of the townhouse, Kevin backtracked a quarter of a mile to a small playground and parked his truck behind a concrete utility shed. For once he was thankful to be living in a place where the media didn't win any prizes for breaking news. Anywhere else they'd have dogged him all the way home from the police station.

The temperature fell twenty degrees with sundown, and Kevin cursed as he made his way along the narrow, snow-banked side streets, Domino at his side. He cut through a neighbor's yard to the back entrance of his place. With the wind chill it felt like five below zero. The wood panel fence bordering his small patch of back garden was six feet tall. The neighbor's picnic table was flush against the fence, a foot of drifted, frozen snow on top of it. He went over the fence with a skillful hand-over-hand rock climbing maneuver, and dropped to his feet on the other side. Domino followed right after.

They walked through frost-stiffened weeds to the kitchen door. He checked the automatic water station and filled the food bowl. He made his way through the rooms in the dark. No need to turn the lights on and announce his arrival to the vultures outside.

The news van's headlights streamed through the front blinds, laying thin stripes on the wall. He gave a hard turn to the lever of the vertical blinds and set them swinging with a "fuck you."

The phone rang and he reached to unplug it, figuring it was one of Kimi's reporter friends trying to get a leg up. Who else would have their private number? But instead he let it ring on and on, enjoying the power struggle—and then he answered. He wanted to see what it felt like to be that person, the one they wanted, the words "no comment" already forming in his mouth.

"Kevin, oh my God, I was so worried," Tracy said. "I called your cell like a million times, but you didn't pick up. Are you all right?"

"I'm fine, Trace."

Playing it down, dismissing the chick drama. He understood the seduction angle of his situation. It wasn't right, but all the same, it did put him in a good position with Tracy. She was not easily impressed, but something this big, he could tell it hooked her.

"Why didn't you pick up?"

"I was with the cops. Not the best time to talk."

"All this time? What happened?"

"You don't know yet?"

"Know what, Kevin? What should I know?"

He pulled the drapes closed, secured them, and hit the remote. His wife's face lit up all fifty inches of his flat screen. Kimi. She looked good. Smiling, taming her long hair in the wind, her diamond ring flashing in the sunlight. She loved Ocean Lake, so he'd taken her there to propose. When she said yes, he'd pulled out his phone for a picture to upload to Facebook, making the announcement before she could change her mind.

Now a continuous newsfeed ran across the screen under that photo, announcing her disappearance over and over, while at the bottom of the screen the words "woman missing woman missing woman missing" scrolled on.

"Kimi's gone."

"What?"

"She's been gone since Friday."

On the line he heard water, the whooshing sound of a hand dryer. Tracy was calling him from a public restroom. The sound of glasses clinking, a track of laughter, random voices rising from a low tide of conversation, bar sounds. She must have broken from the others, taken a private moment and slipped away from the party to call him. She wasn't so worried she couldn't go drinking. *Like Kimi*, he thought, *slippery. Can't keep hold of my women.*

"Oh my God, Kevin, what the hell?"

"Sucks, right?"

"Oh my God."

"Party on, Trace."

"No, Kevin, wait, I'm here in your place."

"You're wasted, I can tell. No problem. I got this. I'm hanging up now."

"No, Kevin. Don't hang up. I'm straight. I'm here. She's been missing since Friday? Four whole days? The whole time we were in the Winds?"

The normally neat bedroom he shared with Kimi was a mess from the search. Every drawer was open, clothes hanging out or thrown to the floor, and all the photos of Kimi—from the bookshelf, the engagement picture that ran on the television news feed, her high school graduation picture—all of them were missing.

"Fuck me," he said.

"What? Are you okay?"

"What do you think, Trace?"

"Do you know where she is?"

"Are you fucking kidding me, asking me that? I've been with you for the last four days. I have no fucking clue where she is. Why does everybody think I know where she is?"

"Kevin, I'm sorry. This is so sick, so totally wrong."

"I'm hanging up now."

"You're right. We shouldn't tie up the phone in case she calls."

"The cops put me through the ringer. It was brutal. I'm done."

"Do you want me to come over? I could listen for the phone while you get some rest."

"I don't think that's a good idea under the circumstances."

"What do you mean? At a time like this you need your friends, Kevin. Don't shut me out."

He stripped and dropped his clothes on the floor, adding to the clutter. Naked and free. He thought of the empty hours rolling out before him; nothing but time to himself, like the old days, before he had a wife to nag him or want anything from him. He felt his spirits lift.

"You know, she's done this before."

"What do you mean?"

"It's not the first time she's taken off."

"Are you serious?"

"Dead serious. Lots of times. She's got a problem. She's seeing a shrink."

"So you're saying this is some kind of joke, and she's going to come back and act like nothing happened?"

"I never said it was a joke, Trace—in fact, I said it was a problem. But whatever. It's not your problem. Go back to the party. I'm sure someone's missing you."

"Don't be mean. Does law enforcement know about this problem of hers?"

"Now they do. She'll be pissed I told them. But what the hell, she's only got herself to blame now. Can't blame me for her crazy shit."

"Oh my God, she left because of the fight?"

"Doubt it. Maybe she got sick of me."

"Tell me she didn't leave because of me."

"She didn't leave because of you, Trace."

"Do you mean that?"

"I seriously mean it. You've got nothing to do with this."

"I can't believe your wife is missing and you're so calm."

"She wants to leave, I can't stop her. I can take a hint."

"But to leave without telling you is cruel."

"Enough. I'm beyond stressed out. My wife is missing, for Christ's sake. Can I get a break here? I don't need any more questions. Seriously, I'm hanging up now."

"You sure you don't want me to come over?"

One part of his body, even under the circumstances, was strongly voting yes. But he had to be smart. "You cannot come here. There's media out front."

"Promise you'll call me when she comes back. I want to be the first to know. You have to promise me, Kevin."

"She's not coming back, Trace."

He was going to play this for all it was worth.

He hung up and immediately the phone rang again. He killed the TV and yanked the phone from the wall, sending the dark, empty house into a vibrating silence.

"*Don't leave town,*" the detective had told him.

He began to worry the police had tapped his phone and were even now getting ideas, forming a story: him and Tracy. Did cops do that? Was it legal? Better not take any chances. He wouldn't talk to Tracy on the house phone again.

He shouldn't have stayed with Tracy on Thursday night. If they found out, it wouldn't look good. He should have checked into a motel. Tomorrow he'd tell her to keep it quiet, keep it between them. Better do it now, before they got to her. He called her on his cell phone. Back to partying already—she didn't answer. The phone went to voice mail, and against his better judgment, he left his message: "Hey, Trace, let's keep it between us, me sleeping at your place the other night. It's nobody's business but ours. Someone could take it the wrong way, if you know what I mean. Our little secret, okay?"

He'd never believed that Kimi actually lost time. What was the word the shrink used? "Dissociating." Lying was more like it. All those times she claimed she didn't know where she was. Did she think he was an idiot, that he wouldn't figure it out? She was lying. She was seeing someone the whole time.

He punched the bathroom door hard and the cheap plywood caved and splintered. Now his hand throbbed and small pinpricks of red appeared on his palm, the tissue already swelling; in the morning a bruise would blossom. He had to get a grip, stay cool; this would look bad.

He ran the shower hot. With the light from his cell phone, he found the white candles Kimi kept for her bath. With a click of his lighter a sweet vanilla scent was released, bringing a vision of his wife, naked and wet, in this room. Too tired to stand, he lowered himself into the bath and stretched his legs out to catch the steam-ing fall of water. A sweet dizziness arrived as he let go. He couldn't remember the last time a simple hot shower had felt this good.

He thought of Kimi and how they used to have reunion sex. Those nights she would cook for him—something spicy, tough wild game dripping with warm sauce, a warrior's homecoming meal. She'd take a small bite first and then feed him from her spoon. And with that thought, he began to miss her.

TUESDAY
DECEMBER 21

CHAPTER 10

I arrived at the Sweetwater Counseling Center, where I run the Sex Offender Group, for the weekly intake meeting. I was hoping that the routine administrative issues would be a break from thoughts of Kimi, who had showed up in my dreams throughout the night, always out of reach.

But Kimi was the main topic of conversation, and the director of the counseling center told me to be prepared to meet with Probation and Parole in the next few days to go over the list of registered sex offenders in the area in connection with my patient's disappearance.

It was a good idea. Was Kimi the latest victim of the serial rapist? All of the victims had been kidnapped from public parking lots as they approached their cars in shopping plazas. He'd ordered each of them to drive to a remote location on White Mountain. As far as they knew, he'd left all his victims alive. *As far as we know.* What if something had gone wrong this time and Kimi was murdered? The victims reported the rapist carried a knife and threatened to use it. Kimi might have fought back, given him a reason to hurt her.

I drove the short distance down College Hill Drive to my office, hoping an afternoon of seeing patients would help to put thoughts of Kimi out of my mind.

I was shedding layers in the warm office when Marla came in. "Detective Antelope's here to see you. He said he'll be quick."

I'd met Antelope the previous winter. Because of my work with sex offenders, I'd been recruited as a consultant in the early stages of the case to develop a profile of the serial rapist. It made sense to look first at the known offenders in the community. Most of the men in the group had committed crimes against family members, and it was a sad truth of deviancy that a predator's behavior could escalate to become more violent and impulsive. At the police department's request, I'd reviewed the profiles of all the registered sex offenders in the county and, using the accepted evidence-based instruments, rated the likelihood of reoffense for each one.

Antelope had taken over the investigation from a retiring senior officer. It was his first violent crime investigation since making detective, and he was on it like a pit bull. I was down with the flu but agreed to a brief meeting at home because of the seriousness of the case.

Antelope met me at home, and we worked at the kitchen table while a fierce wind rocked the house and snow came in under the door.

It must have been the combination of my fever and the illusion of intimacy in the cozy room that broke me. Whatever it was, when Antelope asked how I ended up in Rock Springs, I gave him the unedited version.

It wasn't a pretty story. I was married to a psychiatrist who was murdered by a jealous patient. She discovered him with his lover and shot and killed them both. I was the one who found the bodies. The woman he'd taken as his lover was also my friend and colleague.

As soon as my fever broke, I regretted confiding in Antelope.

For a while he tried to make a friendship work. I'd been taking riding lessons and wanted a horse of my own. He helped me find a handsome Appaloosa horse I named Soldier. But as soon as I had the horse, I wanted nothing to do with Antelope. It'd been six months since I'd talked to the man.

Now he filled the doorway, looking taller than I remembered. I took in the bronze skin, his almond-shaped black eyes, the cleft in his chin. He was a handsome man, but I felt nothing.

"I'd ask you to sit, but Marla said you wouldn't be long."

"Hello yourself, Doc. I've been fine. And you?" His smile indicated he wasn't holding a grudge.

"I have a patient waiting. What do you need?"

"I don't need anything. Just wanted to give you a heads-up that we'll be working together again soon. There'll be a meeting with Probation and Parole as soon as they get their computer issues sorted out—they're guesstimating Thursday."

"I'm aware. It was discussed at the counseling center meeting."

"Unnecessary stop, I guess. I'll get back to you when we lock down a time." He nodded, turned, and walked out the door.

I was being ungracious, I knew, but all I could manage to call after him was, "Good-bye, Detective."

CHAPTER 11

Cass had been out of the office yesterday. Today she'd have the weekend mess plus whatever Monday had already served up. Antelope pictured her at her desk, hair in a twist or coiled at her neck, classy dark suit, riot of red lipstick, off-the-charts beautiful.

If he had more courage, he'd be at her office instead of calling her on the phone. He tried to tell himself he was following professional protocol, but the truth was he couldn't watch her face take the hit when the news landed; he knew it would be like a punch. There was still the chance she'd tell him Kimi had been with her in Salt Lake or she knew where Kimi had gone off to, but his gut told him it wouldn't go that way.

So, he did it—he punched in Cassandra McKnight's office number at the Probation and Parole office. Again. But this time, she answered.

All he said was hello, and she came at him all morning-after husky. She answered in her personal voice, raw and Native, not the professional passing voice he knew she used at work—the unedited version, customized for him. It was worse than he'd imagined.

"What is it? I'm not here a minute and you're hitting me up? I haven't got caffeine in me yet."

Same old Cass—her full-on, irresistible bitchiness launched straight as an arrow at him.

"Slow up, Cass, this is business. I got something I need to ask you."

"So you're telling me it was work that made you dial my number no less than six times yesterday?"

"What does it take to get a call back from you?"

"Bad need of a booty call, Beau? *Six times* you hit me up, I mention that?"

"I was calling on official police business. You ever consider it might have been an emergency? You want to hear it from someone else, I'll hang up now."

"Quit your drama, Beau. I didn't see the missed calls until this morning. I'm back from Salt Lake and the whole Christmas shopping thing. So today is my Monday. I don't need to tell you what that means. You got me now. Go ahead with your big emergency that couldn't wait until I got back—actually, hold on a minute. Let me get these aspirin down. I've got a headache that won't quit."

Not long enough later, she was back on the line.

"Done. Spill it. I'm looking at a real busy day."

"Was Kimi with you in Salt Lake?"

As soon as the words hit the air, he felt the hope in them fade like the lost light of trailing fireworks.

"No. What made you ask that?"

He laid it out for her in the standard format of law enforcement: step one, build the foundation; step two, deliver the information; step three, orient to solution. Though it was designed to bypass emotional reaction, it rarely succeeded.

"We got a call from one of her coworkers yesterday, and we haven't been able to find anyone who's seen her since Friday. I'm hoping you can help narrow down her activity last week. When was the last time you saw her?"

"Kimi's missing? Since Friday, you said?"

"As far as we know, she was last seen at 8:00 P.M."

He heard a clunk as the receiver dropped onto the felt blotter on her desk. He waited in the silence while the empty minutes passed. Finally, the buzzing murmur of the dial tone told him Cass had nothing to say to him for the moment.

He hung up and seconds later his phone rang. He briefly considered not picking up, but he owed her more. This was a woman he'd once loved.

"This is the way you tell me, you bastard? On the freaking telephone? You should have been at my place this morning when I rolled in. You know me, Beau, and still you did it this way. Fuck you."

"Cass, I have questions—"

"I bet you do. Don't come here now," she said and hung up.

CHAPTER 12

Dawn was breaking as Diego rolled into the mobile home park. After driving all night, he was exhausted and longed for a warm bed, but he felt too guilty and selfish to sleep inside with his sister lost in the dead cold of a Wyoming winter, so he slept in his car in the shadow of the trailer.

He'd do anything to have her back. *Anything?* the ancestors asked. *Give up the comforts of his modern life?* So he'd bargained, given up the warm bed, slept in the GTO under the weight of his camp blanket. And now he woke to weak winter light at the window and air so cold it hurt, and reality slammed his mind like a prize fighter's fist. In his mouth a bitter taste, like salt, or sorrow.

His father's ghost roamed the quiet house, so he wouldn't be going in there.

The hospital had called the previous night and told him of his mother's admission. Could his mother have had something to do with Kimi going missing? Crazy as she was, he couldn't imagine her hurting Kimi. But her voices had told her to do some strange shit in the past.

He needed coffee, food, and fuel. He turned the key, and the car's engine growled to life.

■ ■ ■

At the Flying J on Elk Street, a fine deluxe truck stop, Diego found everything he needed, and a shower, too. An hour later he was behind the wheel again, headed north. The road was clear and the desert glowed; the remains of the snow from the night before sparkled in the noon sun.

He thought back to Sunday night a week ago. Kimi, so strange and so normal at the same time. Impossible to believe it could end up being the last time he would see her in this life.

It had been meat-locker cold, and his car's heater had been going on and off. Diego blew on his fingers to keep them warm. Kimi rubbed her hands together in the silly blue gloves that left her fingertips bare.

"What's the point of those?" he asked.

"Cell phone dialing. Frostbite or phone, take your pick."

"What's my problem, having a damn car with no heat?" he asked his sister.

It had been giving him a problem all week, but his plan was to wait until after the holidays to throw money at it. He needed cash for Christmas. Little James had his heart set on a new game system, and he wouldn't disappoint his kid just so he could keep warm. The sweet lesson of parenthood he kept learning over and over: once you had a kid, they always came first. It was a lesson his mother had skipped, only one of her many failures in the parenting department, so it meant all the more to him, pumped him full with pride, whenever he came through for his own son.

"Your real problem is having a sister who needs to go for a drive in a damn car with no heat."

"So tell me. What's on your mind?"

"Drive a little bit. I want to get away."

He took a right onto Elk Street, headed north and out of town, away from the mobile home park they'd lived in since the second half of their so-called childhood began.

"Afraid she'll hear us? Her hearing's not so good these days," he reminded her.

"She hears things we don't say," Kimi insisted.

"She'd like us to believe she's a mind reader, but she's just an ace snoop," he said. "It used to be she'd just read the mail, but now she's figured out how to crack the passwords to my e-mail and voice mail."

"Would she go through my phone?"

"If you left her alone with it."

"That's all I need." Kimi scrolled and deleted.

"What's to see?" he asked, craning his neck to look.

"In a minute," she said, and held up her hand to block him. "Keep your eyes on the road before you wreck."

She was taking control the way she always did, making mystery out of the smallest thing.

He shifted and pushed it. The GTO complained but responded, lifting and roaring, his good little land jet. He was happy being with his sister. He realized he'd missed her. She hardly came around to the house anymore, and she never invited them to her place. She lived in a different world now. He'd have to take what he could get.

"You're going mysterious again. I can never figure you out, sister."

"My secret power."

This could take forever, Diego thought. He'd had plans to meet up with a woman he'd met at the bar. She'd been with a guy last time, but she let him know she'd be back alone. He wasn't scheduled to work but would take the drive over. He figured she'd wait.

"Who's the guy?" he said, and gave a slight tug on his sister's hair.

"Quit it," she said and slapped his hand away. "Did I say there's a guy?"

"It's always a guy, or a girl. What other kind of trouble is there?"

"Money, evil spirits."

"Can't help you with evil spirits. I already sold my soul. I can help with money if you need it."

"It's nothing that simple. I don't need your money."

"I hear divorce is costly these days."

"Don't be a smartass." She made another slap at his head; this one he dodged, but the distraction caused him to lose control of the car for a second—long enough for a brief tailspin. He reacted quickly and set them straight again, but it was enough to scare Kimi. She let out a scream and slapped him, a real slap this time.

"Might be worth it, though," he said as if nothing had just happened.

"Damn it, Diego, grow up."

The little incident spoiled the mood between them, and they rode in silence for a while. The wind wailed and rocked the little car along, and he enjoyed being there with her, even if she was mad at him.

After the silence had gone on for a while, he spoke. He wasn't a patient man, and he knew if he left it up to her she could push it to the limit, maybe not speak to him for the rest of the night.

He reached over and put his hand on hers. She startled at his touch.

"Talk to me," he said, his voice a whisper. "Come on, Kimi, talk to me. You got me out here, now spill it."

"I can't tell anyone but you, brother," she said.

Minutes passed and he drove on. She wouldn't say a word until she was damn ready, that much he knew.

"I got myself in some trouble."

He smoked and drove. Kept everything still, inside and out. "What is it?" he asked. "You got trouble at home? Some other dude?"

"You have a one-track mind. You would say that. You hate Kevin. You're so predictable." She pulled her hand away.

He was irritated. Why couldn't she speak in straight sentences?

"Did you ever have a situation where no matter what you decided to do, it would all end in heartbreak and chaos?"

"You mean something more specific than the destiny I was born into?"

The minute the words hit the air between them, he knew he'd made a colossal mistake. Her question had scared him, and he'd gotten flippant in response. He might as well have been driving a corpse around. His sister had gone away—had shut her soul in a tomb, safe from him.

He gave it one last try. "Are you going to tell me?"

She stayed silent, and he didn't press her. None of his business anyway. He'd rather not know.

After a long while she said, "The moment passed. Another time, maybe."

Across the short distance, her sadness had claimed him.

As children, they'd been so close it felt like they shared the same heart. He'd had enough of sorrow. They'd been through enough as kids with their mother's random men.

Now Kimi was missing, and more than anything, Diego wished for a second chance to listen, to have that other time she'd promised.

There was nothing to do but drive and hope he found her.

■ ■ ■

The Wind River Reservation was one hundred miles away, and, like a homing pigeon too long away, Diego ached to be there. It hadn't been home for a long time, but it would always be home. He drove for hours, up to Pilot Butte and down the long, winding mountain road.

When he got as far north as Wyoming Highway 28 and the county line, he made a wide U-turn, leaving angry tire marks on the crumbling concrete. He wanted to press on to the reservation, hated that he couldn't. It was known to be the most violent reservation in the country, a place sadly familiar with brutal murder. But he couldn't chance it. He was still on parole and tied like a dog to the boundaries of Sweetwater County.

On the way south to Rock Springs was the small settlement of Reliance; he pulled into the gas station where his buddy, Troy, worked. Tucked behind the station was a fifth-wheel trailer. As he approached, there was the wild sound, like a rutting elk, of Troy's rhythmic snoring. No wonder he'd never had a woman in his bed. But besides Kimi, Troy was the only person Diego had encountered in his twenty-four winters of living that he would even consider trusting. They'd shared more than most men ever did in the strange, unwanted kinship of the sex offender group. That, and they shared the status of being the only two minorities in the group.

Troy could pass for white if you didn't notice the Asian eyes, surreal and startling, in his pale face. At first Diego had seen the guy as a mutt, but after a while things had taken another direction. Diego knew Troy would never share with the group. He doubted their group leader knew that.

Diego wanted only to rest for a minute, maybe indulge in a quick smoke to take the edge off the slicing panic of Kimi being gone. All it took was one rap on the door to wake his pal. After you've slept in jail, you never sleep deep again.

Troy turned the gas on under a pot of old coffee, made it good with a shot of some decent whiskey, and bent to light a blunt with the flame. He passed it to Diego.

"You first, brother."

When Diego took the blunt, Troy grabbed a blanket from the bed and draped it over his thermal underwear, then tossed another one at Diego.

"Colder than a witch's you-know-what in here. Drink up," he said, taking an extra hit straight from the pint bottle and handing it to Diego.

Diego threw back the shot and shivered in agreement. "That thing work?" he asked, pointing at the space heater in the corner.

"I'll spark her up for you. Don't like to chance dying in a fire in my sleep."

"No question why I'm here?"

"I figure you want me to know, you'll eventually spill it. If not, doesn't matter what I ask."

"That's why we're friends," Diego said, raising the bottle.

"Straight up," Troy said. "This coffee's piss. Can't remember when I made it, could be a week."

"You hear about my sister?"

"Kimi?"

"Only got the one."

"What, then?"

"It's all over TV and creation. She's missing."

Troy opened his arms angel-wing style. Diego caught a whiff of his underarms. "You see a TV anywhere? I got no use for the world and its fame and woes."

"Well, she's having her fifteen minutes right now."

"She left him?" Troy held his coffee mug up in a toast, made a beeline to the couch, and threw himself down.

"Why would you come out with that? Who says she's leaving him?" Diego asked. He opened the refrigerator. "Mind if I have some of this orange juice?"

"I heard some things," Troy said. "Help yourself—what's mine is yours."

Diego opened a quart of orange juice and drank from the bottle. "Who's talking?" He pulled an empty milk crate over to the couch and sat close to Troy's face. He felt hot—a combination of the toxic coffee, the whisky, and a flare of rage at Troy or anyone else who might be trash-talking his sister.

Troy sat up before he answered. "Cedric mentioned a few things. Bullshit or wishful thinking. Forget it. I never should have said anything."

"Was he running his mouth?"

"No need to lose it, my friend. The man worships your sister. Nothing was said in a bad way."

"I'm the judge," Diego insisted. "What was said? I want to know, need to know. It could be important. Seriously man, she's missing. He might know something that could help me find her. Bullshit or not, you have to tell me."

"Maybe you should talk to him yourself."

"Maybe you should finish what you started here." Diego felt his muscles tighten. He could take a swing, except he had no need to hurt Troy. All he wanted was to know what Cedric said, an end to this maddening back and forth.

"I knew this was a mistake," Troy said.

"Look at me," Diego said. He pointed both of his index fingers at his eyes. "Look into my eyes. I'm fucking serious. Don't make me do something here. I'm serious, man, what the fuck did he say to you?"

"Kimi wants out."

"Is that right? And how is it the two of you are talking about my sister's private business? Why would he tell you? You don't even know her!"

"Come on, man." Troy pushed up off the couch and past

Diego and stood in the kitchen. "I know Kimi. We've talked at your mom's place a couple of times. And Cedric's family, he knows whatever he tells me won't get spread around. As far as Kimi goes, he likes hearing himself talk about her. But I gave him a reality check and some tough love—told him not to get his hopes up. If she ever did leave her pretty-boy husband, she wouldn't be looking his way, the certified freak he is."

"When did this heart-to-heart take place? You never mentioned it to me."

"I can't recall. It's been a while since I saw Cedric. It wasn't relevant. And the way you are about her, I didn't want to stir anything up."

"It's relevant now she's missing. What do you mean about him being a freak?"

"The man has strange tastes. I've never known him to have a woman. I never said in the group who it was molested me when I was a kid. I didn't want to give up his name, but Cedric—he messed with all the nieces and nephews. Nobody said anything. I don't like this." Troy turned his head away, but not before Diego noticed his eyes had filled with tears. "Now you know," Troy said and gave a two-finger salute.

"I need to find her," Diego said.

"I'm going to tell you something else. But you have to promise you won't tear out of here destroying folks and landing yourself inside."

"Don't hold back. I need to know everything."

"Don't go off half-cocked," Troy pleaded.

"Tell me what you know."

"I don't know anything, for certain. Remember, this is Cedric's version of reality. Take it for what it's worth."

"I got it. Now tell me."

"Take a close look at the sheriff."

"Bullshit." Diego stood up abruptly. "That'll be the day. Kimi's got more sense than to go for a man like Scruggs, or any lawman."

"I'm on the clock in two hours. Got to catch some beauty sleep. Stay as long as you want."

Troy turned off the space heater and made his way back to bed.

CHAPTER 13

Marla told me she'd scheduled Kevin Cahill into a time I normally reserved for paperwork. He was frantic and insisted on seeing me as soon as possible.

Kimi had brought him to a session with the hope it would help him understand her dissociation. He had found credit card receipts for travel expenses out of town, and when told she didn't remember being in any of those places, he'd accused her of having an affair. That was in October, and much was still to happen. *Arrogant* was the word that came to mind when I thought of Kevin Cahill. In the waiting room that day, he rose so slowly from his chair I thought he was injured. It was like watching the glacial unwinding of a boa constrictor. His handshake had a matching coldness. In the consultation room, he took Kimi's usual place in the middle of the couch and sat with his arms on his thighs. He had large hands for a small man; his long fingers were splayed open on his knees, ready to make a point.

Kevin took his time and appraised the room. He didn't look me in the eye, which could signal poor social skills, evasion, or arrogance. His body was physically relaxed, not something seen often in a psychotherapy office. Most people experience some level of anxiety at the first meeting. He looked bored, and nothing in the room got his attention.

Kimi sat huddled in one corner of the couch, and he sat well away from her, taking center stage. They looked like strangers waiting for a bus. Nothing passed between them. He never touched her once as I explained the clinical symptoms she was experiencing and the possible psychological issues underlying them. The whole time, Kimi protected herself with folded arms and kept her eyes on the distance. I thought she might dissociate right there in the office. Kimi didn't feel she was safe with her own husband, and it was easy to see why. He was a man who didn't recruit people; no smile, no sign of interest.

In an earlier session, Kimi had said, "Kevin demands to be loved. To him, it's a birthright."

Before meeting Kevin, I got Kimi's permission to share her trauma history with him. She was wary because she feared he might use it against her, but without knowing what she'd been through, I knew he'd never understand why she developed dissociative symptoms. It was a hard sell. Kimi hadn't even wanted him to know she was in therapy before now.

As I told Kevin about her childhood, Kimi tentatively placed her hand in the space between them on the couch. Kevin didn't reach out. When I finished talking, he raised his platinum blond eyebrows like a skeptical customer impatient for the good part of the deal. It was quiet in the room for a long time.

"You can fix this, right?"

"That's why I'm in therapy," Kimi said.

"Always freaked out about ending up like your mother, and now it's happening."

He turned his wedding ring around and around. Kimi looked like she was about to bolt out of the office. She was a survivor. Her fight-or-flight reflexes were kicking in.

How did the two of them manage intimacy with his narcissism and her hypervigilance?

"That didn't take long," Kimi said, her voice flat, defeated.

"Fair question, though?" Kevin asked and looked at me.

I explained the difference between posttraumatic stress disorder, which was based in experience, and schizophrenia, which was a biological brain illness. I described the treatment process, interventions, and rates of progress.

"Kimi's symptoms are stress related. They're not common—only about three percent of people in outpatient therapy have them—but they are treatable, and definitely not psychotic or crazy."

"You're guaranteeing she won't end up like her mother?"

"Kimi's problems fall in the neurotic spectrum of mental disorders. I've been told her mother is diagnosed with schizophrenia, which is a psychotic disorder—different diagnosis, different causes, and different prognosis. Posttraumatic stress disorder does not develop into schizophrenia. Kimi's psychological structure is different than her mother's. She's not schizophrenic. We'd know by now."

"Explain this: How come she got worse after talking to you?"

"It often happens that way. In psychotherapy, patients look more deeply into things that have caused them pain. The process can be painful, and as more memories are uncovered and defenses against the pain weaken, existing symptoms can intensify and new symptoms can appear. It's part of the process. Eventually, it leads to healing."

"This is quite a gig you've got here. People come to you with problems and leave in worse shape? How do you stay in business? If I went to my doctor with a broken bone and he made it worse, you can bet I'd be filing a malpractice suit."

"Sometimes the bone needs to be rebroken before it can heal correctly."

I was dumbing it down, anything to help him get it. His support could end up making a difference in whether Kimi continued this treatment she so desperately needed.

"This is different, Kevin," Kimi broke in. "You've never been in therapy. That's why I wanted you to meet Dr. Hunt, so she could explain it better than I could."

"Sign me up," Kevin said.

No wonder Kimi had sought out a lover, I later thought when she told me about the affair. Her husband had no empathy.

But what did Kevin want now? The chimes of the grandfather clock in the waiting room rang four times. I went out to greet him.

Kevin wore expensive ski clothes; every piece of his clothing was marked with a famous logo. A perk of his business as a back-country ski guide? Or just vanity?

He settled into the middle of the couch and carefully removed three layers of clothing. When he got down to black latex ski pants, he stopped. He kept his ski hat on.

"I found this in the closet with her Christmas shopping. I'm wearing it until she comes back. It's a tribute," he said, tapping the red wool at his temple. "I never wear this color. It's Kimi's signature color."

The room felt empty without Kimi.

Kimi had been missing for days. To my knowledge, she'd never had a dissociative episode last this long. Still, it was possible Kimi was in a full fugue state—one in which she had lost all memory of her life. Possible, but not likely.

Kevin leaned back into the couch, arms up, hands in fists, first one and then the other hitting the wall behind him. It wouldn't take much to do real damage with those hands.

"You wanted to see me."

"You know she's gone, right? Of course you do. Everyone knows. I can't believe it though."

"She," not "Kimi," not "my wife," I noted silently. "Yes," I said. "I know."

In psychotherapy as in design, less is more.

"Isn't this where you ask me how I feel?"

Kevin wanted something. He wouldn't have come here otherwise. I decided to wait him out. That was a skill that required patience and self-control, but after years of practice, I had it locked down.

"I'm pissed off," he finally said. "I can't go anywhere without reporters and newspeople at my heels."

I'd seen him on television as I drank my coffee and waited for the Jeep to thaw. It hadn't looked like he was bothered by the attention. Close by his side was a muscular young woman. It had to be Tracy, the woman Kimi worried about. She emitted an animal attractiveness with her lion's mane of hair and focused predator eyes. When Kevin walked away from the interviewer, Tracy followed, claiming him with her hand on his bicep, the small of his back, briefly on his cheek. In all her movements, there was a sense of stealth and ease, like something wild maneuvering a tended garden, owning it. If Kimi were watching, she would surely know the woman's intentions.

"How can I help?" It had been only a few minutes, but already I was bored. Boredom, the true diagnostic test for narcissism.

"I don't need your help. She does. But apparently, she's not getting it. Apparently, she had another one of those dissociating things, or whatever. What the hell happened, Doctor? I thought she was coming here so you could fix her."

The first sign of life on Planet Kevin.

"When was the last time you saw Kimi?"

"That's the question. Same question the sheriff asked me. This is confidential, right? Because I didn't tell him the truth, but I'll tell you. Are you ready? *I can't remember.* I mean, besides the two minutes I saw her on Thursday night. Sucks for me. We've been kind of separated. Did Kimi tell you? I wouldn't be surprised if she didn't. You don't know her like I do. She doesn't always tell the truth. Have you figured that out? We had a screaming match on the phone Thursday night. Against my better judgment, I went home and we kept at it. She took off. I thought she'd come back, but she didn't. So I gave in and texted her, but she didn't text back. That got me mad all over again, so I took off too. I haven't seen or talked to her since. And I have a lot of questions, Doctor. Where did she go? I want you to tell me everything you know about my wife."

"I can't talk about Kimi's treatment."

Kimi had been clear about what she would let me tell her husband. Only historical material. All the current stuff was "off the record," Kimi's own words.

"I'm not just anybody. I'm her husband. Doesn't that mean anything? Do I need to get the sheriff? Will you talk to me if I haul the sheriff in here?"

Kevin stood up and bounced on his feet several times. He started pacing in circles, looking agitated, possibly on the verge of a panic attack. His face was flushed. He grabbed his hat to fling it off, then stopped himself—tribute. He pulled it back down, leaving some stray blond hairs sticking out at the bottom. He shoved his fists under his armpits to keep from punching something.

I kept the Beretta Nano in the top drawer of the table to the left of my chair. Five seconds to draw, point, and shoot. It was there for a reason—for people like Kevin. People who lose it.

"Until there's evidence a crime has been committed, I can't talk to anyone, not you and not the sheriff."

I decided not to tell him the sheriff had already tried.

"You talked a lot more when I was here the last time," Kevin said.

"At Kimi's specific request, I talked about her symptoms and the history that was the likely cause of her current symptoms so you'd know what she was dealing with and how therapy would help."

"The detective, Antelope—did you know he's Kimi's cousin? Go figure, small world, right? Maybe we caught a break there, and he'll try to find her. He said you might've been the last person to see her. Did she say anything about me?"

"I'm sorry, but I can't tell you that."

"Even if you know something that could tell us where she is?"

"What is shared in this room remains confidential."

"When I was here before, you wanted to help her."

"The last time, she was here."

He sat down, but it was an effort for him to stay still. "Did she tell you she was cheating on me?"

"We're finished here."

Kevin took a deep breath and blew it out. He stretched and put his fists under his arms again. "And just when it was getting interesting." He gave me a look that made me glad I had a gun just inches away.

I waited for him to see the session was over.

"So that's it? That's how it is? You're not going to give up his name. Even if it means saving her life?"

Minutes passed. He tried to stare me down. When it didn't work, he began putting on layers, getting ready to head out into the weather again. The sky darkened to a deep purple as the sun disappeared behind the mountain.

"Back to my volunteers," he said. "The whole town's rallying for my damn wife. Because she's gone, she's some kind of angel. What would they say if they knew her like we do? The Holiday Inn's donating the space. Drop by later. It's the place to be seen."

When the door closed behind him, it was as if he had never been in the room. Talking to him was like talking to a picture in a catalog, an image rendered in single dimension, too flat to contain the beating heart of a human.

Seconds later he pushed the door open and said, "You know who he is, the one she's been lying about. And he's the one who knows where my wife is. How will you live with yourself if she ends up dead?"

CHAPTER 14

By the afternoon, Antelope had a copy of Kimi's credit card receipts for the previous three months and the first three weeks of December. The card had last been used on Friday, December 17, at 8:30 P.M.—a twenty-four-dollar charge at the Get & Go Convenience Store in Reliance, five miles north of Rock Springs. Antelope was on his way to talk with the cashier who handled the purchase.

Five miles north of the city of Rock Springs, Reliance was a separate community with a population of six hundred, named for the Reliance Coal Mine. Paint curled off the weathered white shingles of the old storefront that housed the Get & Go Convenience Store. A closed-circuit television camera was mounted above the entrance and faced the single fuel island. Antelope hoped the tape from Friday night had not been erased.

The store, only about forty feet square, was crowded with sagging shelves. Tube lights blinked frantically from a low tile ceiling. On the back wall, a perspiring freezer worked hard to cool beer, milk, and soft drinks behind dewy doors. Lottery tickets from neighboring states and a variety of tobacco products lined the counter. The owner, Antelope thought, was likely a shrewd miner's descendant who was making sure the residents of Reliance didn't have to travel down to Rock Springs for necessities or pleasures.

The security alarm buzzed a sharp squawking sound when he opened the door. A woman who resembled Mrs. Claus sat on a stool behind the cash register, working the *Rocket Miner* crossword puzzle. She was dressed for the season in a red sweater, a halo of white hair under a Santa hat. As he got closer, he saw she had strange-colored eyes, the color of new pennies. Huge copper eyes magnified by bifocals in black frames.

From a television mounted high on a wall, K2TV shouted at rock concert level. Kimi's engagement picture graced the screen for a moment, like a butterfly, there and gone.

"Detective Antelope, Sweetwater County," he said, and placed his badge and ID on the counter in front of her.

She lifted her glasses and, squinting, looked him up and down.

Ever since he'd made detective and got to start wearing street clothes at work, he had gotten a thrill from seeing the surprised looks when he showed his badge. Today he was dressed in his fur-lined black leather coat and an Italian wool suit; the temperature was fixing to be brutal again, and before his day was over, it would be something minus zero for sure.

She offered him her right hand and said, "Clarice Johnson. What can I do for you?"

"I'm investigating the disappearance of Kimi Benally."

She tapped at the remote control and muted the television. In the sudden silence, dusty portable heaters wheezed and pinged.

"Too quiet," she said, and pressed the play button on a portable CD player. Patsy Cline singing "Crazy." She smiled. "That's better."

It was one of his favorites. The satin and sugar voice stirred something private; Cass came to mind.

He'd give anything not to be standing here talking to this woman about his missing cousin. For a moment, Antelope indulged his fantasy about living in a sweeter time, back when murder was for passion or money, before the term "serial killer" was created to describe the crimes of Ted Bundy and the other monsters who followed.

"We traced her credit card to this location," he said. "It was used here last Friday, the night she disappeared." When Clarice didn't say anything, he reminded himself he hadn't yet asked a question. "The purchase was made at 8:30 pm. Did you work that night?"

"I'm the day shift. That's way past my bedtime for sure. Early to bed, early to rise, etc., whatever. And now that you ask me, I recall I was off that day. I had a doctor's appointment up in Casper and couldn't travel back because of the storm. I didn't get back home until Saturday around noon. I went up there to see a special doc, got tested to see if I'm gluten sensitive, which I highly doubt. Always been able to eat anything, until recently, that is. The doc is threatening bypass if I don't slim down a bit. You can't tell these doctors anything anymore. They're all about their tests. But enough about me, you're not interested in me. I can see that."

"You spent the night in Casper?"

"Not my first choice for sure. Checked into the Economy Lodge Motel, which let me tell you, the name is not accurate at fifty-nine dollars plus tax for a night's sleep on a hard bed."

"I noticed you have a security camera out front. I'm going to need a copy of Friday's tape."

"It starts up the first of the month then resets itself. Hold on and I'll get it for you now. We're all about cooperating with the law."

She slid off the stool and disappeared through a louvre door into a closet-sized room packed tight with surplus. Outside, a red truck stopped at the pump, and the driver got out and began fueling. As he pulled away, Clarice came back and handed Antelope the tape.

"Might be kind of boring for you. We don't get much trouble out here."

"Who was working Friday night?" he asked.

She bent sideways, her long nails on a clipboard of curled pages—a handwritten work log. She inched it crab-like across the counter, using the most minimal effort possible. It was all Antelope could do to stop himself from grabbing it.

Clarice lifted up the frames of her glasses and set them back on her face again. She ran her index finger down the ledger and tapped at the name beside Friday's date.

"Troy Kinney. Four to midnight shift."

Antelope wrote the name in his notebook. He recognized the name and a red flag went up: Kinney. He was one of the county's registered sex offenders.

"Have you ever seen her in here before?"

"Her?" she asked, eyes on the television corner again.

"Kimi Benally," Antelope clarified. He had to do that much for her, make her real.

"Could be. I can't say for certain. I'm all business when I'm working. And I'm not into ladies. Now, *you* I'd remember." She swiveled her gaze back to him. "I'll tell you what happened. A girl like that, no doubt she had man trouble. She took off and left him. That's what I'd do if I wasn't happy with my man. You'll find her in Vegas if she hasn't already crossed the border, that's my two cents."

"Do you have a home address for Troy Kinney?"

Another slight head movement indicated a location in the general direction of the television.

"He lives out back. In the Airstream. It's our version of employee housing, you could say."

"This is your place?"

"Mine and my hubby, Daryl. It's all ours, and we've got the mortgage to prove it."

Antelope nodded. "Would I find him there now, Clarice?"

She turned her watch face toward him. The Mickey Mouse dial showed three forty-five.

"Alarm's going off as we speak. Wait on him a bit. He's due in at four, and he's never late. I can say that for him." Clarice rolled her eyes, indicating she had other things she could say.

"He's got a pretty short commute."

"That's a good one," she said. "I'll remember that one when it's time to raise the rent. Part of the benefit package, if you know what I mean."

Antelope wasn't feeling patient. He walked back to the Airstream and pounded on the aluminum door. The fifth-wheel trailer shook under his fist. He heard movement inside—clink of a belt buckle, boots on a vinyl floor, a smoker's cough, hacking and spitting, a toilet flushed—and then Troy Kinney was at the door, red-faced and scowling, angry at being hurried in his waking-up ritual. Half a foot shorter than Antelope, barrel chested and sturdy, he held his ground with pit bull confidence: shaved head, a stubble of dark beard, and hooded Asian eyes. In a red flannel shirt and denim overalls, he was a cross between Paul Bunyan and Buddha.

Antelope showed his badge and gave his name. He told him he was investigating Kimi's disappearance, and Kinney said, "What do you want from me?"

"I need to ask you a few questions."

"On my way out. Follow me."

Kinney pulled on a fur hat with earflaps, slammed the trailer door shut, and jumped the stairs. Antelope followed as he headed in the direction of the store. Behind them, clumps of ice dropped and shattered on the wooden steps. The day was turning bitter cold. Underfoot the pavement was slick. Kinney kept losing his footing like a new skater; his leather boots added a few inches in height, but they weren't made for the weather.

Behind the store, propane tanks and industrial-size dumpsters huddled together, pipes and wheels tethered in ice. If Antelope decided there was cause, it wouldn't take long to get a warrant to search the dumpsters.

At the door, Kinney stopped and said, "Talk out here. I've got five minutes before I clock in."

From an inside pocket he pulled out a cigarette and cupped it in his hand. He lost three matches to the wind before it lit.

"I cleared it with Clarice. She'll cover for you."

"I don't need anyone covering for me, or clearing things for me, either. What do you want to know?"

"You worked 4:00 P.M. to midnight last Friday?"

"You already know the answer. What do you want with me?"

"Did you see Kimi Friday night?"

"We established I was here working. I wasn't out seeing any women." Kinney took a long drag on his cigarette.

"She stopped for fuel here. You must have seen her."

"Kimi was here? That's news to me."

"Her credit card receipts put her here at eight thirty."

"She must have paid at the pump. No reason to come inside."

"Wouldn't she come in to say hello?"

"She didn't." Kinney tossed his cigarette and crossed his arms over his chest.

"How do you know Kimi?"

"Freezing my balls off," Kinney said and turned his back to the wild slapping wind.

Antelope indicated his white Cadillac sedan, taking up two spaces at the side of the store. On the far side of the lot, Kinney's Dodge pickup loomed, casting a feral shadow over the Airstream. "Yours or mine?" Antelope asked.

Kinney chose the Cadillac and walked toward it.

Inside the car, Antelope took off his leather gloves, turned on the heater, and cursed the crappy late-model heating system. He'd floor it on the ride back into town to get the juices flowing. The wind roared and cradle-rocked the big car.

"How did you meet Kimi Benally?"

"A friend introduced us," Kinney mumbled, his face turned to the window; he seemed to be going for bored, but Antelope sensed he was getting edgy.

"If I have to work this hard, we can do it at the station," Antelope said. He slapped his gloves on the steering wheel. "What's the friend's name?" he asked. He shifted the Cadillac into drive and hit the gas hard, releasing a blast of tropical air.

"Whoa . . . what the . . . Wait, wait . . . where are you going? I have work now."

Antelope hit the brakes and sent Kinney flying forward. He didn't get to play these power games too often, and he was enjoying it.

"You want to dance, we're going in," Antelope said.

"Her brother Diego's a buddy of mine. I've been to his house. Kimi comes by every once in a while."

"You're not trying to hide anything, are you? Like, maybe you've got something going with her, but Diego would take you down if he found out about it?"

Kinney gave him a look that Antelope had only ever seen on ex-convicts—a psychopathic mixture of contempt, self-hatred, and primal fear.

Antelope put the car back in park. "When was the last time you saw her?"

"Who?"

"Who else are we talking about? I'm done playing with you," Antelope said. His right hand moved toward the gearshift again.

Kinney put his hand out to stop him. "I can't say for sure. It wasn't here Friday night."

"Ballpark it . . . a year, a month, a week or less since you last saw her?"

"More like a week, maybe two."

"At her mother's house?

"That's what I said."

"You never saw her anywhere else?"

Kinney crossed his heart. "On my honor. Diego would kill me. I don't know the girl."

"Friday night's security tape. You sure I won't see you talking to Kimi?"

"I swear I never saw her here."

Kinney brought out the Marlboro pack and lit up. He cracked the window open an inch and tossed out the match. Smoke danced in a zigzag pattern before disappearing.

"So it's a coincidence your friend's sister was here Friday night. You might have been the last person to see her before she went missing. What will Diego do with that information?"

"I've got his back and he's got mine," Kinney said. "Diego knows who I am."

"Now would be the time to talk, if you know what I mean. I'm not just talking about Diego here. This is a respectable, married woman, a professional in the community. Everybody is going to want this woman back in her home fast. If you know anything could make that happen, you'd only be seen as a hero."

CHAPTER 15

Antelope sat across from Tracy Hopkins, Kevin Cahill's guide partner at Wyoming Backcountry Sports, in a booth at the Dairy Queen on Elk Street. He'd left Reliance hungry and wouldn't see the end of his workday for hours. She'd agreed to meet for an early dinner.

He ordered a chicken sandwich, fries, and a shake. Tracy said she didn't have much of an appetite, what with everything Kevin had going on.

The waitress brought their drinks, and he watched as Tracy drank down the super-sized sweet tea, her full red lips working the plastic straw like a porn star. Antelope could see how Kevin might be tempted by her Renaissance beauty—the wild mane of yellow curls, skin like cream, and those lips. She grabbed a handful of hair to tame it, shook it free again, and gave him an innocent girl-next-door smile. Something about the timing told him she was hiding something.

"It's going to snow," she said, giving her hair a tug and him a wink. "My hair always tells me." The pride of ownership was in her voice. "I was surprised when you called me."

"I have a few questions for you. It shouldn't take too long."

"Not a problem. I'm all yours, Detective. I was napping when you called, could you tell?" When he didn't answer, she took a deep breath and began again. "I was up early this morning to meet Kevin and the crew at the ballroom of the Holiday Inn. A sad way to spend the day, especially when we all planned to be in the backcountry. I hate to say it, but I know that's what all the crew thought. So selfish, none of us caring about Kimi, poor Kimi, and poor Kevin, too. At least I get to go home for Christmas Eve. By tomorrow afternoon, I'll be on a plane and out of here. I hate to leave Kevin all alone. But it's not like there's anything I can do here, beyond what I've already done, setting up the call center at the buttcrack of dawn. I sat there all day waiting for the phones to ring. The silence was kind of scary. At three o'clock I called nap time. And now here we are." She spread her hands out in a ta-da motion.

Liquid voice like bourbon on ice, lingering on vowels, the softening effect of money. Not as strong as Kevin Cahill's redneck country accent, but unmistakably the woman was from somewhere below the Mason-Dixon Line. "Where's home for you?" Antelope asked.

"Atlanta, Georgia, I'm proud to say. I'm a Georgia peach."

"Same area as Kevin Cahill?"

"Not far at all. I grew up in Atlanta proper. He's about twenty miles north in a suburb I can't remember the name of."

"Did you meet Kevin back in Georgia?"

"Let's say I knew 'of' Kevin." She made quotation marks with her fingers. "He's a little bit of a celebrity where we come from. Not too many of us are hardcore into mountain sports— small pond/big fish thingy. I was looking to get into guiding. Someone said try contacting Kevin, so I did, and voilà! I'm guiding! My dream come true! Networking rules, I guess you could say."

"How long have you worked with Kevin?"

"*For* Kevin," she corrected. "I'm his assistant, his second-in-command. This is my second season. I came out in October last year. We did the interview on Skype but didn't meet until I showed up for work. We came in on the same plane from Denver. He and Kimi had just gone away for their honeymoon . . . oh, here I am rambling and that poor thing is out there all alone and God knows where. So what's happening? I didn't get a chance to turn on the news. Rolled out of bed and into my clothes to get here on time. I know," she said, pulling her black fleece jacket away from her ample breasts and patting it down again, "my mother would have a fit if she saw me out in public like this. It's true, I've gotten lazy. I live in ski clothes now. That's Wyoming for you."

"The investigation's ongoing. So far there hasn't been anything definite to go on. What kind of boss is Kevin?"

"The best, bar none. Believe me, I've had my share of bad bosses. I lucked out with this one for sure. I call him my bad-ass boss because he's the best. Kevin loves what he does, and as long as you love it, too, and do what it takes to make it go the way it should—and by that I mean perfect, nothing but perfection for Kevin—you don't have a problem." Tracy snapped her fingers to summon the waitress. "I changed my mind. I'm going to have a Blizzard after all, make it Oreo, and some curly fries, please—hold on." She held up a finger and downed the rest of the tea, ran her tongue lazily over those lips, handed the empty glass to the waitress.

The girl picked up the glass with a practiced left hand, slid her right middle finger slowly over her eyebrow. She blushed when Antelope saw what she had intended to be a silent protest to Tracy's entitlement and hurried off to place the order.

"Sorry, I'm starving. Haven't eaten much since yesterday."

"How well do you know Kimi?" Antelope asked.

"I hardly know her at all. We've only met twice. The first time was at the airport. She was so happy and all focused on Kevin, whatever. I got it. And then at the end-of-the-season party last year. Oh, and I guess another time, too, a smaller thingy, in the summer sometime. But it was always just hello, how are you. Nothing else, nothing real."

"So you wouldn't have any ideas about where she might have gone or why?"

The waitress placed the Blizzard in front of Tracy, and she dug into the whipped cream topping like it was the first food she had seen in a month. When she was done she licked off a cream moustache and smacked her lips.

"Me? No idea. Sorry. I wouldn't know."

"Did Kevin talk about any problems in his marriage?"

She shook her head, and her curls scattered and rippled in a spray of gold light. "He's all business."

"Most people tend to share a little bit about their personal life at work, especially with the people they're close to."

"I guess that would be me. I mean, I know Kevin and I are close. But I honestly can't remember anything. I'm no help at all. I bet you're sorry you asked me to meet you." She grabbed a handful of hair and held tight.

"Tracy, at this point we have nothing to go on, not a single lead. If you know anything, you need to tell me. Kevin and Kimi fought the night before she disappeared. We know Kevin slept in his truck Thursday night."

"He told you?"

Antelope nodded and gave her a look that said nothing was more important than what she had to say and he would wait as long as she needed him to wait. Her eyes darted under lowered lids, back and forth, before she looked up at him, a little less certain and confident than before. What nerve had he just hit? It was a sign something wasn't right, and he'd learned to notice such things, trust them. Everything counted—subtleties, nuances, shades of gray, a hint or a whisper, all clues. He'd thought she'd been telling the truth when she said she didn't know anything, but now he wasn't so sure.

"You have to know Kevin to know that when he doesn't want to talk, he doesn't talk," Tracy said. "That mental strength he shows on the mountain? He's always that way. Like I said, he'd never talked to me about his marriage. If I hadn't found him sleeping in his truck Thursday night, I doubt he would have mentioned it at all."

"What time was it when you found him asleep in his truck?" Antelope asked, working hard to contain the kick he felt at this contradiction to Kevin's story.

Tracy shrugged. "I woke up and had to use the bathroom. That's when I noticed him parked under the pine tree. I pulled on boots and a jacket and went out to him. He was real upset. I'd never seen him like that before. That's when he told me that Kimi had left him. And he would have stayed out there all night alone, but I made him come in with me."

Clearly, Kevin had put a spin on the argument with Kimi and her walking out that he hadn't mentioned to Antelope when he told Tracy about it.

"That's tough news," he said. "How did he handle himself on the trip?"

"Kevin's a trooper. He threw himself into it like usual. He was in a great mood, living the life. Kevin comes alive in the wilderness— he's in his element. We skied the back country and camped for three glorious days. Then we got the radio call to come back down."

"How did he react?"

"Not well. He didn't know what it was about. The office said the sheriffs would be waiting and to come down quick. Everyone was all confused, and no one was happy, that's for sure. Kevin and all of us, completely bummed out. But we had no idea how bad it was. Poor Kimi—and poor Kevin. They always look at the husband first. That's what Kevin said. Is that true?"

Antelope nodded and slid a notebook and pen across the table. "I'm going to need your Atlanta contact information in case I need to reach you."

CHAPTER 16

At 4:00 P.M. the night closed in like a cave. Before Diego set out on another mission, he walked two lanes over to borrow his cousin Moxie's car. Diego didn't want his little silver GTO in the sheriff's rearview mirror.

From the couch, high on weed and deep into *Grand Theft Auto*, his cousin tossed him the keys.

The Pinto rode like a jumpy colt; it was a shaken and stirred ride that threatened to spin Diego's anxiety into the danger zone. The three quick Red Bulls for dinner weren't helping either, but he had to stay alert. He couldn't indulge in real rest until he found her.

It was a good cover car, though, with a quiet motor and a flat-black primer finish that disappeared into the gloom of night— perfect for prowling. Moxie hadn't even asked him why he wanted the car. *You can always trust a stoner not to care.*

He couldn't leave the county without permission as long as he was on probation, and he'd had to find a way to stand being haltered in pasture like a broken horse.

When he got out of prison, all he'd wanted to do was drive. He got stopped a lot those first sweet cruising nights. With his name newly added to the sex offender registry, the local cops smelled fresh meat. They enjoyed making the point they knew who he was and all the no-good he was capable of. It didn't matter what he was guilty of: making love to his underage girlfriend, something most of them did for fun back in the day.

But things went different for this Native and the white girl he'd wanted. He'd done three years at the Riverton Farm, Wyoming's medium-security prison, for having consensual sex with Charlene, who was fifteen at the time of his arrest, too young by Wyoming law to consent. They'd gone at it for months, crazy in young love, until her old man noticed—and damned if it wasn't right after Diego had turned eighteen.

At first he thought he'd lose his mind, locked up for no reason that made any sense in his world. He loved Charlene, and she'd given every sign she loved him. But she didn't wait for him. Instead she married the part-time help at her father's auto body shop. A white dude a few years older than Diego, it turned out. But he put a ring on it, and that was what mattered in the end.

Learning about it in lockup, he felt himself dropping like a rock into deep water. When he got out, he went looking for her, needing to see her walking through her life without him and being okay with that. He watched her house, waiting for a chance to catch her alone—but his luck clearly hadn't gotten any better, because her old man was watching *him*. He caught a voyeurism charge and landed back at the Honor Farm for another full six months. Worse, when they sprang him, the combined charges added up to a Level One Sex Offender label for life.

He thought of his time inside as his education for life—not quite a badge of honor but a definite rite of passage. Now he was serious, a man schooled in everything he needed to know about making his way in the world. But by far, the most important thing he knew was how not to go back inside.

Lockup taught him the world was a series of walls and fences, and he knew what side he wanted to be on. Any place could be a prison; it was the mind that trapped or freed you. He'd never been a rule follower, but by the end of his time inside he knew that following rules made you invisible, and invisible was another word for free.

Soon, his parole would be over. He welcomed the end of his weekly aftercare group, which was just a couple hours of shooting the shit with other ex-cons, all of them lost and falling into trouble. Ordinary guys who'd been unlucky enough to pull a blend of bad genes, bad luck, and bad choices—a toxic cocktail that had landed them on the broken-down side of human. He felt for all the sad stories that led to sad endings.

A few of them, though, had been born sick, and no one had figured out how to fix them yet. The doctor said it wasn't their fault; still, Diego had trouble relating to guys who got turned on by little kids. Charlene had been young the first time they did it, but she was no child—and Diego had been young too. This past year, they'd had a rapist in the group. Diego had stared the guy down and wouldn't talk during the two sessions he was in attendance. His mind had filled with images of Kimi meeting up with that pervert every time he saw him.

The group never knew why the rapist was sent back to prison. *Good riddance*, Diego thought, and gave a thumbs-up to the group leader, Dr. Hunt, when she delivered the news. He would be glad not to look into those dark places every Tuesday night. Dr. Hunt always pushed for self-disclosure, but he kept his own stuff boxed tightly inside.

Diego thought about Kimi and the way her job might have brought her to the attention of the sicko who was raping local women. He rolled down the window and felt the scrape of arctic blast. He had to pee; he used a milk carton to relieve himself. Would the sheriff ever take a break? They'd been cruising in the Christmas shopping traffic for an hour already. The guy drove like a restless bat, weaving tight circles and quick, tilting detours. Diego might need Dramamine if he kept it up.

It had been a useless tail. It was a crazy idea, the sheriff and his sister, him grabbing her and stashing her away somewhere. Troy and Cedric had got it wrong. Had to be. So what if Kimi had been seen talking to Scruggs? She was a reporter on the police beat. It was work and nothing more. So why was he following Scruggs?

What if her whack-job husband thought different? Could Kevin lose it big-time? Maybe. With the right motivation. Kimi was a star and a prize. Kevin didn't want to lose her. And Diego didn't know a guy who wasn't capable of killing, given the right circumstances.

CHAPTER 17

When I left the office, crimson and violet flares were lighting up the wide sky. White Mountain cast an indigo shadow over the Western Addition homes below. I drove home in the twilight as the day surrendered to shadows and secrets.

Home was a brown-shingled ranch in the curve of a cul-de-sac, square and compact, built at the edge of a steep shale ledge overlooking an older section of Rock Springs. Many houses in the city, including this one, were built over abandoned mine shafts, vulnerable to subsidence cave-in. But my house sliding down the hill and landing in pieces on Elk Street wouldn't be the worst thing that ever happened to me. The possibility didn't bother me, because I no longer believed in security.

Besides, I liked that forty feet below, the two main thoroughfares of the city intersected and carried commuters across and out of town for the ten-minute rush hour at the end of the workday. The view of all those lights at night was worth the risk.

I'd found this place a year and a half earlier, and now the sprawling, hardscrabble town was home. The city was laid out in concentric tree rings, making it possible to date the age of the houses. Small miner's cottages, trailer courts, modular tract houses, and log cabin mansions sat side by side with drive-through chain restaurants, auto parts stores, and grocery superstores. It was a boom-and-bust oil town without charm or glamour, plain and steadfast, with nowhere to hide.

I poured cowboy coffee in a glass mug and added a shot of whiskey and heavy cream. I headed to my study on the sunporch at the back of the house—a room built on wooden pilings set into the hillside overlooking town—lit the gas stove, and wrapped myself up in a woolen blanket in the leather chair, the one piece of furniture I'd moved from Cambridge. Outside was the familiar sound of the wind. The houses and lanes below resembled a village of toy blocks, scattered and forgotten. On any other night, it would be a peaceful place.

But I couldn't get Kimi's last session out of my head.

She'd been afraid in the last session. She'd twirled her hair and bitten her nails. *All the way home I felt something out there, coming for me, following me.*

I shivered remembering her words. Outside, in the dark of night, everything was hidden, lost in the shadows. *Was* someone following her? Over the last few weeks, Kimi had become increasingly anxious and had dissociated more frequently.

I could relate to the dread and paranoia Kimi felt. Because of that, I worked hard to keep my own issues out of the therapy room. Before I knew the truth about Zeke's betrayal, I felt paranoid. But the sense of danger lurking had been confirmed in the end. It wasn't paranoia, was it, when the threat was real?

Kimi had stopped seeing her mystery man months ago. Kevin had been suspicious. He could have hired someone to follow her. Kimi wasn't happy in her marriage. *Did she take the easy way out and drive away?*

Kimi had never spoken the name of her lover. "This is about me," she said. "He's just a man who has my heart. I owe him his privacy."

I sipped Irish coffee and looked at the frozen wilderness spreading out beyond the city limits of Rock Springs. Could Kimi be out there somewhere, watching things unfold, waiting for the right time to return? She'd been missing for five days. She'd never had a dissociative episode last so long before, but that didn't mean it was impossible.

Who was Kimi's lover? Was he worried about her? Was he

missing her? Had they run away together, leaving their unhappy marriages behind? Was she planning to meet him on Friday night after her session? Did things go wrong between them? It wouldn't be the first time a lover turned violent, killing someone who couldn't be kept.

All through the evening a hard wind raged, rattling the windows, unsettling my nerves. At ten o'clock I went to bed and closed my eyes to the sound of wind, like wolves at the door. But just after midnight I woke up, lonely and uneasy in the quiet house. An hour later, when it was clear I wasn't going to sleep again, I decided to make productive use of the time. I got out of bed, put sweats and boots on over my pajamas. The middle of the night was a perfect time to review the sex offender files before the profiling session at the parole office in the morning."

I still wrote therapy notes in longhand. The idea of consigning patients' thoughts to an electronic medical record was something I planned to put off for as long as I could. I pressed the remote starter and waited ten minutes while my Jeep warmed up enough for the five-minute drive to the office.

When I slid into the driver's seat, the dashboard's digital clock showed the time and date: "1:10 AM 12/22."

I was staring at Zeke's death date.

I felt it like a punch to the gut. How could I have forgotten? I remembered to breathe, pictured Soldier in his winter pasture, and in a few minutes I was back where I needed to be. Overhead, stars on fire and a polished moon like a rare pearl. I might never leave this place.

■ ■ ■

The gray-shingled building was hidden in the shadows of the tall black pines behind it, only the casement windows shone like silver mirrors in the moonlight. Across the road was the modern campus of Western Wyoming Community College, where everything was in darkness, all the buildings deserted for the Christmas break.

I parked, and as I approached the front door, my footsteps cued the halogen security lights. My key wouldn't turn in the lock, and I realized the door was already unlocked. Someone had been careless. In the morning, I'd have Marla check with the other offices to see who had forgotten to lock up. We'd talked about installing a security camera, but so far, no one had taken any action.

I flipped the switch for the fluorescent lights, and the hallway turned bright as a beach at noon. My office was the last one on the left, a large corner suite facing Hilltop Drive. When I reached my office, the door was open.

My heart went wild. I had locked up for the night; I knew I had.

Darkness and silence waited on the other side of the door. I held my breath, my heart loud in my chest. The last time I'd walked into a quiet office alone at night, I'd found Zeke dead. I knew I shouldn't go in.

With a slight push the door swung open into the still room. The light from the corridor showed everything as I'd left it. I closed and locked the door behind me. Moonlight showed empty chairs, undisturbed in the waiting room. Marla's desk behind the glass partition was neat, all its drawers locked up tight. But when I switched on the gooseneck lamp, the reason for the break-in hit me in the face. All the drawers of the file cabinets were open; a mess of papers was on the floor.

From the back of the building a low sound came—a soft click—as the emergency door closed, eased into place by a careful hand. I killed the lights and got down on the floor. Outside there was a low growl, the sound of a big engine catching. Through the window a large truck escaped with a cargo of silver light. It traversed the arc of Hilltop Drive and sped down into the desert with its running lights off, wrapped in the camouflage of night.

The flashback hit me like the trailer for a horror movie. Monsters on a speeding carousel with no off switch. The images merged into one dark entity that circled the room. The circling thing had claws. I was burning hot and dizzy. I stumbled to the bathroom and shoved my wrists under cold water. I filled the basin, took a deep breath, and sank my face into the icy water. I held it as long as I could and came up gasping for air. It was a test

I'd devised for times when I thought I didn't want to live. Faced with imminent death from drowning, I chose living every time.

In the mirror, my face was red and swollen, wet with tears and water. I let the water drain out and away. I now lived on the western side of the Continental Divide; the water swirled counterclockwise, as governed by the laws of physical science. It was gone to join a river, become the ocean, a floating cloud, and then to be released as cleansing rain to do it all again. The simplicity of this endless cycle brought me some peace.

WEDNESDAY
DECEMBER 22

CHAPTER 18

I called Beau Antelope because the truth was, I didn't trust anyone else. It took him less than five minutes to get to me. He was all business, immediately called for the crime scene techs to come. We both knew this was no random break-in.

After the forensic crew completed their work, I made a quick search of the files and discovered that Kimi Benally's file was missing. It would take hours to sort through every file and determine if anything else had been taken. But one thing was certain: the thief believed there was something in Kimi Benally's records that he—or she—wanted to keep hidden.

I locked up the office and was back in the Jeep headed home to give sleep another try when Antelope called and invited me to join him for breakfast at the Village Inn. I knew I should say no and put a stop to any thoughts he might have of rekindling a friendship. But I was hungry, and knew I wouldn't be able to sleep after the disruption of the break-in.

The Village Inn stayed open all night and catered to the oil field crowd—stacks of pancakes and sausage, steak and eggs, fuel for the working man's day. Crystal, the night waitress, raised the sunglasses she always wore and said, "It's been a while since I've seen the two of you in here."

"Hello, Crystal," Antelope said. "We'll have two specials with the house coffee."

It was one of the things I found annoying about Antelope. He was always quick to make assumptions.

"Orange juice for me, please," I said. "I haven't slept yet and I'm not ready to give up on the idea. And I'll have oatmeal instead of the special, thanks."

Outside, giant snowflakes twirled in a slow, lazy pattern.

"Do you believe this?" I said and pointed outside.

"It's looking to be a hard winter."

I met Antelope in the crushing cold last winter, my first Wyoming winter. He'd shared his survival strategy: an annual February road trip to Mexico, an easy overland trip. The drug dealers did it all the time. I closed my eyes and pictured myself on a beach, and I immediately felt warmer.

"Are you falling asleep on me?" Antelope asked.

"Borrowing your coping mechanism and hallucinating a Mexican beach."

"Works for me," he said, and held his coffee cup up. "To breakfast. What can you tell me about my missing cousin?"

"You know the answer to that. But in case you've forgotten, I can't tell you anything. Everything I know I learned in psychotherapy sessions, which makes it all privileged communication."

"Different rules in my work. I can tell you everything I know. Unfortunately, everything amounts to nothing right now. She didn't leave a trace. The sheriff wants to focus on her husband. I disagree. It's too soon to narrow the field."

I suspected as much. The news would have had it if there'd been anything new.

"Have you met Kevin Cahill?" he asked.

I nodded. "It's hard to imagine Kevin getting his hands dirty."

"Agreed. What else can you tell me about him?"

"I've already said more than I should."

"I'll have a court order tomorrow. You'll have to talk to me then, Doc."

"Bad timing on the records, though, burglar beat you to it. Someone suspects I know something incriminating. I wish they'd let me in on it."

"Any other records taken?"

"I can't say for sure. I'll tackle that tomorrow and let you know."

We had slipped back into a familiar sparring cadence I remembered from working together in the early stages of the rape investigation, trading "sound bites." The man was as guarded as I was, careful not to give too much away. It would make intimacy tough going.

I stopped that thought from developing. This was business.

"Off the record, Doc, what are your thoughts?"

"Given my relationship with the missing woman, there is no 'off the record' for me."

He waved his napkin. "Okay, white flag. How's the oatmeal? Big tip for Crystal today— pancakes have never been better."

He held out his forkful of pancake dripping with syrup. I didn't take the bait. He smiled and popped it into his mouth. If I'd been trying to get to him, it wasn't working. The man had too much confidence. It bothered me.

"You said Sheriff Scruggs considers Kevin a suspect?"

"It's a little too soon to get single-minded, but I have some inside information, family gossip mostly, that supports his view."

"Isn't that a conflict of interest for you?"

"I'll work my way through it, pull out if I need to. Her mother and mine are sisters. Estella likes the Whirlwind story. It's an Arapaho legend I pulled into service to save Kimi from the haters and bullies who said she was crazy."

Estella had told me this, but I couldn't disclose this to Antelope; my psychological evaluation of Estella, like my treatment of Kimi, was confidential.

"Speaking of conflict of interest, would you be comfortable coming in as a consultant on this case? It would be great to have your help."

"I don't know. I'll give it some thought. She's my patient. And there are other complications and relationships to consider."

Kimi's brother, Diego, was in the sex offender group I worked with. That made three members of one family I had a professional relationship with. Licensed psychologists are scarce in rural Wyoming, and because of that the usual standards of practice had to be relaxed.

"Sleep on it. Maybe we'll all get a surprise and she'll come home soon," Antelope said and quickly looked away. "I hate the thought of her lost out there. It won't quit snowing."

"So you protected Kimi?"

"She's my little cousin, seven years between us. There wasn't anyone else to do it. Diego was a scrawny mutt, not up to fighting her battles. That part came later." He sighed. "If Kimi doesn't turn up soon, this thing will blow up big. It isn't the first time a pretty wife disappeared before Christmas. Echoes of the Laci Peterson case, circa 2000. Except Kimi's not pregnant—at least as far as I know—so no extra media points there."

I noticed the careless, offhand way Antelope was talking about Kimi and thought he must be defending against all the sadness and worry he must be feeling about his cousin.

"So why is the sheriff so focused on Kevin?"

"Scrugg's hell-bent on keeping the department from becoming the media's Christmas present. Kevin's already lied to us. He told us he slept in his truck in back of The Astro Lounge on Thursday night, but his guide partner said he slept at her place."

Again, I thought that Kimi had been right to worry about Kevin and Tracy.

"It makes sense the sheriff would be suspicious."

"If the regional media picks up the story, it could mean a lot of exposure for you as her therapist. Are you ready for that?"

"Show me a court order, Detective."

"That was a personal question," he said.

Fatigue hit like a hammer. My patient was missing. Someone had broken into my office. The cold hand of panic gripped the muscles in my back. I had to get to my bed fast, pull the covers over my head, and try to shut it all out.

"I'm not ready to go there, Detective."

"Still in love with your Appaloosa?" he asked, changing the subject.

"Soldier's great. I don't know how I made it thirty-five years without a horse. It's a different life. He's in winter pasture at Marla and the sheriff's place up near Lander."

"You ride up there?"

"I'm on that horse as often as I can be."

"Equine therapy, that's what you called it, right? Doesn't surprise me. I've known horses to have healing powers. I could tell you some stories. Get close enough to them, you get changed. We don't have a name for it on the reservation, but the magic happens anyway."

"Riding gave me my life back. Like a miracle. I can't explain it, but I'll take it."

I was doing it again, oversharing with this man I hadn't spoken to in six months—this man who had the ability to get me talking when I didn't want to talk. That's what had made me pull away from him back then. He seemed like a trustworthy man, but unfortunately, I'd decided never to trust a man again. It wasn't worth the risk.

"Are you doing okay?"

"I'm doing fine, Detective."

"I wanted a friend. Thought you did too, then you shut down."

"I didn't shut down. I had nothing more to say. And can we not do this, please? My patient is missing, my office is trashed, and my records are gone. I'm running on empty."

"I guess I was wrong. I thought it meant something when you opened up to me about why you came out here."

"That was a bad decision on my part. You know some facts. You don't know me. I apologize for dumping my baggage on you last year. You caught me at a bad time. I've regretted it ever since."

"Thanks for clearing that up."

"I'm sorry if that sounded harsh."

We ate in silence. I didn't like the sudden tension that settled between us, but it was preferable to anything else that might be said. It wasn't his fault I had absolutely no faith left in the male half of the human species.

"Time to say goodnight, Detective. I'm heading up the hill before it turns to black ice."

"You going to be all right alone?"

"Mind your business, Detective Antelope."

I didn't mean to be cold to him—he was trying to be nice—but I didn't want him getting too close. It was a fine line, and as tired as I was, the effort needed to hold the line was irritating my frayed nerves.

"Your welfare is always my business. At your service, courtesy of Sweetwater County."

"Alone is good. I'll be okay. I need to get some sleep."

"Call if you need anything."

Crystal came over and slapped the check on the table.

I grimaced. "I ran out without my wallet."

"We'll put it on the county tab," he said. "If I'm lucky, you'll be on the payroll soon anyway."

I told him he didn't have to, but Antelope followed me home anyway, up the steep, snowy road to the subdivision and into the cul-de-sac. Behind the house, ice-blue light edged the eastern horizon. A new day was coming; the world wouldn't stop. In the rearview mirror, I watched the Cadillac make a slow circle, then roll away.

I walked through the silent house, not bothering to turn on any lights, enjoying the soft tones of dawn coming in at the windows. I headed straight to the back of the house, drawn by the magnetic pull of my bed.

But the house was freezing. Cold air blew in through the open French doors to the study. Inside, shattered glass, snow, and white papers on the floor.

Another flashback. Zeke on the office floor. I shook my head, scattering the images, erasing the bloody scene.

Whoever had come in had tossed every file and left disappointed. There was nothing of Kimi's in here, nothing about any patient. But of course, whoever wanted my files wouldn't know that.

I called Antelope. He was barely out of the subdivision, so it didn't take long for him to get back. He made a quick report while I packed up a few things, and followed me back down College Drive and over to the Holiday Inn, where I checked into a room as the day shift was arriving for work. I'd been awake for over twenty-four hours. I handed over my credit card and paid for a bed behind a locked door.

I left Marla a message that I was closing the office for the next few days because of the break-in and asked her to call and reschedule patients to the following week. I turned off my cell phone and unplugged the landline.

The blackout curtains did their job. In the absolute dark, I was invisible, unreachable, and safe. I wanted instant sleep, and I wanted to know who was after my notes.

The break-ins hit me hard; they were a menacing violation, one that set me back. No one had the right to my therapy notes. My patients trusted me to keep safe their private thoughts and conflicts, the difficult situations in their lives. That's why I recorded only the barest elements necessary to be in compliance with professional standards. In all likelihood, if Kimi didn't return, the sheriff's department would go for a subpoena, but now I had no file to surrender. Whoever this thief was, they thought my notes contained something incriminating.

I fell asleep wondering what I'd missed.

CHAPTER 19

Antelope had been seeing too much of the station and not enough of his bed. After dealing with the break-ins at Pepper Hunt's office and home, he managed to get two hours of sleep before heading back to the station. That was what was required, working a case like this. But the fact it was happening during Christmas added another layer of misery for all concerned. He wouldn't make it over to Ethete on the Wind River Reservation to see his family for the holiday, that was certain. He'd miss his mother's wild game stuffing and fry bread.

His mother. She usually gave him a hard time about his long hours. He had a job to do, and it came first. She always said he was married to his job, and she wasn't off the mark. But this time the work involved finding someone so close, a member of his own family, and she hadn't said a word about him working too much this time.

It had been a while since he and Kimi had been close; still, it cut to the bone that she was gone. He understood the whole family was counting on him. His shoulders ached from the tension he carried, the physical weight of the enormous responsibility, like a buffalo robe pressing down.

He went straight to the sheriff's office. Scruggs looked as tired as Antelope felt, with dark circles under bloodshot eyes. A pot of oily black sludge was heating on the two-burner stove. Scruggs poured himself a cup and offered some to Antelope, who shook his head and held up his Starbucks travel mug. Scruggs reached into a greasy brown bag and pulled out two glazed doughnuts. Antelope declined again.

"When Marla asks why my sugar's up, I'll blame you," Scruggs said and bit into a chocolate doughnut. "You look like crap."

"I was up most of the night dealing with a burglary at Dr. Hunt's office."

"Someone looking for drugs? Office in a medical building is a prime target for that. How'd you get involved?"

"She called me from her office just after midnight. It wasn't drugs they wanted. For one thing, she's a psychologist. She doesn't prescribe medication. Hers was the only office in the whole medical complex that was hit."

"It's not like anyone would know she didn't have drugs in there. To your average layperson, especially your average dumb criminal, a doctor's office equals drugs. What was she doing at the office at that time of night?"

"She went to work on some files and interrupted the burglar. She saw a truck leave the parking lot, black pickup. She didn't get the license plate."

Scruggs was working on the second doughnut now. "I'm Dreaming of a White Christmas" played on a radio in the squad room. Antelope thought that was one dream he could count on coming true. Bringing Kimi home, on the other hand, wasn't looking too promising.

"But there's another thing makes it clear it wasn't a random break-in or someone looking for drugs. A few hours later, there was a break-in at her home. And both times the main focus was her files. Crime scene units secured the sites, pictures and prints were taken inside and outside both buildings. Dr. Hunt will do a thorough check of both premises today and let me know if she finds anything missing. When she looked last night, the only thing missing was Kimi Benally's file."

Scruggs opened a drawer, found a bottle of antacid tablets, and popped a handful in his mouth. "That's a lot of effort for one file," he said as he crunched the pills. "What do you make of that?"

"Whoever took the file believes there's something incriminating in there, possibly something that could link them to Kimi's disappearance."

Scruggs swept crumbs and sugar into the bakery bag and tossed the bag with an overhand shot into a wastebasket across the room.

"Good shot," Antelope said.

"Still got it. I could use a few hours on the court."

"Name the time, I'll be there," Antelope said, though he doubted either one of them would take any time away from the investigation. With every hour that went by and Kimi was still missing, he was personally letting his family down.

"When we wrap this one up, I'll get back to exercising and eating right."

Both men had been captains of their high school basketball teams—Scruggs in Lander and Antelope at Wind River High School in Ethete—and both had earned all-state honors. The love of the game was the first thing they'd bonded over.

"The intruder thought there was something in the files—and he's got those now, but what about the doctor herself?" Antelope said. "She knows what's in the file. She could be in danger."

"My gut tells me she knows something. Damn confidentiality," Scruggs said, rubbing his chest.

"Do we have the budget to bring her on as a consultant? It might give us an inside route to valuable information she might not realize is important. And I like the idea of keeping her close to the investigation."

"I'll take it under consideration. I'll have to justify it to the county."

"Might be cheaper than a police guard to keep her safe," Antelope said. He knew he was going out on a limb and his logic didn't hold up. But he thought if he could work closely with Pepper, he could keep an eye on her and make sure she didn't come to harm.

"I said I'd think about it. Meanwhile, make sure she knows to keep her eyes open and her doors locked. Is there no other way to get her to talk to us?"

"Psychologists can be compelled to cooperate with law enforcement in the investigation of a serious crime."

"I don't like to say it but if this were a murder case instead of a missing person."

"Find a body, all bets are off and she'll be free to speak. Murder trumps doctor/patient privilege," Antelope said.

"Is that where this is heading?" Scruggs asked, hand on his chest, thumb rubbing the same spot over his heart. "Hell of a thing to hope for." He rattled the bottle and shook out more pills.

"She's been gone five days. It's the dead of winter. People are losing hope of finding her alive."

"With her history of going missing, it's tempting to believe she'll come back."

The strains of "I'll Be Home for Christmas" drifted into the room, and Antelope felt a tug at his heart at the nostalgic words. He thought Scruggs might have felt the same thing, because he got up and closed the door, shutting out the sounds. Antelope watched as the sheriff moved slowly, bent over at the waist. Before he reached his desk, he stopped, closed his eyes, and grimaced.

"You okay?"

Scruggs opened his eyes, blinked quickly. "Chest pain, heartburn. It'll pass. It's this damn case—right in the middle of Christmas, and we haven't got one sure thing to work with. Let's talk about Cahill."

"When I questioned Cahill, he said he partied at the Astro Lounge on Thursday night. He claimed he drank too much to drive home, so he parked out back of the bar and slept in his truck. But Tracy Hopkins said she found him parked outside her place sometime in the middle of the night, so she brought him inside to sleep. And that's not the only inconsistency. He told me he and Kimi fought and she took off and never came back. He didn't like it, but he wasn't worried. He headed out to the bar to meet up with his pals. But he told Tracy something different: he said Kimi left him."

"So he lied. What else is he not telling us? I had my eyes on him the whole time you questioned him. He's a shifty one all right. He didn't take it near serious enough his wife was gone. Not the typical reaction you'd expect from an innocent spouse. Take a look at this."

Scruggs handed him the lab report from the evidence samples the crime scene technicians had taken from Kimi's residence. "It's mostly a lot of nothing but take a look at the second page, last paragraph. In the bathroom trash, a pregnancy test, one of those things you can get in the supermarket pharmacy, and there was a semen-filled facial tissue in the bedroom trash."

"She was pregnant?" Antelope looked up from the report. "That's the first we've heard of it."

"We're running a DNA test on the semen. Find out if Cahill had sex with his wife before he left and if he knew she was pregnant. We need his DNA. He didn't mention anything about her being pregnant. One more thing to talk to him about."

Scruggs tossed a newspaper, and Antelope caught it on the fly.

The photo had front-page placement in the Tuesday evening edition of the *Rocket Miner* with the caption, "Who is this woman?" The byline on the accompanying story was Cedric Yee. The gist of the article was that a secret female visitor had been caught on camera as she exited Kevin Cahill's home early Tuesday morning.

Antelope handed the paper back. "Tracy Hopkins, Cahill's partner. When I asked her yesterday, she denied there was anything going on between them."

"Everybody lies. Especially in cases like this. When you talk to her again, mention the penalty for obstruction of justice. Works like a truth serum, I find. Pictures don't lie, Antelope. Kimi's husband's been screwing around on her, and here's your proof in black and white." Scruggs dropped the paper on his desk and tapped the photo. "Do this for me. Find out if Cahill was cheating on her. That's number one in the motivation department for wife endangerment and murder cases. She could have found out about his cheating. The two of them argue, Cahill loses it, and she ends up dead. That's the definition of manslaughter in these domestic situations. I know what you're thinking, it's a lot of supposition. But that's why this one's yours. Give me a reality check here."

"Cahill's been working his public image, present all day,

every day at the volunteer hotline. How long before we get serious media coverage?"

"I'm surprised they haven't hit on the story by now, to tell you the truth. It hits all the media high notes: beautiful woman missing, cheating husband, Christmas. And when word gets out about her being pregnant, put on your best suit, because it's *Good Morning America* time. We'll be getting requests from all the national networks and have no time left to do our jobs. You've never been through anything like that, but I have, and trust me, you don't want to know what's coming our way if we can't find out what happened to Kimi real soon."

Antelope folded the paper under his arm and stood up. "I'm on it."

He opened the door to the sounds of "Blue Christmas."

"Antelope."

He turned around. Scruggs leaned back in his chair, his hands behind his head. For the first time since Kimi went missing, he looked like he might survive the investigation.

"Now that I think of it, signing Pepper Hunt on as a consultant will play well with the media. You've got the go-ahead. Bring her on."

■ ■ ■

Antelope caught up with Tracy Hopkins in the parking lot of her apartment building at Kimberly Place. The three-story brick building was on a service road at the southern boundary of town, across the road from the Holiday Inn and the volunteer headquarters. Open desert and railway tracks on one side and the interstate highway on the other.

She was lifting her luggage, a matched set of designer suitcases, into the open hatchback of a little red car he recognized from the Dairy Queen parking lot. He was glad he had thought to ask her for her travel itinerary that night. She was right on time, getting on the road two hours before her scheduled flight out of the Rock Springs airport.

The wind out of the desert made a high keening sound as

he crossed the icy surface, obscuring the sound of his approach. Tracy was pulling her head out of the trunk when he spoke.

"Going somewhere?"

She jumped and turned to face him, hair pulled back in a tight knot, pale moon face squinting in the sun.

"Detective, you scared me. I'm on my way to the airport." She gave him a brilliant smile, then pouted her red lips when he didn't smile back. "What are you doing here? I'm not in trouble, am I?"

Antelope waited. In his hand, the *Rocket Miner* pages snapped and fluttered.

Wary eyes narrowed, scanning the landscape. She wanted to run. It was a hint of another Tracy, tricky and feral.

He opened the paper and tapped the front-page picture.

A quick glance at the photo.

"Want to take that home to show the family?"

"You think this is me?"

"Do you deny it?"

"I don't have to answer that." She crossed her arms and pouted for real.

Antelope stabbed at the paper. "This man's wife is missing. This is you coming out of his house. Without your cooperation, I can connect the dots any way I want. Lying in the course of a police investigation is obstruction of justice and carries a penalty of up to three years in prison."

Tracy dropped her arms and lost the pout, leaned against the car, and stared out at the desert. Wind came off the open land, knocked at Antelope's back, settled in the sleeves of his leather coat, and unraveled Tracy's curls.

"Shit! What do you want to know?"

"The truth. How long have you been sleeping with him?"

"It's private between me and Kevin. He warned me you might ask."

"If you're withholding information, we have a big problem. How long?"

She didn't answer right away, and Antelope figured she was

considering her options, trying to sort out whether what she had going with Kevin was worth prison time. A plane sliced the light blue sky overhead, white plume of contrail mixing with tangled clouds.

"He needed a friend. I let him sleep in my bed. He was a mess. I was being supportive."

"You lied when you told me you found him sleeping in the truck. He came straight to you, isn't that right?"

She nodded yes and looked away. She had lied to him in the course of a serious investigation, a life-and-death search for someone he cared about. His right eye twitched—a dead giveaway that he was angry. But Tracy wouldn't know that.

"He called me from the bar. Kimi had left him and he didn't want to go home or be alone."

"What did he tell you?"

"She walked out on him. It was all over. She wanted a divorce. I held him, tried to comfort him. I didn't mean for it to happen. Neither of us did. It was just the situation. Kevin was right. I should never have said anything. He was afraid it would look bad, him being at my house."

"Kevin told you to lie?"

"He told me not to bring it up. It wasn't important. He didn't want it to look like it had anything to do with Kimi disappearing, which it didn't." Her mouth twisted in a smirk. She was confident again, red lipstick too bright for midday.

It would give him some pleasure to tell her she wouldn't be going home for Christmas this year.

"Did Kevin tell you his wife was pregnant?"

"She's pregnant?"

She kicked a ball of ice and dirt into a pile of plowed snow. When it rolled back down, she kicked it again. From the look on her face, it was clear she wasn't happy with Kevin.

"So you didn't know. Would it have mattered?"

"Stop trying to make me the bad person here. I didn't do anything wrong. I didn't break any laws."

"Obstruction of justice, possible accessory to a crime," Antelope said. He folded the paper and slipped it into his coat pocket.

"The sheriff has ordered you to stay in the county until further notice."

"You can't do this. I told you, I'm about to get on a plane."

"I'm here on the sheriff's orders. He wants you to make yourself available to the investigation by remaining in Rock Springs. If you choose to ignore that request, I'm authorized to place you under arrest for obstruction of justice."

He waited while she phoned her mother, who consulted with the family attorney, who advised she cooperate with the sheriff's department and cancel her travel plans. She was holding back tears as she opened the trunk and took out the bags.

"One more thing. I'll be bringing Kevin in for more questioning. Don't give him a heads-up we had this conversation."

"This totally sucks."

She stomped away, dragging the roller suitcases behind her over ruts of packed snow and into the apartment building, where she would spend Christmas alone. Antelope smiled.

He thought about swinging by Kevin Cahill's place but decided it was better to confront him in the interview room, where he could record the meeting on video camera. He left messages on Kevin's landline and cell phone, asking him to come into the station at his earliest convenience.

CHAPTER 20

Traffic on Dewar Drive was stalled, with back-to-back vehicles clogging the entrance to White Mountain Mall. Antelope pulled into Wendy's, ordered a grilled chicken sandwich with french fries and a chocolate shake, and took his time with lunch. In the patio dining room the noon sun streamed in through tall windows onto giant potted palms. He thought of his favorite beach in Baja, Mexico—white sand, turquoise sea, timeless, windless.

Back in the car, he managed to find a station that wasn't playing nonstop Christmas tunes. Listening to Bob Marley, he felt content on the slow ride back to work.

Kevin Cahill was already at the station. He stood at the top of the wide concrete stairs in a silver quilted parka and red ski hat, his right leg bent and braced against the stone building.

"I was about to leave. I've been here twenty minutes already."

Antelope motioned for him to follow and led him to the first-floor interview room. It was stale with the previous occupant's body odor.

"When am I going to get my stuff back?"

"What stuff are you referring to?" Antelope asked.

Kevin turned his chair around and straddled it, leaned his arms on the chrome trim.

"Computers, pictures—everything your deputies hauled out of my place the day they trashed it."

"I'll check on that and get back to you," Antelope said and moved toward the steel table. "A few things have come up."

Kevin Cahill took off his hat, and wiped his forehead with it. He unzipped the silver down jacket, stretched his arms, and cracked his knuckles before leaning in toward Antelope. The two men faced each other in the hot, close space.

"You didn't sleep in your truck outside the Astro Lounge last Thursday night."

"Is that a question, Detective?"

He didn't like the guy's attitude. The sheriff was suspicious of Cahill, and Antelope could see why.

"I'm making the point you lied in the course of a police investigation. Makes it look like you have something to hide."

"I've got nothing to hide."

"You slept at Tracy Hopkins's place."

"My private business is none of your business."

"You had sexual relations with Tracy Hopkins."

Kevin shot a quick look at the mirrored wall. Anyone watching would catch the sneer.

"What does any of this have to do with you doing your job and finding my wife?"

The room got so quiet they could hear the buzz of the overhead light and the random hiss of the radiator.

"Let's go back to the last time you saw Kimi. What did you fight about that night?"

"We're going to do this again? The same old bullshit, recycled. She was jealous of Tracy. I threw it right back at her, told her I didn't believe her lies about dissociating, not knowing where she was. She's screwing around and that's why she's suspicious of me."

"Kimi was right, though. You did cheat with Tracy."

Kevin flashed a look Antelope had seen many times, seconds before the gloves came off and the serious blows were thrown.

He was enjoying putting pressure on Kevin, seeing him squirm. All for Kimi, the same way he used to knock around the

bullies who bothered her. He'd been trying to remain neutral, not
letting his personal ties to the victim bias him. But he knew as well
as the sheriff did, nine times out of ten when a woman went missing, it was a good bet her husband had a hand in it.

"I figured if I'm going to be accused of something, I might
as well enjoy it."

"Your marriage is in trouble."

"You think?"

"How bad?"

"You know what they say, if it's got tits or tires, sooner or
later you're going to have trouble," Kevin said, and smiled.

"Did Kimi threaten divorce?"

Kevin glared at him; both fists came down on the chair. "Yes,
she did. Why are you busting my balls? Things aren't bad enough
for me—you have to do this now?"

"A kid on the way complicates things," Antelope said.

"What'd you say?" Kevin dropped his hands and leaned
toward Antelope, eyes wide open and wild. Antelope knew Kevin
wanted to hit him. He wanted it too: bare fists slamming Kevin to
the ground, knuckles crashing into cheekbones, blood staining the
snow.   He'd enjoy pounding the hell out of this lying prick for
killing his cousin. He shut down the impulse. Time to catch his
breath and turn the screws. "Why didn't you tell me your wife is
pregnant?" he said, his satisfaction growing in signal strength.

"What kind of bullshit is this? No way is she pregnant."

"A positive pregnancy test was found in the bathroom trash.
I thought she must have told you before you left. You never mentioned it, which seemed strange. But it makes sense if you didn't
know. I'm sorry."

The radiator hissed and released steam into the overheated
room.

"Right. Fuck you."

"You don't seem happy about the news," Antelope said,
unleashing a part of him he usually kept under strict control, vestiges
of something primal, called into action when needed.

"I find out this way? Are you freaking kidding me? She's

gone and you expect me to be happy she's pregnant? This is so fucked up."

"So your marital problems didn't stop you having sex?"

A harsh sound, a cough or a laugh, and Kevin shook his head again. "You've got some nerve." He unzipped his black fleece, pulled it over his head, and threw it to the floor.

"Did you have sexual relations with your wife Thursday night?"

"We fought. She left. I never saw her again."

"Do you remember the last time the two of you had sex?"

"What's your point?"

"What I just said hit a nerve. You said Kimi was screwing around. You worried it might not be yours?"

"This is some perverted line of questioning. If you know something I don't, you better tell me quick," Kevin said, his breathing coming hard and fast.

"I know our techs found semen on a tissue in your bedroom. Is it yours?"

"Bullshit. They didn't find shit. I don't have to listen to this. You're trying to break me." Kevin stood up and kicked the chair behind him. When it screeched on the tile floor, he turned and kicked it again and sent it crashing into the wall.

"Calm down."

"Fuck that, calm down, you're telling me my wife had sex with another guy in my bed. But you're wrong. Kimi wouldn't do that to me." He was on his feet, pacing in small circles, hands safely tucked under his arms. He stopped, his back against the wall, and glared at Antelope.

"It's been entered into evidence and sent for DNA testing. You need to go to the hospital lab today and provide a sample for comparison."

"Can this get any worse?"

"Right now, I'd bet yes. You had relations with another woman. In our book, that gives you a motive to murder your wife."

In slow motion, Kevin scooped his sweater from the floor and reached for his jacket. He smoothed the red cap over his skull and walked to the door—where he paused, turned, and said, "Where's her picture? I want my wife's picture back. Get me her goddamn picture or I swear I'm going to lose it."

"I'll check with the evidence room and see what the status is. It might not happen right away."

Kevin was breathing heavily, his face flushed and sweating. Antelope didn't think the guy was stupid enough to take a swing at him, but there was no telling how violent or blinded by rage he might become given the right circumstances.

"I'll say it again: You need to calm down. This is Week One. We could be at this a while. Trust me, it will go better without threats."

"She's my wife and she's gone. I need that picture back. It's mine. Just like Kimi—she's mine, too. So do something useful: do your job, find her, and bring her back to me."

CHAPTER 21

It was late afternoon when I left my office to drive to the Saddle Lite Saloon on Bridger. The day had been cheerless and overcast, the clouds like coiled steel wool in a restless sky. The Christmas lights hadn't come on yet, and the seasonal decorations along Dewar Drive looked like cheap jewelry on hungover women.

Antelope had gotten the green light to hire me as a consultant. Talk about conflict of interest, but that's how it was in Wyoming, with limited resources to combat the rampant mental health and substance abuse problems.

Antelope wanted my help with Diego, who had no use for his cousin when he put on the badge. Tonight would be the first time the two had talked face-to-face in years. The plan was for us to all meet at the Saddle Lite Saloon, where Diego worked.

On the drive across town, I passed six other drinking establishments. Not too long ago you could buy a mixed drink at a liquor store drive-through—no open-container laws applied. And most nights, serious drinking was done at the Shooting Star Tavern, the place to be for oilmen and cowboys.

I bought Antelope a drink at the Shooting Star the day I bought my horse. It was a warm evening in April, and the sweet smell of sage was in the air. When we left a few hours later, snow was coming down in big, soft flakes.

Returning my thoughts to the present, I parked beside Antelope's Cadillac and headed inside the bar. It was dark as a cave. Two senior citizens sat hunched over beer mugs at the end of the bar, baseball caps beside them, matching bald heads turned to the flat screen at one end. Diego was behind the bar with his back turned to Antelope. When the local news led with Kimi's story, he grabbed the remote and switched to ESPN.

Diego resembled Kimi: deep-set black eyes, a high forehead, and sculpted cheekbones. His long black hair was caught in a rawhide clip at the base of his neck. On someone else it would look feminine, but he wore it like a warrior. At five feet eight inches, his narrow frame supported serious muscle. He wore a black, sleeveless T-shirt and black jeans.

I had never seen him dressed like this; it would be inappropriate dress in the sex offender group, but here it fit. On his right bicep was a tattoo of a girl in a feather headdress, index finger over lush red lips and the word *SECRET* in gothic letters.

If Diego was surprised to see me, he didn't let it show. I knew things Diego kept to himself—things Antelope, who'd grown up beside him in the transparency of reservation life, would never know. I knew Diego loved his sister more than life itself. I knew the exact place where his stepfather's knife had stabbed his chest and carved a scar below his heart.

"Diego," Antelope said.

Diego raised his chin in a standard, tough-guy, nonverbal greeting I recognized from group.

"You two drinking?" he asked.

"I'll have a club soda with ice." I was on the county payroll, and therapeutic listening required paying attention to the music, not just the words.

"Jameson's," Antelope said.

Diego put the club soda on a napkin and set the shots up in two hard slaps on the wooden bar. The men threw them back, and Diego quickly refilled the glasses before placing the bottle between them.

He leaned back with his hands in his pockets, legs crossed

at the ankles—his usual posture during the group sessions. When group members gave feedback, he always looked defensive.

I realized I had never seen the man at ease.

"It took you long enough," Diego said.

Antelope's jaw jutted forward, but he said nothing. He'd told me he'd try to avoid letting "the old bullshit" get between them tonight. Diego had a natural distrust for the law, and when Antelope had made his career choice, it had pretty much severed the ties between them.

"I guess you can't ignore it now," Diego said.

He wasn't looking at Antelope; his head was turned to his sister's face on the television news. Someone had changed the channel again. He walked to the television and unplugged it.

At the sounds of protest, Diego emptied his pockets, slapped coins on the bar.

"TV's off for the night. Play some goddamn songs," he called out to no one in particular. Then he looked at Antelope. "Your boss, the sheriff, came by the house yesterday to question me. When he had no cause to arrest me, he left. Haven't heard anything since. What are you doing to find her?"

"We've been working around the clock," Antelope said. "I'm here now." His face was still. He was working hard to keep his composure.

Diego looked at me. In the therapy group, we'd been down the rabbit hole together, touched a place of trust, and bounced back whole. "She told me she was seeing you. Is that why you're here?"

"Dr. Hunt's here as a consultant," Antelope said.

"County's getting fancy," Diego said. "Sheriff needs all the help he can get, I hear."

"It's proof he's taking her disappearance seriously."

"I'm not impressed with your work so far. For what it's worth, it helps the doctor's here. Otherwise, I wouldn't be talking to you."

I felt the tension ease between the men.

"You know your sister better than anyone," Antelope said. "You may know things no one else knows."

"She'll be mad as hell when she finds out I told you anything private."

"You want me to find her, don't hold back. Every second counts."

I watched the two men square off. I hoped Antelope knew to let Diego tell the thing at his own speed. My experience in the group told me the man couldn't be rushed, had to have control of the story.

"You're the lawman, so it's your show?" Diego filled his glass and drank the whole shot down.

"This is about your sister. If you know something, now's the time to tell me."

"Might be another guy sniffing around. Maybe you know more about this than I do." Diego spit out the words, his face looking like he tasted something sour.

"Did Kimi mention another man?"

"Not exactly."

"What did she say?" I asked.

"It wasn't what she said so much as how she was acting. Like she knew something was going to happen. She wanted to tell me something, but she never got to it. I thought it was man trouble and didn't want to hear it. We grew up on that, and nothing good ever comes of it. If your mama didn't teach you that, mine sure did."

"When was this?" I asked.

"Sunday last. I didn't take it well. All the crap we lived through, the crazy dudes my mother brought home, Kimi should know changing out men doesn't do a thing. She got what was in my head. I didn't have to spell it out for her. She shut down. I've been kicking myself about it since."

This was the most I had ever heard him utter.

"She said she was seeing another man?" Antelope asked.

"Kimi talks in code. Did you forget that, too?"

Diego was on his third shot now, a major parole violation. How much alcohol would it take before he lost his edge? So far he was in total control of himself. Antelope poured another shot for the two of them. He must have been thinking the same thing as I was, hoping to get Diego to open up more.

Diego picked up his shot glass and the bottle and headed to a table at the back of the bar. We followed him into the darkness, and in moments, the dark corner became a confessional.

"I should have taken care of her," Diego said.

"You can talk to her about that later," Antelope said. "Did you notice anyone new hanging around?"

"I don't know who she hangs with anymore. Check with Cass. I don't keep tabs that way. And if Kimi wanted it secret, it would have stayed secret, even from Cass."

I noticed Antelope flinch at the mention of Cassandra. "What do you know about Cedric Yee?" he asked.

"Only what Kimi tells me."

Diego's eyes shifted to the left, and he smoothed his right eyebrow with his index finger, a sign he was holding something back. "He said something to a buddy of mine. It pissed me off."

"What was that?" Antelope asked as he reached for his notepad.

"I was about to tear him a new one, but my buddy said he's harmless."

"What buddy are we talking about?"

"It's nothing. Forget I said anything," Diego said, and rubbed the back of his neck.

I finished my club soda as I watched the two men spar. They were managing to keep it civil. Someone who liked Brad Paisley had dropped a lot of quarters in the jukebox. Another melancholy love song, "Is it Raining at Your House," brought Kimi to mind.

"If you want me to find her, quit playing games. Give me a name. Let me do my job."

Diego looked at me before he answered. "Troy Kinney."

For the last year, I'd watched the two of them, Diego and Troy, vying for the alpha male position in the sex offender group. Raw competition, no sign of male bonding. I should have known both men were too clever to let a friendship show. It was against the rules of Probation and Parole for felons to associate while under supervision. The aftercare group supported those rules and prohibited fraternizing among group members. Of course they would have kept it hidden.

"How does Kimi know him?" Antelope asked.

"She's been there a few times when he's been at the house."

Diego looked at me again. Troy had graduated from the group when his parole ended six months ago; he was free to socialize with whomever he wanted. But Diego was still bound by the rules of parole. This was another violation. But who was counting, under the circumstances? I'd have to deal with it after Kimi came home.

"What's his interest in Kimi?" Antelope asked.

"He has no interest. Not if he wants to stay breathing. Troy knows what's good for him."

"This is your buddy?"

"One thing has nothing to do with the other."

"Sometimes people will fool you, though," Antelope said.

"Troy has nothing to do with my sister."

If the words had been typed out, they would be in bold print, capitalized, and italicized. The only times I had seen Diego this agitated, it was about Kimi.

"What did Troy tell you?" I asked.

"Some bullshit about Kimi and the sheriff. Don't ask me why it's any of his business."

"She's a crime reporter," Antelope said. "Everybody in the department knows Kimi." He sounded defensive, and his right eye twitched, a sign that he was angry. Did Diego know that about his cousin?

"She's too classy to go for a lawman. She was raised better than that," Diego said and downed another shot.

"What do you know about her marriage?" Antelope asked.

"He put hands on her. That I know. I saw the evidence. His fingerprints on her arms."

I recalled seeing the same bruises. Kimi had minimized the violence, explaining that she and Kevin often wrestled with each other and sometimes things got a little rough.

"You let that stand?" Antelope's right eye twitched again.

"Did I say I let it stand?" Diego slapped his shot glass on the table so hard the whiskey splashed over the sides. He wiped the surface dry with his arm, drained the remaining liquid from the glass.

"I had a talk with Kevin. No more bruises. What can I say? Some guys scare easy. Kevin's one of them. I never had to touch him. Can't make any promises now."

"How long ago was this?" Antelope asked.

"Last summer some time. It changed things for her. It showed in her face, like a cloud over the sun. I could see it wasn't the same for her after that. Maybe she thought another guy would be different. Goddamn." Diego turned his head away, caught the tears before they fell with his fingers.

"How's Estella holding up?" Antelope asked.

"I'm sure she'd be glad to answer that question herself, cousin. All you have to do is find her."

On the dance floor a couple did a slow waltz to Brad Paisley's "Nothing on but the Radio."

"Anything else we should know?" I asked. After years of doing therapy, I'd learned that people often left the most important thing until the end.

"Whatever happened to Kimi, it's got something to do with a man, and it's complicated or she would have worked it out on her own," Diego said. "It won't be easy. It never is with Kimi."

CHAPTER 22

Antelope watched Pepper Hunt drive off to another night at the Holiday Inn. They said good night outside the tavern under a bright neon sign that turned her hair the color of sugar maples in autumn. He was attracted to her, but he had to put that aside for now. He was glad she opted for the hotel again instead of going home to her empty house.

They still didn't have any leads on the break-ins. So far it looked like the intruder had only been after the records of Kimi's treatment. Pepper said there was nothing in the file that would incriminate anyone or give any clues to Kimi's whereabouts. He worried that the intruder, frustrated by what wasn't in the file, would come after Pepper.

He'd thought about asking her to join him for dinner, but his gut had told him not to push it. Sitting side by side in the bar, he had watched her face in the mirror—power-drill concentration, hazel eyes like a cat in the night, calculating. Her perfume smelled like new grass and the summer prairie.

Last April he had taken her to the wild mustang auction in Riverton. The air was soft with spring. From hundreds of horses, she'd chosen Soldier that day. He'd seen her smile for the first time when she put down the cash and claimed the horse for her own. He'd taken a picture with his phone. A tall, slender woman dressed in black beside a wild gray-and-white Appaloosa. The two of them already a pair—standing close together, like stray puzzle pieces connected.

He hadn't been looking for anything serious, but she'd gotten spooked anyway, skittish as her new horse. From his perspective, one day she was there and the next day she was gone. He called and texted a few times, but when he didn't hear from her, he let it go. It usually went the other way with him and women, so he was at a loss. After a while, he'd dropped it. No sense playing the fool.

About the same time, he'd fallen back into a tangle with Cass and gotten distracted. Maybe Pepper had heard about that? What could you ever know with a woman? There'd been eight months of radio silence until this case brought them together.

He got to the Burger Bar just before closing and took his cheeseburger to go, unwrapped it immediately, and ate it in the car. The lights went off in the Burger Bar, and he sat alone in the quiet, dark alley. He could go back to the station and catch up on paperwork, or he could go home, have an early night, and get some sleep for a change. He didn't like either option. He was restless, and his muscles jerked with the sting of tiny electric impulses.

He couldn't stay still any longer; he pulled onto Bridger and took a right onto Elk Street. It wasn't until he cleared the intersection that he knew he was on his way to see Estella. Diego's last comment had stung him with guilt.

His aunt's crazy spells had frightened him as a child, and he'd kept his distance. As a result, he'd never developed much of a relationship with her, which was a strange thing in a Native family, where all the grown-ups tended to look out for all the young ones. When he'd gone to the hospital to tell Estella about her daughter being missing a couple of days earlier, she'd seemed pretty lucid—saner than he'd anticipated given she'd been admitted to a psych ward the night before.

He hadn't talked to Pepper about whether Estella could have had anything to do with Kimi's disappearance. He was afraid to speak the words out loud. It was hard to admit that when the sheriff first told him his cousin was missing, Estella was the first person who came to mind. One day she could be crazy and the next day

appear perfectly sane. He thought that must be the living definition of schizophrenia. The thing that gave him comfort was not
being able to come up with any reason why Estella would want
to hurt her own daughter. Diego was the problem child; Kimi
brought nothing but sunshine and blessings.

It was still early, just past seven o'clock, when he entered the
mobile home park. Every modest dwelling was decorated to the
hilt for Christmas: tinsel and garlands everywhere, and strings
of lights along rooflines, around windows, and on porch railings.
Outlined in the extravagant colored globes, the trailer houses and
fifth-wheel campers looked like gingerbread houses. *In a warm
kitchen with Diego and Kimi, sugar frosting on fingers, gumdrops sticking to
wisps of hair.* Once in a while his memory ambushed him with a
stunning clarity that raked his heart raw.

Estella's place was dark. He parked beside Diego's GTO and
killed the lights. If she was asleep, he shouldn't wake her. But he'd
made the effort to come, so he might as well finish the job. He
opened the storm door and knocked, three quick halfhearted taps,
then listened for sounds of someone moving inside. The night was
still and clear around him. The recent snow softened all sounds of
life in the houses and winding lanes.

He waited some minutes in the cold, watched his breath take
form and disappear like magic. In the car he wrote out a note: *I
was here, your nephew Beau.* He stuck it in the door frame, closed the
door, and clicked the latch tight to secure it.

It had been tough from the start. Another man might have asked
to be taken off the case. But he was not another man. He took whatever fate sent him and stood it, focused on work during the day, work
and nothing but. He was good at that, had honed his skill at compart-
mentalizing personal life and work life. Daytime, Kimi was a case he
was working, not his sweet cousin, the jingle dancer. At night, he saw
Kimi in her red jingle dress, feathers and spangles, a sparkling girl.

All the bars on Elk Street had their doors open, lights and
music blaring, an open invitation. He could take his restlessness
inside any one of them, but he kept driving, in search of something
he couldn't name.

Sobriety was a requirement. He could only drink so much because at any moment his phone could ring with news of a break in the case, putting him behind the wheel. He knew himself, knew what he could tolerate, and he meted out his pleasures—food, booze, sleep. Most days, he achieved only a teetering balance. He hadn't slept much since Monday, and his exhaustion was pushing his winter depression, that stark, hardscrabble landscape, closer to the surface.

He thought about Mexico in February, his annual two weeks of rest and recuperation, and hoped this business was done by then—and not just because he wanted the vacation. The more time went by without a lead, the more likely they would be finding Kimi's body.

And that was best-case scenario. The possibility existed they wouldn't get even that. And without a body and its payload of clues, it was less likely the killer would ever be caught.

He was on White Mountain Road. If he took a right, he would be on the switchback road leading up to where the four women raped in the past year had been taken.

He made the turn, and when the light changed, he found himself on an incline he knew was deceptively tame at the lower elevation but would turn challenging, then daunting as he made his way up the mountain.

The ice on the road shimmered silver in the radiant moon-light, evil disguised as beauty. At four different spots along this way, women had experienced pain and fear. And he was no closer to finding the person who'd brought them to this barren place.

Cedric Yee believed the rapist had come for Kimi, was drawn to her because she wrote about him. Antelope knew those things happened, that the twisted minds of violent offenders, murderers and rapists, led them to construct a different, distorted reality. Kimi's job as a crime reporter connected her to the rapist; he came alive in her words. Perhaps that provoked a dangerous longing.

Early in December, when the winter storms had hit day after day with no sign of stopping, Antelope had put winter chains on the Cadillac. Still, he drove carefully on the icy turns, relieved every time he felt the tires grip and hold tight to the mountain. Below him the city looked strangely beautiful, white streetlights snarled in a haphazard layout, twinkling like fallen stars.

The idea that Kimi had been taken by the rapist was something he couldn't rule out. But it got them nowhere. The sheriff's department had no suspects for those earlier crimes and no suspects in Kimi's case, either.

His mother called every night on speaker phone with a pack of relatives, all of them smoking and drinking around the warmth of her giant space heater—the modern equivalent of a campfire. They wanted facts so they could step back from their desperate dangle at the cliff's edge of the unknown. Victims' families always wanted to know what happened, thought that not knowing was worse. But some of the cases Antelope had worked had left him wondering if that was true.

Every night, he disappointed them. He never had anything to tell. He'd told his mother that talking about the investigation could compromise it, and that he would call her when there was something real he could say—but as usual, the ideas and ways of the white world didn't translate well in the world he came from.

Why was he driving this treacherous mountain in December? Was he looking for the rapist, hiding in the harboring granite? Was he looking for his cousin, asleep in a secret grave? Was he a desperate small-town detective searching for answers he'd never find?

He parked at the peak and walked out onto a wide rock ledge at the mountain's highest point. Below him the mountain vanished in a steep drop-off. Wind, like a ghost, an invisible chill, rose up from the chasm below. The air at the edge felt colder and meaner—a quick, hungry spirit waiting to grab him. He felt a flash of vertigo and took a step backward, retracing his steps as his heart beat fast against the wall of his chest.

It would be easy to die up here, miles from town, where no one in their right mind would risk travel for months. His tedious frustration had brought him to this landscape fit for rapists. If he ran out of gas, or got stuck in the snow, it'd be a gamble getting down. Far away in the southern sky, murky shapes stirred and swarmed. He watched as their slow-moving mass overtook the moon and its light. The world around him went black.

He waited for shapes to emerge from the darkness. Rocks and trees gradually distinguished themselves. Then his white car revealed itself, showing him the way out of there. He drove down the mountain with even more caution than he'd exercised coming up. He felt he'd been changed; it was as if every one of his cells had been altered, stained with the fear and violence the mountain had witnessed.

CHAPTER 23

Diego left the Shooting Star as soon as his shift was over. Any other night he'd have been throwing back the drinks, his eye out for the next woman who'd be willing to take him home, but his known world was shut down. Since Monday he'd lived a new reality—one where everything counted. He tried to come across as normal, while in his soul wild dogs prowled and switchblades slashed in alleys.

He'd put the word in his cousin's ear. But he couldn't trust Beau to do anything with it. He was still stuck in the county, waiting for the word from Probation and Parole to let him loose so he could head up north to the reservation. He might as well stick with his own tail on the sheriff.

He parked down the block from the sheriff's department and waited. It was 11:00 P.M., and he knew Scruggs didn't waste any time hauling ass out of there at the end of a shift. At three minutes past, the black Chevy Tahoe came out of the parking lot and turned left. Diego waited, another truck pulled out of a side street, and Diego followed. At the intersection, both trucks turned left onto Dewar Drive in the direction of the mall. Stores stayed open late this time of year to catch the last-minute shoppers' business.

He thought about the rapist's pattern of grabbing women as they came out of stores at closing time. Tonight would be prime hunting. Maybe Scruggs thought the same and was doing his job, trolling. Scruggs skirted the mall parking lot, pulled in, and took a tour past the main aisle along the storefronts. *Great minds think alike,* Diego thought and laughed out loud at the idea that he and the sheriff could have anything in common.

Back on Dewar Drive, Scruggs headed for the entrance to I-80 West, joining the stream of eighteen-wheeler traffic racing toward Green River and points west. Diego dropped back three car lengths to keep the sheriff from noticing the tail.

He thought back to that Sunday night. Kimi beside him in the bucket seat, her legs folded under her. Him driving too fast, racing away from town, the GTO's engine screaming. Fear coming off her like the cracking and branching of pond ice before it separates to reveal the depth of black water below. He'd felt it and turned away.

"I need to tell you something," Kimi had said.

Her voice that night had belonged to his Humpty-Dumpty-on-the-edge-about-to-crack sister from the past.

Could the woman have been any clearer? Like a jackass, he'd missed it. Did he ask her what it was she needed to tell him? No, he did not. Instead, he turned up the radio. He hadn't been in the mood for Kimi's drama.

She'd turned away and watched the frozen landscape, tugged at the sleeves of her navy sailor's jacket, gold buttons shining in the dashboard lights.

Something bad was on its way, an underground force ready to erupt, right there on the seat beside him. She took the cigarette from his hand and lit one of her own. The touch of her hand grazing his skin was insanely thrilling and familiar. When he'd tossed the cigarette butt into the wind, bits of hot ash had flown back and stung his cheek, and he'd slapped at the pain. *Women and their damn love,* he'd thought then. All of them . . . his mother, Charlene, now Kimi, the last and only good one, all freaking slaves to the heart. The music went loud again, and he didn't know which one of them had turned it up.

The taillights ahead made him sleepy, hot charcoals scorching his eyes. It had been a long day and his body ached from being confined in the car. He yawned and stretched; hands in the air, flying free, a kid on a bike.

He blinked and the deer was there, coming at him with giant horns, wild eyes, gold flanks, and fat rump. It hit and bounced, dropped off and was gone on a gallop of long legs, back where he came from, still breathing in the winter night.

Diego braked and turned. The animal was alive and so was he. Mere seconds' difference and the two of them would have been wandering a prairie together in another universe.

Shot with adrenaline, his chest heaving, the tears broke out from where he'd stashed them. A sound came from him, the sob of someone tortured and broken, but it didn't matter. He pulled onto the shoulder and watched the cars and trucks zoom past on the highway until the crying jag passed and he could see straight again. That goddamn lucky deer. He wished Kimi the same good fortune.

A few minutes later he caught up to the sheriff, who signaled for the first Green River exit. Diego slowed and followed him down into the deserted weeknight streets. At the bottom of the off-ramp, the sheriff stopped short, forcing Diego off the pavement to avoid a crash. The Pinto shuddered and stalled in the soft ditch.

The sheriff was out of his truck and bearing down on him, fast.

"What are you after? You've been riding my ass since I left the station. Get out of the car."

The two men faced off in the ravine. Wind snaked around them with a low whistling sound, a sleeper's sigh in the night. Diego felt the cold grab hold of him, and he began to shake, still in shock from his encounter with the deer.

"I asked you a question. What's with the tail?"

"I'm looking for my sister."

"So that's it. You're going to be the one to set things straight? Don't make me laugh. She is priority number one for the sheriff's department, on my orders."

"She's still gone, though."

"You're wasting time following me. You think I know what happened to her? If I knew where she was, I'd haul her back home myself. That's for damn sure. Now leave me alone before I decide to throw you in jail for the night. And don't ask me what for. For no reason at all. Because I can. Because you're pissing me off. And keep that mother of yours off the streets while you're at it."

For a few minutes they held their places. Then Scruggs broke from his rigid stance and placed his right hand on Diego's shoulder.

"I know your sister. I will not let this case go cold. That's a promise."

All the way back to Rock Springs, the lights of the sheriff's truck flared in his rearview mirror. Diego played with the idea of hitting the brakes, giving the sheriff a jolt of fear and making him back off a little. But when he thought of the sheriff's promise, he felt grateful for the kindness. At Elk Street he turned off to go home, and the sheriff didn't follow.

CHAPTER 24

Scruggs drove north out of town on the road where he'd first met Kimi.

Three months had passed before he saw her again. The first of January dawned, a gray morning that promised nothing. A lazy snow came down, haphazard and teasing at first, then serious. By the end of the first shift, the world was white, the air opaque with zero visibility. Wild snow flew sideways, swarming and stinging. On days like that, it was easy to lose your bearings. And a dense new fear was growing in the city already, pushing down on everyone like a low-pressure weather system. Kimi had called him to say she would be covering the story for the paper, so anything the department wanted to share, he could send it straight to her.

Travel warnings closed the interstate. The storm gave him good reason to stay on the clock.

He'd found Kimi coming out of the dark courthouse after finishing up her police beat assignment. He told himself he wasn't stalking her. Her little Honda was already buried under snow; there was no way she was making it out of the parking lot.

She spotted his truck, smiled as she walked toward him through the blizzard and over icy ground with animal precision. He reached over and opened the passenger door, and she climbed in beside him. Her hair was tucked away under a bright purple cap.

He offered to drive her home. And that should have been that. Except it wasn't. The heater was blasting sauna air. She took off her hat and shook out the snow and wet. The sight of her released hair was too much to bear. Ten minutes from her house, he said, "Sure you want to go home?"

The words came out before he knew he was going there, and he immediately felt like a fool. He didn't know this woman.

"Get me a hot chocolate," she said. "I like that when it's snowing."

That was a surprise—one that made him smile.

The Loaf and Jug was on College Drive near her place. He left the truck running, and they went in together. In flat Native boots, she slid sure-footed across the ice ahead of him, laughing over her shoulder at him as he slowpoked after her in his county-issue boots.

They were the only customers, obvious and anonymous at the same time. The hot chocolate was machine-made and dangerously steaming. She grabbed her half-full cup and topped it with whipped cream like a greedy kid, then did the same for him.

Back in his truck they sat in silence and listened to the muted rumbling of the engine. It seemed that for once the citizens of Rock Springs had listened to warnings and stayed put inside. It had been a long winter, and not halfway through it they'd had some local travel casualties that made road safety feel real. But he knew from experience the fear wouldn't last. He had a long night ahead of him, no plans for sleep. There would be stranded auto calls and maybe some domestic violence, too.

"Ride with me," he said. "I could use the company."

It was half statement and half question. It took her a while to answer, but finally she said, "That sounds good."

"Husband won't mind?"

"He's gone up to Jackson skiing."

He drove out of the parking lot onto the slick highway overpass. "Tell me when you've had enough excitement."

He made a lazy patrol through empty streets. The radio stayed quiet. The two of them were the only people alive and awake on the planet, or so it seemed. They cruised for hours, talking and laughing. Then he felt her hand on his arm, and when he turned to look at her, she said, "I want you to take me home now."

He responded immediately, took her words as an order—made a sharp U-turn and headed west to her place.

"Can't wait to get rid of me?" Beside him she was smiling, her head tilted, giving him a look that he read as playful and flirtatious.

"Nothing of the kind," he said. "It's been a real pleasure. I can't remember when I talked so much."

They were a half mile from her place when the storm ended. A riot of stars sparkled in a clear black sky. He turned onto her street and kept the truck idling in front of her place. She made no move to leave. The flirtatious mood was gone. She looked solemn and certain. He didn't want her to go, didn't want the time with her to end. He looked away so she wouldn't see what he wanted.

She touched his cheek and turned his face so he was looking at her when she said, "Come home with me."

CHAPTER 25

Antelope had to shake off the scare that followed him down off White Mountain. He couldn't face going home alone, and he didn't have the energy to hook up at one of the local places. So close to Christmas, only the desperate ones would be at the bar. Cass's place was on his way home, a short detour if you wanted to miss the four-way on Bridger. If he found the windows dark, he told himself, he would drive on by, make do alone for the night.

A white artificial tree, decorated with silver ornaments and blue lights, sparkled behind lace curtains in the front room. The year Cass moved to Rock Springs, the two of them had hauled it out of Walmart and over to her new place at ten o'clock on Christmas Eve. A small wave of excitement rose in him. Then he remembered this was in no way a sure thing. He told himself he had a reason to be here. He had questions he needed answers to that couldn't wait any longer. He was taking a risk showing up expecting anything, but it was a risk he was willing to take. After everything they'd been through, all the breakups and bullshit, there wasn't much more damage he could do.

How long had it been since he'd stopped by this house? A hot night and his shirt sticking to his chest, a sudden roll of thunder, white light flashing at the window, hard rain like nails on the tin roof. A cool night breeze coming across the room to find him in her bed. So, June, then, the summer solstice and the night of the first summer storm.

When she opened the door, he saw right away it wasn't a mistake. She had taken Kimi's disappearance hard, in the way only an old friend's trouble can slam you. A thin gold chain at her neck held a charm, a jagged half of a broken heart. Kimi owned the other half and would still be wearing it wherever she was in the world.

"Where you been so long?" Cass asked, the words coming slow. She put her arms around his neck and kissed him.

Barefoot in a long white dress shirt, holding a bottle of Courvoisier in one hand and a full glass in the other. Was the guy who owned the shirt waiting in her bed?

"You always answer the door like this?"

"Only when I'm waiting on you."

"Can I come in out of the cold?" Antelope said and took a step toward her.

She took him by the arm and kicked the door closed behind them. The mixed aromas of burning sage and onions and garlic frying up—the warm scent of home—surrounded him.

"You hungry?"

He shook his head.

"Still killing yourself with fast food, am I right? I got something on the stove, but I can't seem to get hungry enough to eat. Better turn it off before I burn the house down like an old reservation lady."

She disappeared into the kitchen, and he walked over to the Christmas tree, where he carefully adjusted strands of tinsel. The twinkling lights and the simple task were a good distraction from the serious thoughts filling his head.

Back from the kitchen, Cass was beside him, the snifter of cognac still in her hands, the bottle gone.

"I came to talk."

He was surprised by the sound of his own voice; the words came out soft as a whisper.

"You got more game than that," Cass said. She bent down and placed her drink on the floor. She stood close, just inches from him, and her hands found his shoulders with a light touch, small birds settling on branches. He felt the old vibration, years of history and hurt, quivering and humming, alive in the room with them, held captive and ready.

"I've got questions that need answers."

"Later. Can't you see I'm drunk? Take advantage of me, Beau. Isn't that why you came here?"

"Don't say that. It's not like that."

She leaned into him, let her full weight fall against his chest; cognac and rose water, sweet, clean hair. He bent down and cradled her in his arms. She swayed in a slow, mournful motion. After a long time, she came to her senses and stepped away from him.

With a soft touch, he wiped tears from her face.

"Our girl is gone. I'm so sad. I've been a bad friend lately." She slid to the floor in front of the tree. "Sit by me."

He sat down beside her. Cold air stirred the curtains at the old wooden windows.

"She left me a message last week, and I never got back to her. I can't stop thinking about that. I should have called her back."

"The way the two of you are, she must have understood. Don't fret. When was the last time the two of you went away on a girls' weekend?"

"Are you kidding? I wish! That all ended when she got married. Why?"

"Kevin told me different, that the two of you go off on shopping trips."

Why would Kevin lie? And then it hit him. Maybe it was Kimi who lied.

Cass took a long drink and tucked her hair behind her ears. "What now?"

"I need to catch up." He took the glass from her hand and drank the liquid down in one gulp. Hot, magic cognac straight to his brain, every ugly, evil thing melting away. "Can I get another one of these?"

She took the glass from him and walked on tiptoe into the kitchen, showing off the saucy swing of her wide hips. She stretched up to the cabinet for the liquor. It was all he could do not to grab her from behind and take her right there on the cold linoleum floor. He thought she wouldn't resist, but didn't want to risk losing his chance. Now that he was here in her nest, stirred by the sight and scent of her, he couldn't bear it if she sent him home.

A few more drinks and he'd have her laughing and wanting him again, or at least wanting what she remembered of him, what they'd had and lost. Either way he wouldn't fall asleep alone tonight. And wasn't that why he'd come here? He wasn't sure what she wanted. But for the moment, it didn't matter.

She came back with the bottle and a glass for him. They drank and watched the lights twinkling on the tree. It felt like old times, the two of them suspended in a moment.

Without warning, she hit him in the stomach, all the force a slender drunk girl can muster behind her fist.

"You have to find her. Don't let me down."

He put his arms around her and pulled her close. He held her down and felt the blood beating in the veins of her wrists and knew the sweet certainty of being alive again.

■ ■ ■

Dawn was breaking when Antelope woke, darkness resolving around them. In the still room, the only sound was an ancient clock ticking like a heartbeat. He allowed himself a minute to absorb the peace that had settled over them in the night. Cass slept curled around a pillow, her small hands folded under her chin as if in prayer, her long, loose hair falling across her small breasts. She looked innocent, childlike, and he was reminded of her as a girl, barefoot in the reservation summers, brown legs running in tall grass.

She'd turned in her sleep all through the night beside him, making murmurs and small cries. At one point, he'd been sure she was awake when she sat up in bed and shook him hard. He rose up alarmed, asked, "What, Cass?" But she fell back down in a heap, dead asleep. Nothing new; it was always a challenge getting any real sleep in Cass's bed. They would talk again.

Though he longed to stay in the warm bed with her, he rose and dressed in the mottled light, careful and silent so as not to wake her. He didn't want any words to pass between them this morning, wanted only to keep last night's dream a dream. He left her and closed the door behind him.

THURSDAY
DECEMBER 23

CHAPTER 26

When Antelope stepped out of the warm cave of Cass's bungalow, the wind hit him in the face with a heavyweight punch. The thermometer on the door registered two degrees Fahrenheit, but with the wind chill factor, it felt more like ten below.

Tall pines lined the streets of the Old Town section of Rock Springs, like a straight row of soldiers standing at attention in the dark street. Beyond them he saw a mass of swollen clouds turning in the dark sky.

On the two-way radio, there was talk of closing the interstate. They'd be stuck with stranded holiday travelers, all the bars and motels choked with guests dumping money and frustration. Just what they didn't need if they wanted to make any progress on this land mine of a case.

He went straight to the station, and when he walked inside, he shivered. He took it as a sign something bad was about to happen.

If Kimi was found dead somewhere in the state, they might never know about it. Wyoming didn't have a shared database to keep track of people who went missing. A person could disappear in one part of the state and turn up dead in another and be buried in an unmarked grave. There was no easy way to identify the dead without coordination between the counties. Scruggs was standing at his desk, one hand on the phone, the other on the mouse attached to the desktop. He motioned for Antelope to come in.

As he walked into the office, he picked up the metallic odor he'd come to associate with Scruggs's anxiety.

"I got a call from KATV down in Salt Lake. CNN picked up the story. Our case is going to be on national news at noon. Forget about Christmas with the family. Marla will have my balls. Who do I hang for this? This wouldn't have happened if Kimi wasn't media herself, damn it. Cedric Yee's escalated this, I bet."

"I'm sure Kimi's family's got the worst of it."

"This bitch has gone viral now," Scruggs said.

For a second Antelope thought he was referring to Kimi, and then realized he was referring to the way the story was spreading.

"Anybody who works for me has 'no comment' if asked by any of those media hounds. That goes for you, too."

When Scruggs talked like this, Antelope knew better than to engage in conversation with the man. It was a survival tactic he'd learned growing up around all the angry old men on the reservation—men who wanted to hear themselves talk and nothing from a punk kid like him. It worked equally well with his boss. So he waited. He knew Scruggs would wind down soon. There was work to do, if he wanted this thing over.

"Say something," Scruggs ordered.

"Waiting on you."

Phones rang like Christmas bells in the outer office. Scruggs looked sick, his skin dulled to a gray pallor Antelope had never seen before.

"I don't need this." The sheriff's right hand rested on his belly. He rubbed it with his thumb, grimacing every few seconds on the down stroke.

Anyone else and Antelope would have asked him if he was okay.

"I don't need this," Scruggs repeated.

Antelope was quiet. Though the day outside was menacing, the office sported Christmas cheer: pine boughs draped the windows, and someone was brewing mulled cider. The cinnamon smell lulled Antelope into thinking things would be okay. It was a short-term anesthetic, he knew, but he went with it.

No matter what, Christmas was hard to take down. As if reading his thoughts, Scruggs reached across and swatted the tiny Charlie Brown–style Christmas tree on his desk into the trash can. It made a tinkling sound when its single red ornament hit the rim and shattered.

"This is not the time to go mute on me."

"Yes, sir."

"I'll have my hands full managing the media. I need someone on the street. You know the street better than anyone. Not because she's Native. Don't listen to any bullshit rumors—you know it better than anyone."

"Agreed."

"This one's yours. Take it and run with it."

Antelope nodded. Scruggs motioned for him to lock the door. When he turned around, there was a shot glass on the desk.

"Drink up, son. This isn't going to happen again."

Antelope threw the shot down fast, another reservation lesson learned.

"Hard luck, she's family. Don't go soft because of it, use it."

"Yes, sir."

"There's something you should know. Hell, maybe you already know it. But you haven't heard it from me yet and that means you haven't heard it."

Antelope waited. It was going to be just the one drink. The pint and the glasses went back in the drawer. The sheriff didn't need much artificial courage.

"It's been ten years. A young woman by the name of Lisa Bennett disappeared without a trace. Native American. Married. What will the media do with those coincidences? I was the lead investigator and I didn't deliver. She was never found. The case ruined me. Hell, it's the only reason I'm sitting here talking to you. If it hadn't been for that case, I'd have made sheriff in Lander."

"What went wrong there?"

"What didn't? A true forensic clusterfuck. First responders disturbing the scene, leads not followed, evidence compromised or totally lost. Investigative lines got crossed when the Feds came in early on a tip about a serial rapist relocating to Wyoming up from Colorado. If I made a mistake, it was in looking deep instead of wide. I focused on the husband. He looked good for it, but in the end, he wasn't." The sheriff pulled open the drawer and poured himself another shot. "This case is worse. Too many suspects and not a single piece of evidence pointing to any one of them. The cheating husband and his lying mistress covering for him. A sex offender brother who introduces her to his sex offender pals. A serial rapist we have no leads on. And the mother's a mental case, schizophrenic or something—you know, she's your aunt. What I want to know is if she was hearing voices that told her to harm her own daughter. You know the saying, with friends like that, who needs enemies? It fits in this case."

Antelope nodded. "This afternoon I meet with Dr. Hunt and Cassandra McKnight at Probation and Parole to review all the registered sex offenders and prioritize according to level of risk."

"We need to cover all the bases, scare all the snakes out from all the rocks. Get Probation and Parole earning their keep for once. Tell Cassandra McKnight I want her to meet with each one of the men she supervises and put the screws to them, see what turns up. But don't let up on Cahill. Right now, he's our Mr. Number One."

Pride, gratitude, excitement, and fear mixed with acid in Antelope's gut as the weight of the responsibility settled. This was the career-making case he had been waiting for. But he'd need to temper his enthusiasm, given the circumstances. Any sign of arrogance as he took charge, and he'd lose all he valued on the Wind River Reservation.

"I appreciate you putting your trust in me. I won't let you down."

The thought of Kimi in a Jane Doe grave sickened Antelope. "I'm still hoping to find her alive," he said.

CHAPTER 27

Cassandra McKnight had no business being a probation officer for sex offenders. She was a drop-dead gorgeous Native woman, black hair pulled into a bun at the base of her neck with a few loose tendrils gracing her face. She couldn't hide her figure with the tailored suits that made up her professional attire. If her parolees ever saw her in Native dress, their fantasies alone would get them locked up again.

I was impressed, though, with the way Cassandra handled herself professionally. Her motto for surviving as a woman in a world of male ex-convicts was to keep better boundaries than a barbed wire fence.

When I arrived at the Probation and Parole office, Cassandra had the files pulled and piled on the conference table. It was another Sweetwater County public building erected in the 1970s with oil field profits—all rock walls, tile floors, and oak furnishings. From the inside, the county didn't look too shabby.

There was a touch of obsessive-compulsive disorder in Cassandra's organization. She had ninety manila jacket files arranged in groups according to offense. I knew the statistics. I treated only a small percentage of the sex offenders in the county in the aftercare group, the ones currently on parole. Still, ninety was an astounding number in a county of sixty thousand. Most of the cases involved family incest; these were offenders unlikely to go outside their comfort zone of easy-access victims. Those offenders with crimes against strangers made a smaller but still disturbingly impressive pile.

"So how are you doing with this?" I asked. I knew Cassandra was Kimi's friend from way back. Kimi spoke often of her in her sessions.

"Me and her are best buds. Between us, it's been tough. Thanks for asking. Kindness tends to be in short supply in my business." Her face hardened. "Now that we've got that out of the way, I'm going to need to shut that door to get through this."

"Sounds like you've got a plan."

"Here are all the offenders she knows."

She pushed a small pile toward me.

"Good idea."

"Antelope's orders: take a good look at the perpetrators known to her before we look at anybody else."

We decided to work separately, hold comments, and compare notes after the first run-through. I would review the sex offender evaluations, noting static factors—the events that defined the offense and contributed to the unchangeable historical factors of the case— as well as the change factors: stability in a long-term relationship, a clean and sober lifestyle, full-time employment, and participation in community supports, such as counseling or church affiliation.

We worked in silence, and the morning hours passed quickly. Before long the sun was gone from the east window, leaving the room in chilly shadow.

Cassandra got up to turn on the overhead light. She stretched and yawned. "It's noon. I need a break. How about you?"

"I need to meet someone right about now—Cedric Yee. He left me a voice mail earlier asking to meet in exchange for a free lunch at his family's restaurant."

"The Wonderful House. Yummy. But Cedric? I'll pass. I'm going to kick it out of here and hit the twelve-twenty spin class at the Rec Center."

"Can I bring you back some takeout? I promise to leave Cedric there."

"No thanks. I'm saving my calories for alcohol these days. Want to meet for a drink later?"

"I'm at the Holiday Inn. There's a fundraiser for Search and Rescue in the ballroom. Want to meet at the bar?"

"Good idea. It'll help me get through the afternoon. Do me a favor though, don't mention it to Antelope. I'm in the mood for girl talk. I've had my fill of testosterone for a while." She pointed at the files in front of her.

"Our secret," I said. I put a clip on the page I'd been reading to mark my place before I headed out the door.

■ ■ ■

I walked the three blocks to the restaurant. It felt good to be out in the fresh air and away from the morning's dreary reading material.

The Wonderful House was two blocks over, in the Carlyle Hotel in Old Town. Dozens of goldfish swam in dizzying circles in a large pool at the entrance to the dining room. Not much had changed since it opened in 1947, from what I could tell.

I spotted Cedric across the dining room. He stood perfectly still, his hands folded in front of him. When he saw me, he bowed and came to me, took my right arm, and led me to a private nook enclosed in velvet drapes.

He didn't look at me. His eyes moved back and forth in the small, confined space. He adjusted his wire-rim glasses, coughed, and scratched his neck with his index finger. When Kimi talked about him in her sessions, she'd described him as socially anxious. But she also admired Cedric. He was the one who'd convinced the paper's editor to make her the exclusive reporter on the serial rapist, arguing that assigning a female reporter would demonstrate more sensitivity to the rape victims. It was a prime assignment for a young reporter, and Kimi had been grateful.

But his attentions had also left her anxious. In a recent session Kimi had confided that Cedric had crossed a line by using her Native name without her permission.

A waiter came in.

"You will trust me to choose something delicious for our luncheon?" Cedric asked. I nodded, and he ordered in Cantonese.

I waited for him to take the lead since he'd asked for the

meeting. I hoped to hear about Kimi's state of mind in the days before she disappeared.

"I need to talk about Kimi," he began. "I didn't know who else to call. You're her therapist. I presume that means you know her well."

"I can neither confirm nor deny that," I said.

"Confirmation came from Kimi. It wasn't unusual for her to share some of what she talked about in therapy. Did she never tell you how close we are? I know she met with you every Friday night at seven o'clock. That's how I know you may be the last person to have seen her before she left us."

"I still can't talk to you about Kimi."

"Again, no need. It is I who wish to speak to you about Kimi—off the record, of course. You see, we both have our professional guidelines."

"I'm listening."

The waiter appeared with the food. Cedric carefully served out portions from the steaming plates and handed me a set of chopsticks. "Perhaps it would have been better to have made an appointment, come to your office. I don't know how these things work."

"That would be appropriate if you are seeking treatment. Are you seeking treatment?"

"No, I'm not interested in therapy right now. Like all of us, I have my problems, but I've always been able to deal with them. Maybe another time, I will need treatment." He laughed, a short croaking sound. He put his napkin over his mouth and stifled the sounds. "Sorry. Nervous, I guess."

"You said you wanted to talk about Kimi?"

"You know I was the one who reported her missing. So of course, I'm being questioned. To them, everyone is a suspect. I'm not sure I should tell them what I know."

"How can I help?"

"She trusted you. Maybe I can, too."

"You want to tell me what the sheriff's department should know?"

"You're working with the sheriff's department, correct?"

"As a consultant."

"I didn't mention it before because it didn't seem important at first."

"But you've changed your mind now. What is it?"

Cedric put his head in his hands, and his shoulders rose and fell. He made no sound, but he was crying. I felt sorry for him. He seemed so lonely and isolated.

"Forgive me," he said, wiping away tears.

"It's hard for all of us who care about Kimi."

"I may never see her again."

"Try not to lose hope." Easier said than done. I struggled with the same fear.

"You are kind. Perhaps that is why Kimi so enjoyed her sessions with you."

"I'm listening whenever you're ready to tell me."

Neither of us had eaten a thing. I picked up the chopsticks, but I'd lost my appetite.

"Kimi was supposed to meet me for lunch here on Friday, the day she went missing. But she didn't come and she never came back to the office that day. Detective Antelope asked me if I began to worry right away. He seemed suspicious of my friendship, hinted at something more. I didn't like that implication. It would be a waste of time for him. So I told him I wasn't worried. I couldn't tell him what I'd done."

"What did you do?"

"I couldn't sleep. I went to her house that night. I had to know she was safe. But the house was dark. Her car was gone. I told myself she'd be in the office on Monday. But, of course, she wasn't."

Cedric hadn't picked up his chopsticks and showed no signs of interest in eating.

"I wasn't the only person looking for Kimi. The sheriff showed up not long after I did. He checked the door, looked in the garage. Why he was there?"

CHAPTER 28

I waited for Antelope in the cold under the green canvas awning outside the Probation and Parole offices. Snow melt dripped onto the sidewalk from the roof five stories above. When the sun went down, the walkway would be treacherous with ice. Across the street, in a gazebo near the unused railroad tracks, children lined up to visit Santa's Depot. I was thinking about what Cedric had told me when Antelope appeared.

"Are you waiting for me?"

"I want to tell you something Cassandra doesn't need to know."

"This is getting interesting."

"I had lunch with Cedric Yee. He held back information when you questioned him the other day."

"Why did he tell you? Why not come directly to me?"

"Something about you getting the wrong idea about him and Kimi. He's not the most direct communicator."

"You can say that again. What did he hold back?"

"He admitted that he went to her house Friday night."

"I asked him about that and he flat-out lied to me. On the face of it, though, it doesn't add much."

"The point is, he claims the sheriff was there."

"On Friday night?"

"At Kimi's house, knocking on the door and looking for her car in the garage."

"I'll have another conversation with Cedric. Cassandra is

coming now. That was a good call, by the way. She doesn't need to know about this."

■ ■ ■

We sat around the conference table, working on the sex offenders' files. An hour into the work, Antelope threw down his pen.

"That's it," he said. "This is giving me a headache. Let's talk."

"How do you want to do this, Beau?" Cassandra asked.

"By the book. Forget for the moment that we know her. I don't want to miss anything because we're making assumptions."

"I'm in," I said.

I was bored reading reports I had written and was ready for a break too.

"Let me grab a candy bar real quick," Cassandra said. "And don't either of you say anything. I worked my butt off at the gym over lunch hour."

Antelope smiled and watched her as she posed with hands on her hips in the doorway.

"Shut up," she said. She disappeared into the hallway and reappeared a minute later with three Kit Kat bars, which she dropped on the table in front of us. "Help yourself. It's on me."

"No thanks," I said.

Antelope took a candy bar and put it in his shirt pocket.

"This isn't a buffet," Cassandra said. "Eat it or leave it . . . no takeout." She reached for the candy in his pocket. Antelope pushed her away and tossed it on the table.

"All yours," he said.

There was that twitch at his right eye. Could he really be angry about that? Cassandra gave a light kick to his calf with the toe of her royal blue stiletto, and something passed between the two of them that I couldn't pin down. There was a flash of play-fulness in Antelope's eyes, and Cassandra licked chocolate from her lip. But seconds later the two of them were staring blankly past each other as if nothing had happened.

"Speaking of takeout," Cassandra said, "how was your lunch with Cedric? He's an odd duck, isn't he?"

"He might have Asperger's disorder."

"Ass what?" Antelope asked.

"Asperger's disorder," I repeated. "It's a form of autism. Intellectual intelligence can range from average to superior. The deficit is in the area of social and emotional relating. I haven't evaluated him, so I can't give a formal diagnosis, but he exhibits many of the characteristics of the disorder."

"What characteristics?" Antelope said. "Paint me a picture."

"Difficulty with eye contact, stilted speech, inappropriate emotional response, repetitive conversation, lack of empathy, inability to read social cues," I said.

"That's Cedric, all right," Cassandra said. "Maybe you can't diagnose him, but I will. Case closed."

"Hold on a minute, Cass," Antelope said. "I'm curious, would a person with Asperger's be able to sense other peoples' emotions, figure out their intentions, and be able to tell who was being straight and who was leading them on?"

"All those things you mentioned, those are the kind of things someone with Asperger's would have difficulty discerning," I said.

"Interesting. So they'd be given to drawing false conclusions, acting on their own wishes and assumptions?" Antelope said.

"You've got it. You're a quick study," I said.

"He is," Cassandra said, and gave his calf another nudge with her shoe.

A frown, another mini-twitch, and Antelope got serious.

"Let's get back to what we came here to do," I said. "What have you got for us, Cass?"

She wiped chocolate from her fingertips and tossed the paper towel and wrapper into a basket under the table. "Ninety registered sex offenders, and if that isn't bad enough, we have to work from paper files. Our computer system is being upgraded, and, big surprise, all the files are temporarily unavailable."

"I'd trust your brain over a computer any day," Antelope said.

"Don't try to charm me, Beau. Watch out for this guy, Pepper. You don't know him like I do. We grew up together . . . though he chooses to forget that sometimes."

Antelope stiffened. I'd never seen the man be so reactive and sensitive. I knew the two of them had a long and complicated history, but it was still surprising.

"It's all right here," he said, placing a hand over his heart. "There's no forgetting. And you shouldn't say things like that. Especially now." He shot Cassandra a dark look.

Cassandra put a hand to her throat and touched the gold charm she was wearing. She returned the same dark look.

I had no interest in being in the middle of their private battle. I considered excusing myself and letting them finish what was going on between them. I could come back when they wanted to work. But Cassandra saved me the trouble.

"Whatever, Beau," she said, "let's get to work. That's why we're here. This is about Kimi. Let's take a look at the guys in your group, Pepper. Kimi's acquainted with some of these characters. Diego, for example."

"What's his status with Probation and Parole?" I asked.

Cassandra checked the file. "Three more months and he's a free man."

"He gets two checks, one for being family and one for being a sex offender," Antelope said.

"Beau, it can't be Diego," Cassandra said. "You know that."

"It doesn't matter what I know. Kimi's missing, and whether we like it or not, Diego is a suspect because he's related to her. And thanks to his insanely poor judgment and impulse control, he's put himself on the short-list for suspects in this case."

"He's her brother, Beau. Have you forgotten that, too?"

"You know the statistics in these cases as well as I do," Antelope said.

"You've got a history with Diego. Are you too close to this?"

Antelope looked at her for a long time. Outside it was snowing, and in the silence ice crystals hit the window like birds tapping—quick, precise. A cold blue light chilled the room. I felt a sense of foreboding as the storm pressed in.

"Don't worry about me, Cass," he finally said. "I can do the job."

His mood seemed to be following the trajectory of the weather, getting lower by the minute.

"Sometimes the job is all you can do," Cassandra said. "At least, that's what I hear from home. There's more to Diego than you'll find in here. Try to remember that." She pushed a stack of files toward him.

"Focus, you two," I said. "We've got a ton of work to do here."

"You're right. Let's do *this*," Cassandra said, and tapped the jagged heart at her neck.

CHAPTER 29

Cassandra had changed out of the gray power suit. She wore white jeans with a silver belt and a blue silk shirt the color of her stilettos. Her waist-length hair was freed from the top knot she wore at work. Tying her hair up was meant to send a message to the felons she supervised that they didn't need to be fantasizing about her, I guessed. I hadn't changed out of the clothes I'd worn earlier: black jeans and a black turtleneck sweater, sturdy boots that had survived New England winters.

I spotted Cassandra's white coat, draped over an empty seat in a dark corner at the far end of the horseshoe-shaped bar, before I saw her. Volunteers packed the ballroom to the right of the bar, their laughter inconsistent with the evening's task: find a missing woman. What was everyone laughing about? On a red, white, and blue banner from a past political campaign, the words *Still Missing* had been spray-painted in silver. The whole scene had a party atmosphere, with the ballroom functioning as an extension of the bar, empty glasses and beer bottles accumulating at the communication stations.

Cassandra was in a zone, lost in her smartphone, and jumped when I touched her shoulder.

"This is the place to be tonight. Here, sit down." She pulled the coat onto her lap to make a place for me.

"Any news from all of this? It looks like the whole town is here."

"Not that I've heard. Kevin stopped by. He's having too good a time, if you ask me."

"What did he have to say?"

The narrow room was packed and overheated from the warmth of all the bodies crowding together.

"He was all about telling me how hard this has been on him. Seemed happy in the spotlight, though. There he is now. He's wearing that blonde like a sweater."

She tipped her head and rolled her big doe eyes in the direction of the other end of the bar.

"Tracy Hopkins?"

"Kimi was onto him. From what I'm seeing right now, looks like she was right." She slipped her phone into a coat pocket. "Enough. I keep thinking it's her. Stupid."

Cassandra threw back the last of her drink, and her eyes watered

"Kevin doesn't strike me as the type to turn away support," I said.

The blond bartender came over and swiped at the clean bar top.

"What can I get you cowgirls tonight?"

Strong western accent, cleft in his chin, a crooked smile—a grown-up Dennis the Menace in a white dress shirt with sleeves rolled up.

"Please, don't insult me," Cassandra said. "I fight for the other side. Bring me another one of these." She smiled and flicked her middle finger, sending the empty glass sailing across the bar.

"Dewar's double coming up," the bartender said, giving a salute to Cassandra. He looked at me for confirmation.

"I'll have the same," I said.

He winked and went off to get our drinks.

"Kevin should put on a better show in public," Cassandra said. "If Diego saw this, it wouldn't be pretty."

"Have you talked to Diego?"

"Once and only briefly. I'm keeping my distance, considering. He's been blowing up my phone, though. He wants me to finesse a temporary order to leave the county. He's the only one who can find her, according to him. His usual protective brother bullshit, tacked on to regular male bullshit, tacked on to Diego bullshit."

"I didn't know you liked him so much."

Cassandra laughed and for a minute it seemed as if everything was all right and Kimi wasn't missing. "The man's got too much testosterone. But he's always been there, you know, right beside Kimi. Back home you never saw one without the other. He made himself her protector from early on. Not that it's a bad thing. She needed it. But he's a hothead with a quick temper, always ready to use his fists. Smart as a whip, but no off switch. If he thinks he's right, he's right. And you don't ever want to cross him. You might see another side of him in group, where he's pushed to be vulnerable and self-disclose. But believe me, bottom line: don't turn your back on Diego."

"You make him sound dangerous."

"He's a registered sex offender; what more is there to say?" Cassandra smirked and scanned the bar. "Where's our guy? I'm getting thirsty here."

"There's always more to say. Especially in this case, where you know the story. You defended him pretty strongly this afternoon."

"I admit he got a bad deal. She was his girlfriend, it was consensual, blah, blah, blah. But—big but—I wouldn't put it past him to do something similar again. Even so, as far as him doing anything to hurt Kimi, it would never happen. Beau's not thinking straight when he goes in that direction. He gets all twisted up because of the way things are between them. But enough about their macho war."

"So Diego wants to search for Kimi himself?"

"That's what he said. And I am going to see what I can do for him. If I don't, there'll be hell to pay. He won't let it drop. He's convinced the sheriff's department isn't doing all they can to find her."

"He might be right," I said. "All this action and still no clue where she is."

In the other room, someone began talking over a loudspeaker. The crowd quieted down, but the speaker's words still escaped me.

"Uh-oh, trouble in paradise," Cassandra said. She'd been watching the room behind us in the mirror behind the bar. She spun around on the bar stool and followed the action at the door to the ballroom.

I looked in time to see Tracy Hopkins pull her arm free from Kevin Cahill's grip and speed walk toward the door, elbows flaring, blond curls flouncing. A serious girl on the move. Kevin tried to play it off by giving a dismissive wave and turning away. But by the look on his face, he was seething. He took a long swallow from his beer, placed the mug on the bar with precision, and followed her to the door and out into the night.

"He's a snake. But not the only thing on Kimi's mind lately."

The bartender arrived with the drinks. I caught him eyeing Cassandra, but she only had eyes for the whiskey he'd just placed in front of her. He left without a word.

"You hurt his feelings."

"Screw him. This new breed of bartenders—excuse me, *mixologists*—with their signature drinks, all trying to court the female customers. Bring me my alcohol—that's all I need, baby."

"Kimi had something else on her mind?"

"That's funny coming from you, you being her therapist. You'd know what's on her mind, what she's worried about, right?"

"It doesn't always work that way. Sometimes the therapist is the last to know."

"She's been spooked lately. That's for sure. She thought she was being followed. I told her to let the law know. Kimi just laughed. She wasn't inclined to do that. I couldn't disagree. I asked her if she ever worried about being targeted by the White Mountain Rapist. You should have seen the look on her face . . . Native girl turns white girl that quick." Cassandra snapped her fingers. "I told her to talk to Cedric about it, but she batted that idea away like a bug. Speak of the devil, here's the man now."

Cassandra summoned Cedric Yee from across the room with a long, wide wave, like she was stranded on an island and flagging down a plane. It took a while for her to get his attention. He had a glazed look. He spotted her as she beckoned him with curling fingers; she looked like she was trying to call over a lost cat. He came obediently.

"Are you here on official business, Cedric?" Cassandra asked.

She spoke his name softly, making it seductive, intimate. I knew what she was doing, trying to throw him off guard.

"Yes, I cover everything related to Kimi. I'm on that story around the clock, twenty-four seven."

A stale smell, like a moldy laundry hamper, came off him. I watched as Cassandra registered the unpleasant scent and sat back a few inches. She had a tendency to lean in when she was talking with someone. It was part of her intensity.

"Kimi thought someone was following her. Did she tell you about that?"

"She did seem stressed lately. I wasn't aware she thought she was being followed."

"So who's following her?" Cassandra asked.

"How would I know that?"

"The two of you are close, right? That's what I hear from Kimi." Cassandra paused and seemed to be waiting for a reaction.

Cedric's face glistened with sweat.

"If I had to guess, I'd say the White Mountain Rapist was following her. What about you, Cedric?"

Cedric wiped his forehead with a white handkerchief. "That has occurred to me. I told Detective Antelope about it when he questioned me. He didn't seem to take it seriously, I'm afraid."

"So what'd you do about that, Cedric?" Cassandra asked.

"What did I do?"

"Did you offer to be her lookout? Did you tail her to make sure she was safe? Did you have her back? Well, did you? You didn't let her go around unprotected, did you?"

There was a vicious look in Cassandra's eye I'd never seen before, pleasure in the fear and weakness Cedric was displaying.

"The thought came to me after she disappeared. But Kimi would have been uncomfortable with that kind of action."

"So that's how you work? You let the woman call the shots? It's good to know Kimi had a friend when she needed one." Cassandra folded her arms, resting her case.

She was gunning for the guy, clearly. But I couldn't figure out her motive.

"I'd do anything for Kimi."

"You thought she was losing it, though," Cassandra said. "Going crazy like her mother. She felt that. Kimi felt that when you worried about her being stressed."

"Did she tell you that?" Cedric swallowed multiple times. He looked like he was going to be sick.

"No, she didn't talk about you much."

Cedric had a drink in his hand, clear liquid—vodka or water. He hadn't touched it. Cassandra continued to look at him in that steady, probing way of hers. She wasn't done with him yet.

"You seem uncomfortable, Cedric. Let's change the subject. I'm curious about something. Did you ever hear from the rapist? You know how that happens sometimes, these creeps write to the paper, make threats and all?"

"Are you asking if the rapist is communicating with us at the paper?" Cedric asked.

"What, like that's too crazy?" Cassandra asked. "I'm watching too much TV? That doesn't happen in real life?" She finished her drink and summoned the bartender with a whistle and wink. He was there in an instant, refilling the glass and swiping the bar with a clean towel. Cassandra didn't look at him.

"Well, yes, in some of the bigger crimes that has happened . . . in the larger metropolitan areas. Nothing like that has ever happened at the *Rocket Miner*."

"So no word from our little guy in Rock Springs?"

"It's taking a chance, putting something in writing like that. Those letters are full of clues and often become the vehicle by which the criminal is apprehended. The White Mountain Rapist is smarter than that."

"But if you had heard from the rapist, a telephone call or a letter, you would have told Kimi, right? She would need to know, especially if the letter was about Kimi."

"Why would he write about her?" Cedric asked.

Cedric didn't have the usual emotional responses; more evidence in support of a diagnosis of Asperger's.

"Think about it, Cedric," Cassandra said. "Twisted criminal,

Founded

beautiful woman writing about his sins. Sounds like a psychopath's wet dream to me."

Cedric gripped his glass and stared at Cassandra as if caught in a spell. The bar was packed and noisy. A local country band was playing a cover of Brad Paisley's "Somebody Knows You Now"—a song about intimacy that comes from being seen and known in everyday ways. I thought about Zeke, the only person who had ever known me like that. The problem was, I hadn't known him—a fact I'd been unaware of until after he died. He still had a stunning claim on me.

"You've got as good a handle on this guy's psychology as Kimi does. I mean, you worked with her on the stories, right? Was she in danger?"

"It was a thought. But I assure you, I am no expert. Excuse me. I'm going to leave now." Cedric wiped his face again and with the handkerchief over his mouth moved quickly to the door. A blast of cold air came in, and the room got quiet as the band took a break.

Cassandra rubbed her arms. "Could he be the one?" She tossed her head in a way that reminded me of Soldier.

"What do you mean 'the one'?"

"Kimi's madly in love with someone. You know that, don't you?"

"Treatment's off limits. You can't ask me that. And it's unfair advantage right now. I've been drinking."

"We're in a bar, Pepper. I won't hold it against you if you let something slip. But seriously, you must be having a hell of a time of it—got to be some ethical issues with you being Kimi's therapist, Diego's group therapist, and consulting on the case, am I right? And didn't Beau tell me you got called to the jail about Estella, too?"

"I don't know, did he?"

I didn't like the idea Antelope would be discussing my evaluation of Kimi's mother with Cassandra. As far as I knew, her involvement in the investigation was limited to the sex offenders she supervised.

"Or maybe it came through the grapevine on the reservation. Bad news travels out of there fast. Estella's mental health issues have been a source of gossip on the reservation for a long time. It's why she moved her family down here to Rock Springs—her kids heard too much crap about her, she wanted a fresh start. Can't say I blame her. Living on the reservation can be suffocating at times. Some things I miss about it. But I'll never go back."

Cassandra took another long pull and finished the Dewar's. When she noticed the glass was empty, her eyes traveled the length of the oak bar and settled on the bartender, who was drawing two draft beers. He must have felt her gaze on him, because as soon as he put the drinks on the bar, he came over to us, grabbed the whiskey bottle, and poured.

Something had changed in the dynamic between the two of them. I couldn't place when in the evening's transactions the tide had turned, but it most definitely had.

Cassandra twirled her hair and swayed in her seat to the beat of "Love Her Like She's Leavin.'"

"I can't talk about Kimi," I said, "but I can listen. Tell me more about your friend and what's been going on with her."

"Cedric's got a major crush on Kimi, so she used that, used him, to get ahead. She wasn't into him. Or so she convinced me. But what if she was?"

"She didn't tell you who she was involved with?"

"She clammed up when I pushed her—and believe me, I pushed. Why couldn't she tell me? I'm her best friend. No way would I ever judge her choice and she knew that. Kimi knew that. It kind of hurt that she wouldn't tell me. I let her know about that, of course. It was one of the reasons we haven't seen too much of each other."

Kimi kept the same boundaries in her personal life that she had in therapy. She wouldn't disclose any identifying details.

"You're sure it was love?"

"Girlfriend, I am sure. But something went wrong."

"What went wrong?"

Cassandra looked away. She twirled her hair with her long, narrow fingers and focused on her reflection in the mirror behind the bar. "She was afraid of him when they ended it," she said slowly. "I told her she was crazy to see him again. She was just like her mother, holding on to someone who wasn't good for her. You can imagine how she took those words." Her black eyes brimmed with tears that didn't fall. She still wouldn't meet my gaze. "It needed to be said. What are friends for if not to tell you the truth? Some of the men Estella took up with did some real damage, but she survived. It looks like Kimi wasn't so lucky."

Cassandra grabbed the bar with both hands.

"What's wrong?"

"Whiskey went to my head. I was a little dizzy for a minute. Some things are too awful to imagine." She began to cry silently. "I let her down. That's why she stopped calling me. I was so stupid to compare her to her mother."

I put my hand on her arm, but she pulled away quickly and wiped away her tears. She looked up and down the bar. The bartender was nowhere in sight.

"You tried to help her."

"I love her like a sister. She's my rock. But she can be fragile, too. Damage was done. Like the sand dunes near the reservation. They look solid, but they're always shifting. You wouldn't want to build anything on them."

"Do you mean recently?"

"Always. How could she be any different? What she went through with Estella growing up? The woman was in and out of mental hospitals and jails after Kimi's dad died in a car accident. I never had the heart to tell Kimi, but the way I see it, she and Estella are two of a kind. She lost her husband at a young age and got left with two little kids to raise alone. That's not a new story on the Arapaho reservation—or anywhere else, for that matter. People saw her breakdowns as a natural reaction to the loss. But would she have fallen apart if she wasn't already halfway there? You tell me, you're the shrink. I can't talk about all this without more whiskey."

The bartender had reappeared. She got his attention by pointing and shooting at him with her thumb and index finger. He practically came running.

"Ma'am?" He held the Dewar's over her glass.

Cassandra wagged her finger at him. "Oh, now you're in trouble. Don't come at me with 'ma'am.'"

"I can't get it right with you," he said, grinning at her.

"Pour the whiskey, honey." Her voice was low and husky, and the words came out in a lazy drawl, blurred by a hint of intoxication.

The bartender did as he was told and gave Cassandra a look that conveyed he was happy to follow her orders. Then he looked at me, but I put my hand over my glass. I'd had enough to drink and enough of the crowd. I was ready to leave. He gave Cassandra a sly look, and then he was gone.

Cassandra sipped her drink and followed him with her eyes. "Where was I?" she said.

"Kimi has always been fragile, just like her mother."

"She was afraid of going crazy like her mother. Those spells she had when she was a kid could have been a preview of things to come."

"It's called dissociating. It happens in extreme psychological stress. The individual can't tolerate the stress, so the mind separates from the body and whatever the body is experiencing."

It was strange to be talking about Kimi's psychological symptoms in this place. Stranger still that the music and laughter coming from the ballroom was related to Kimi's disappearance.

"Maybe this time she got so far away from herself she can't find her way back." She was staring into the mirror again and seemed lost in thought. Tears welled in her eyes again. She sniffed and looked at me. "I'm sorry. It's too much. She needs to come home. You're her therapist. Is she in one of those dissociation things? It's been almost a week now. Can they last that long? Or did she lose her mind and get lost in the desert and freeze to death? It's all I dream about. Seeing her dead and frozen in the snow. Tell me I'm overreacting here. I'm about to go crazy myself with these thoughts."

As Kimi's therapist I was bound by confidentiality not to discuss any aspects of my patient's treatment. But I felt conflicted; I wanted to offer some comfort.

"My hands are tied because of my professional relationship with her," I said carefully. "But dissociation and psychosis are the result of two different psychological processes."

"Thanks," Cassandra said. "I'm sure it will make more sense when I'm stone-cold sober."

The band took another break, and the crowd thinned out. I felt a headache coming on. It seemed that Cassandra was done for the moment.

"Now that all the key players are gone, I'm going to call it a night," I said, reaching for my wallet.

Cassandra slapped a card on the bar. "I got tonight."

"Thanks. We'll do this again soon."

"Oh no we won't. You're a lightweight. Can't have you spending all your hard-earned money keeping me buzzed."

"Are you going to be okay to drive home?"

"You sure you want to leave me alone? It could be dangerous. You know what I'll have to do, right?"

"Drink alone?"

"That never works out for me. I'll take my best option."

She tilted her head toward the end of the bar.

The bartender smiled and leaned back against the counter, feet and arms crossed, waiting patiently, like bait ready for the taking.

"I've got someone I want to erase from my mind," Cassandra said. "The bartender should help with that. I could be a cowgirl tonight . . ." She slapped her forehead with the palm of her hand. "Oh my God, I just remembered. Kimi's mystery man called her Cowgirl! Holy shit! Maybe it's him!"

Cassandra was drunk and not seeing straight. A man calling a woman "cowgirl" in a bar in Wyoming was definitely not an incriminating piece of evidence. But she finished her drink and already had her hand up to order another.

"This situation has taken on a whole new dimension," she said. "Before I just wanted to get laid by pretty boy. Now I'm on a mission to interrogate him and find out if he's Kimi's man."

I told Cassandra to be careful and took the elevator upstairs to bed.

FRIDAY
DECEMBER 24

CHAPTER 30

It was Christmas Eve and afternoon traffic was heavy with last-minute shoppers when I drove across town along Dewar Drive to the sheriff's department. I was meeting with Beau Antelope to sign the county contract that would make official my involvement in the investigation of Kimi Benally's disappearance. Antelope had also faxed a copy of the order from the district court compelling me to disclose treatment records to the investigating officers.

To the right of the four-way road was a construction site in winter hibernation, shrink-wrapped in pink Tyvek against a backdrop of lonely sagebrush desert. On the left, a forty-foot wall of red rock flanked the road.

At the sheriff's office, I surprised Antelope, who was deep in thought at his desk.

"We have to stop meeting like this." He smiled.

"Don't be cute. You're wasting taxpayer's money. You're lucky this is a slow week for me."

I was being rude, and I wasn't sure why. My good mood from the previous day was gone. The man had never been anything but polite and professional with me—except when he tried to get close. And I didn't want close.

"I need your signature right here." He pointed and slid the document across the desk.

"I see you backdated it to cover our talk with Diego."

"The sheriff will have my neck if it isn't by the book." He shrugged. "Let's get to work. I need to figure out if Kevin Cahill has the balls to off his wife without giving a crap about the consequences. There's a word for that, but I'm blanking on it. Help me out here, you're the doctor. Narcissist? Sociopath? Am I getting warm?"

He shared his office with three other detectives. Piles of takeout cartons from ethnic and chain restaurants overflowed the wastebaskets. He tossed a ravaged apple core into a small garbage can beside his desk.

"Technically, I'm not supposed to render a diagnosis without the benefit of a psychological evaluation," I said. "But if I'm not being technical, I'd say narcissist is an apt description."

He opened the bottom drawer of his desk and pulled out a Granny Smith apple. "Care to join me?"

"How biblical. No thanks, I'll pass."

"Ah, the apple, as in the Garden of Eden. We could use knowledge about now. As in the tree of knowledge—are you with me?"

I hadn't had an appetite in days; I'd been living on coffee. "So you're willing to risk paradise, then?" I asked.

"In case you hadn't noticed, that's Rock Springs out there. It's nobody's idea of paradise, Doctor. I'll take the risk."

The window behind Antelope's desk overlooked a dry creek bed. The absence of flowing water made me inexplicably sad. Throughout the last year, it had hit me at odd times: I had totally uprooted myself, left everything that had ever been important to me, to live in this ugly, mean little town where the wind blew all the time and there wasn't a real spring to justify its name.

"You've met Kevin," I said. "What's your opinion?"

"Besides interviewing him since Kimi disappeared, I've only been in his company a few times—as a guest at their wedding, some other random social gigs. The day they got married he was high on love and champagne. From what I hear, that didn't last. But does it ever?"

"I know that was a rhetorical question, Detective," I said. "But in this specific case, the answer is no. They got married last

October, and six months later she was in therapy, trying to sort out if it was a mistake."

"She was surprised by that? The honeymoon was over. How long could it last? I know Kimi's a romantic, but she had to know that if it seemed too good to be true, it likely was."

Outside the window, a flock of starlings rose from their perch on a flat garage roof, took flight, and disappeared.

"As always in therapy, there were a lot of layers," I said. "She didn't love Kevin anymore. That was one of the many things she came to therapy to sort out. Can't say we made much headway there. It didn't help that she dissociated whenever anything disturbing came up."

"Back to Kevin. Is he capable of hurting her?"

"Could be. I don't know him well enough to say for sure, but if he felt enough anger and blame when she took something from him that he'd invested in . . ."

"Any other problems?"

"She thought Kevin was interested in Tracy."

I was uncomfortable disclosing the secrets Kimi had shared in therapy believing they would be safe. There was a court order now, and it required me to divulge the content of her treatment, but it didn't change how I felt.

"The plot thickens."

"It's not a plot. It's her life."

"Point taken." Antelope put up his hands in mock surrender. "Newlywed guy doesn't want sex. That'll make a wife suspicious, urban legend of the always-ready male being what it is. So she checks his phone and voilà! He's caught!"

I shook my head. "Kimi never found any evidence he cheated. And Kevin denied anything sexual, of course. No one admits to sex. But emotional affairs are every bit as lethal. Now we know the truth, courtesy of the *Rocket Miner*—Cedric Yee to be exact. That was Tracy Hopkins coming out of Kevin's window, right?"

"How do you stand your job?"

"No two lives are alike. The stories of the therapy room are endlessly fascinating and mysterious."

"So you say."

"Freud said it."

"Pretty standard stuff so far—and, at the risk of being seen as flippant again, stock soap opera. Where's the mystery?"

"Kimi Benally went missing. That's why we're sitting here having this conversation."

"Touché, Doc."

"That's your second French word. Using Rosetta Stone?"

"In plain English, then. Has Kevin got the stuff to do it? That's my question."

"Nothing shouts sociopath."

"Doesn't mean he couldn't do it if she was getting in the way of something he wanted. Am I right?"

"You've been doing your homework on this stuff."

"How'd you come to meet Kevin? It was Kimi who was your patient, right? They didn't come to see you as a couple?"

"Kimi sought treatment for herself. Typically if I'm seeing someone in individual therapy, I wouldn't meet with the spouse, but she was dissociating and he thought she was lying."

"When she did that as a kid, people thought she was crazy like her mother."

"That's what she was afraid of—that her husband would see her as crazy. So she scheduled a session for the two of them, brought Kevin in so I could explain everything to him and answer any questions."

"And that's when you decided he was a narcissist?"

"That was my impression, definitely. Cold, unsupportive, obvious empathy deficit given the circumstances. Nothing I told him touched him in any way."

"And you're pretty good at seeing."

"I'm great at seeing."

"She was sorry she brought him in?"

"We talked about it in the following session. It was a turning point in the marriage. His judgment and calling her crazy, that knack of going right to the heart of the hurt, made her afraid to stay with him."

"You don't need to know Kimi for more than an hour to know that would hurt her. He must be an imbecile."

"Or intentionally cruel."

Antelope stood and faced the window. I followed his line of sight to the still life beyond of an empty creek bed, oak leaves caught in a chain-link fence, tin roofs, and ancient pines. The sky was the color of lead. I felt cold.

"He wanted out and was pushing her to do it," Antelope said. "He fell out of love, but didn't want to tell her or lose his control over her."

"Poor Kimi."

Antelope got quiet then, and his face looked swollen with sadness. He must be remembering the sweet girl who perfected her escape from the shabbiness of her life.

"It was my idea to say that the Whirlwind took her. You know the legend?"

"Tell me."

Estella had told me about it, but I wanted to hear it from Antelope's perspective. He sat down again. The office sounds, phones ringing, murmured voices in conversation, the occasional crack of laughter, all seemed to fade away. The room took on the hush of a confessional.

"It's the story of a boy and a girl, a brother and sister. The Whirlwind takes the girl away. Everyone believes she is gone forever. But the Whirlwind comes again and brings the girl back—temporarily. Soon, it takes her away again. And it goes on and on like this forever. A cycle of continual hope and renewal. What is lost is found again."

"Seems like a good way to describe what happens to Kimi," I said.

Antelope nodded. "We grew up wild, like a litter of puppies. Grown-ups couldn't keep track of us and mostly didn't try. Kimi got lost a lot more often, and for longer, than anyone else. Enough so people noticed and talked. Me and Diego, we beat up anyone who called her crazy. Then I got the idea to use the legend, make it a Native thing, a spirit thing. And it worked. She was special, in a good way—what special used to mean, magical, unique. She transcended her mother. Even the grown-ups bought it. It was my first experience of the persuasive power of narrative. You can put a spin on anything, and if you sound like you believe it, other people will too."

"Kimi's dissociation developed as a coping mechanism in childhood, tapering off as she matured psychologically."

"And she got away from the craziness, don't forget about that."

"That helped. But recently she regressed to those primitive childhood coping mechanisms. That's what our work was about— looking for the underlying causes and bringing them into her awareness so she could be free of those symptoms."

"That wasn't going so well, I guess?"

"She was making progress. Until a month ago, when the periods of dissociation increased in frequency and got longer."

"So she's lost in one of her episodes?"

"At first I thought that was the case. But it's gone on too long. Not that it's impossible— we're talking about psychological symptoms, and psychology is not a hard science. But it feels unlikely."

A gust of wind rattled the windowpane. Starlings rode the shifting currents in a jagged pattern, then settled again on the roof. Antelope's face was as dark as the darkening day.

"If she didn't leave on her own accord, then she's come to harm. Criminology, also not the hardest of sciences, demands we look first at her husband."

"I can't give you what you want, here. I can't diagnose this man without doing an evaluation. It's not ethical."

"It's not a diagnosis I'm in the market for, Doctor. You can save that for the court, when we bring him to trial. Though he'll be lucky to get into court if he hurt Kimi. I can't see Diego trusting the law to avenge his sister."

"You're right about that. It would be self-sabotage at a time when he's about to get his own life and freedom back. But from what I know of Diego, he couldn't live with himself if he didn't do something."

"Some conversation we're having. I'm grateful to have your

help with this—though I wish it had been something else that brought you into my office."

I stiffened. "I need to get going. I'm headed out of town for a few days. Before all this, I made plans to get away for the holiday. It's wrong to say it, with Kimi gone, but have as nice a Christmas as you can. Will you see your family at all?"

I stood up and put on my down coat. The weight of it settled the chills I'd felt while talking about Kimi, the implication that she was gone for good.

"I'll be staying in town. There's only one thing my family wants for Christmas. I'll be working on that. But it's good you're getting away. Tough time of year for you, if I remember correctly."

I didn't want Antelope's kindness. I didn't want to be reminded about what this time of year meant for me. That was the whole point of getting away from the reminders of Christmas.

Antelope thought he knew something about me, but his talking about it was proof he didn't know me at all.

"I'll ride Soldier and it'll just be another day. That's the plan."

"In case Sheriff Scruggs asks, how long will you be gone?" Antelope asked.

"I'll be back on Sunday evening. But the sheriff knows that. Marla offered me the use of their place in Lander. But I'm curious. He didn't want me on the case initially. What changed his mind?"

"He needs a scapegoat to take the spotlight," Antelope said, but when he saw the look on my face, he quickly rephrased. "Maybe that's putting it too harshly. It makes the department look like we're on top of things and taking the case seriously. It was nothing personal, his resistance to bringing you on. He's a stubborn man. Don't worry—you'll be working directly with me. I'm the point man on this case."

Antelope opened the door. Standing beside him, I was aware of his size, a solid giant beside me. I remembered him telling me about his basketball stardom on the reservation.

"That's good. It gets a little complicated with him being married to Marla. She's a friend and she's been so good to me. I don't want to ruin that relationship."

Antelope's cell phone buzzed and he took the call. I felt the change in him instantly. There wasn't one specific thing I could point to, but all of a sudden, I knew the case had taken a new and dangerous turn.

"Hold her there. I'm on my way," Antelope said. Then he turned to me. "Attempted rape, sounds like the same guy. He attacked her as she was getting out of her car. She fought him and got away. I'm going to the hospital now to see what she can tell me."

I took that as a final sign it was time to leave Rock Springs. I said good-bye to Antelope and didn't bother waiting for the Jeep to warm up. The roads looked clear but would be full of black ice later when the temperature fell with darkness. Driving through the canyon would be tricky then.

As I drove north, a serious wind came up. I fought to hold the steering wheel steady as the Jeep rocked and swayed. The unsettled day closed in, and the desert disappeared in the waning light. All I could see in the headlights was the two-lane road ahead of me.

After leaving Rock Springs city limits, there were no other vehicles. An hour later, as I approached the turnoff to the mountain road that would take me farther into wilderness, my thoughts went to Kimi, who also left Rock Springs alone at night.

CHAPTER 31

Just before midnight on Christmas Eve, Diego left the vigil for Kimi at Our Lady of Sorrows Catholic Church—walked out and let the heavy red door fall shut behind him, silencing the voices of the choir and the swelling chords of the organ. Outside the gothic stone structure, Broadway lay hushed in the eerie stillness of the holy evening.

It was the congregation joining in with Christmas carols that had led to his quick exit. He hadn't shed a tear throughout all the crazed days since his sister went missing but knew if he tried to sing, it would be the end of him. In the last three days, he'd crossed the grid that was his sister's world. Like a child in search of a lost pet, he'd hunted all the empty places, called her name into every forgotten corner.

Late in that afternoon, he'd made one last call to Cassandra to remind the woman she was his sister's best friend and if she wanted her found, she had to free him, get him permission to leave the county. She said she'd check and get back to him, a little less cold than he'd known her to be in her usual dealings with him as a probationer. He'd heard back from her just before the county went into shutdown for the Christmas holiday. She'd made it happen. He had the green light to leave the county.

He'd taken his mother to the vigil and put in some face time with Little James because it was Christmas. Not that anyone in the family cared about anything this holiday other than getting Kimi back where she belonged. But now, with his mother and son busy at church for the next several hours, he was free to search for her in their old stomping grounds.

He hated asking for favors, but was forced to ask Troy for the loan of his Dodge Ram before heading out of town. There was too much damn snow to count on his GTO on the backcountry roads. With the truck, he'd be able to scour the countryside from the top of Pilot Butte down, and then cruise all the reservation roads. He and Kimi had their special places out toward Ocean Lake and Pilot Butte Dam. The need to touch familiar soil was strong now. Maybe she'd felt it, too.

It was the first clear night he could remember for days. Overhead, the brightness of December's "Long Night Moon" illuminated the snowy desert for miles. From his vantage point cresting the rising landscape, the streets of Rock Springs below resembled coiled strands of Christmas lights.

Tonight, he would find his way to her. He was sure of it. His mind turned with memories and images of Kimi, a nonstop sister film festival playing in his mind. His gut burned from acid and the grease of fast food. In the pit of his stomach was a god-awful loneliness he couldn't seem to fill.

On the approach to Ocean Lake, the straight dirt road rolled out endless and wild and pocked with frost heaves. The truck was a bullet speeding to its target, his sister. On the steep turns, the tires ground into the cold earth, shot up a mean mix of gravel and hard snow. Speeding now, Diego pushed the big engine for a small bit of fun to break the nauseating monotony of searching.

The dashboard read 12:00 A.M.; it was Christmas. Sudden clouds eclipsed the waxy sphere of moon and left a lethal darkness. Venus flashed her red hooker light in the southwest sky, enough illumination for his Native vision. Out of the corner of his eye, the glint of something metallic, the smallest man-made flare. He hit the brake hard, and the truck bucked into reverse.

Then he was out and running, slipping as rocks gave way under his feet. Below the tree line, her car waited for him. The license plate, SECRET1, sent his heart into overdrive. Yanking open the driver's side door, he released the breath he'd been holding on his scramble down the hill. The interior light revealed nothing alarming. The car was empty of everything except the cloying brew of pine air freshener trapped too long in the closed space. His throat constricted with the intake of the sweet chemical scent. But she was gone from the interior of the cold car.

One more place to look. His hands shook on the trunk. One click and he would know. He found his courage, as he always did for Kimi, and the trunk popped open. It was empty except for a tire iron and spare tire.

Diego retched without warning, an automatic purging of the ugly images that had risen in his mind before he saw the vacant space of the trunk. He turned away fast, careful to toss the mess away from the car.

He took a breath of icy air and read the landscape. Her Honda sat under a sheltering grove of junipers flanked by a towering rock. The silver sedan was expertly parked. No way she went off the road and landed daintily in this nest. Someone had planned this. He hoped it was his sister, before she left for Vegas or Alaska, escaped with her tricky lover, whoever the hell he was.

He slammed the trunk, and coyotes, roused from sleep, set up howling from every corner. The soulful sound stopped him long enough for him to spot a small glint of silver in the snow, a miniature fallen star. A silver ring with a small turquoise stone. It had been his gift to her when she graduated from the university; the Navajos called turquoise a piece of the sky. Kimi had put it on that day and promised she would never take it off.

He cradled the fragile circle in his palm and breathed on it to warm it. He pushed it past the knuckle of his little finger and knew for certain she'd left it there for him to find.

He didn't want to leave her car alone out there, but he had to. No signal on his cell phone so far out from town. A mad scrabbling over the rocky incline and he was back in the Dodge, pushing it to full power, racing from the land of wild horses and the lost territory of his people.

SATURDAY
DECEMBER 25

CHAPTER 32

I woke before dawn on Christmas morning after my first good sleep in weeks. The house phone was ringing in the kitchen. Silver light from the setting moon reflected off the snow, and I walked through the house without turning on any lights.

Antelope skipped the usual pleasantries and told me to turn on the television. I complied.

Diego had found Kimi's car, abandoned on the road to Ocean Lake. The search began at first light, and the local news showed a caravan of county vehicles surrounding the lonesome place where Kimi's car rested in a camouflage of rock folds. It was the last connection to Kimi we had, and it might hold some clue to finding her.

The county forensic crew was set up at the remote location. Weak sunlight defined the horizon at the discovery scene, where a bloated sky waited to release more snow onto the desolate landscape. Then there was the slow journey of the flatbed trailer down Route 191 from Ocean Lake—harnessed like a dead animal, chained to the trailer, the abandoned vehicle on its way to the county garage.

The discovery of the vehicle drew attention to the story of Kimi's disappearance from the regional media. Kimi had officially escaped the anonymous pile of adult missing persons, their stories misfiled and forgotten in the course of routine police work. The idea that she had driven away in a dissociative episode could no longer give her family hope. She might have abandoned the car and proceeded on foot, but it wasn't likely.

My hands shook as I made coffee. I wasn't prepared to accept that Kimi was dead. And while the discovery of her car didn't absolutely correlate with a tragic ending, it pushed things in that direction. Like all trauma survivors, over the last year I had adopted the philosophy that it was better to anticipate and prepare for the worst outcome than to expect the best and be disappointed. As a psychologist trained in cognitive therapy, I knew that reasoning was flawed, but it promised a measure of control.

Within ten minutes, I was packed and ready for the drive back to Rock Springs. Christmas was unlucky for me.

I was certain now that Kimi had come to harm. Her fear in the last session hadn't been paranoia but a primitive signal anxiety alerting her to danger.

I stopped at the barn and fed the horses, making a mental note to call the local man who usually cared for them to tell him I wouldn't be staying on at the house as planned. Then I went to Soldier and stroked his flank, moved closer into the warmth coming from his strong body. I placed my head against his neck and felt pure peace. "I'll be back soon. We can celebrate Christmas then."

I closed the barn door, securing the horses, and stepped out into the morning.

A meager light fell through the tall pines that surrounded the small ranch house. The still, reverent scene was like a fine ink drawing, every bold shadow and subtle gradation rendered with precision. It took my breath away. I didn't want to leave.

I transferred my gear into the Jeep and turned on the heater. When I left the loop road, it was just after seven. On the horizon, the sun was a vibrant pulse of light in the gray, waiting sky. I took a minute to mourn the quiet day lost to this dire development.

It was a cold and cheerless morning, the sky edged by a crop of risky clouds hovering at the Idaho border. I turned left onto US 191, the intercontinental highway from the US-Mexico border in Arizona to the Canadian border in Montana. I was tempted to bypass Rock Springs and drive straight through to the anonymity of the Baja Peninsula.

For the next hour, the scenery was an unchanging moonscape, mile after mile of scrub land and tufted sagebrush dusted with new snow. To the left, the snow-covered Wind River Mountains flanked the desert floor.

I plugged in my phone and waited for service. When I got it, I called Antelope, who told me the sheriff wanted me in Rock Springs as soon as possible. He ended the call before I could ask about his meeting with the latest victim.

A few miles north of town, I passed the Search and Rescue vehicles making their way north to the discovery site. The volunteer crews would pick up where the county search crews left off. The radio news was reporting an expanded search and the use of divers in the shallow saltwater of Ocean Lake, which was currently the only unfrozen body of water in the state of Wyoming.

C Street was bustling with reporters huddled in groups on the street corner like aging teenage gang members, balancing phones and coffee cups in the cold wind. Cedric Yee stood alone in the doorway of a closed convenience store. He seemed to be in the background all the time—an official member of the press with a special interest in the Kimi Benally case.

Inside the station, the squad room was packed. It looked like every officer had been called in to work some part of the developing case. Antelope was alone in his office. He looked like he hadn't slept since I saw him last.

"Change of plan," he said. He took me by the arm, led me through the station and out the back door to an unmarked county car. He turned right out of the parking lot onto Broadway. The street was clear of reporters. The early Mass was letting out, and he sped up to get ahead of the line of cars exiting the parking lot. I waited for him to let me in on what he had planned.

"We're going to Cahill's place. Scruggs doesn't want to haul him in here. He doesn't want it to look like he's closing his options like he did the last time."

A block away from the church the streets stood empty, and

he accelerated to get through the light at the intersection. I noticed the set of his jaw and realized that finding Kimi's vehicle had changed the case for him. He must have been holding on to hope she was safe somewhere and would come back to them.

"He's not at the search site?"

"He's at home. I called to make sure."

"Don't you find that strange?"

"They're dredging the lake. What if she's in there? Would you want to be there when they pulled a body out?"

"When you put it that way . . ."

"It's his right. But he's also not your typical loving husband. We know that. He had Tracy in his bed the same night he learned Kimi was missing. What does that tell you?"

"I keep forgetting to ask about the latest victim. What did you learn?"

"The good news is he didn't rape her. She managed to get away from him. That's another reason we're paying Cahill a call this morning."

Antelope adjusted the lever for the heat but nothing happened. It was freezing in the car. He had the windshield wipers going at top speed to clear the frost.

"Something tells me you've left out some critical piece of data here, Detective."

"Good catch, Doc. The county's getting its money's worth hiring you. It was Tracy Hopkins who was attacked. And I was the one who told her to stay put instead of going home for Christmas."

"What's going on here? We have two women close to Kevin Cahill, and both of them come to harm within a week of each other. What did Tracy tell you about the attack?"

"It happened close to midnight. She was coming home from the Search and Rescue fundraiser. If this is the same guy, it's later than his usual time. She was attacked outside her apartment building. All the other women had been abducted from parking lots of major stores and forced to drive up White Mountain in their own cars, as you know. But the method of attack was the same: he came at her from behind as she was getting out of her car and put a knife to the neck. This time, though, in the struggle to force her back into the car, he dropped the knife. She got a hand free and set off the car alarm. That spooked him, and he took off running. She ran into her apartment and locked the door and didn't begin to think about coming out until daybreak. Then it took her hours to get up the courage to open the door and drive herself over to the hospital."

"I saw her at the fundraiser. It was more like she was putting in time at the after-party. She was arguing with Kevin. She walked off angry, and a few minutes later he left."

"They fought because she wouldn't lie for him. Though that's not entirely true—she lied at first. But she gave me the truth when I confronted her with the picture of her leaving his house."

"Was she able to describe the man who attacked her?"

"She says no. Couldn't give me much except he wasn't a big guy. When he grabbed her from behind, she went for his eyes, felt the ski mask before he jerked his head away."

"Like the White Mountain Rapist. How tall is Tracy?"

"Tall for a woman, about five feet nine inches give or take."

"Kevin Cahill's height."

"Five feet ten inches is average for American males," Antelope said.

"Where's Tracy now?" I moved the levers, trying to coax some heat out of the vent that was still blowing frigid air.

"At the hospital on observation status with a police guard at the door. She was in pretty bad shape—mostly psychological, I'd say, though I'm not the expert here, but there is some bruising on her arms and torso. I figure she could still be at risk from the rapist, hence the guard. Her family's coming in today to be with her and take her home when she's cleared to travel."

"Could Kevin have attacked her?"

"That was the sheriff's first thought. For some reason, he seemed to want him in the fire. But if Cahill attacked Tracy, why would she make up a story about a rapist?"

"You said she didn't get a look at him."

We stopped at the light. The heat came on full blast and

blew a cloud of dust into the air. Antelope fanned it away. "Could Cahill lose it, come unglued under the stress of handling a wife and a mistress?" he asked.

"It's an old story. I can't say if it's Kevin's story. Honestly, he didn't seem the violent type. He manages his roaring testosterone levels with his manic participation in extreme sports."

The light turned green and Antelope made a sharp left. The plan was to interview Kevin and get his reaction to the news of Kimi's car being found. We turned right onto Mountain Road past the hill at Overland Elementary School, already busy with kids trying out new sleds, skis, and snowboards. There'd been so much snow that week that sledding was actually possible in town. Usually it was lost to wind and evaporation in the dry air.

In the short time it took to cross town, the weather had shifted. Clouds covered the sun and giant snowflakes spun in the air, cuing Christmas morning. It looked innocent, but the dashboard read five degrees. Another storm was on its way. Kids in bright-colored jackets filled the playground.

"Let's see if we can shake anything loose," Antelope said as we approached the house. "I've had the sense he's been holding back. Whoever hid the car has got to be worried now that we've got it. If we're lucky, we'll pull some prints or other evidence."

A Channel 5 KGWC news van was parked in front of Kevin and Kimi's townhouse. Antelope parked behind it and raised a hand to the reporter who was exiting the van, microphone in hand, signaling this wasn't the time. The news crew would be there when they emerged, waiting for the latest information, hoping for a sound bite more interesting than "No comment." They wouldn't get one, but they didn't know that.

Kevin had the curtains pulled over the front windows. He opened the door for us but stayed out of sight of the newspeople. In the dark living room, the muted television flashed pictures. He stooped and grabbed the remote from the floor, clicked and dropped it, and the screen went dark.

"I may never watch that shit again," Kevin said.

We followed him to the kitchen, where for the first time I got a look at his face: Someone had done a job on him, turned his left cheek and eye a deep purple, the color of a ripe plum. His split lip was crusted in dried blood.

He pointed in the direction of the empty bar stools. Outside, a dog began barking. He opened the door, and Kimi's border collie, Domino, came bounding into the room. Kevin gave a command to sit, and the dog obeyed immediately. She seemed to be waiting for him to say something else, but when he didn't, she curled into a ball at his feet.

Kevin filled his coffee cup and gestured with the pot. We both declined. One of the hazards of working an ongoing police investigation was ingesting too much bad coffee. Kevin poured a good amount from a pint of Maker's Mark 46 into his mug. I sat on a stool at the island, and Antelope remained standing. He was so tall he blocked the light from the overhead fixture in the living room behind him.

With the blinds closed and only the small light from the stove, it was hard to see. It seemed Kevin was partial to dim lighting; it went well with hangovers. The house smelled like a frat party.

"What happened to you?" Antelope asked.

Kevin waved his hand as if dismissing the question.

"It's nothing. I finished some unfinished business."

"With who?"

"Cedric made the mistake of talking to me when I'd had a little too much to drink. He likes my wife too much. He surprised me by fighting back . . . This is bad news, isn't it? Finding the car, I mean? I have to quit hoping she's going to come back like nothing happened."

"I wish I could tell you otherwise. But that's what it looks like."

Kevin fell back against the counter and covered his face with his hands. Then he yawned and opened his eyes wide and shook his head. "So what's next? What do you do next in a case like this?"

"The crime scene techs are going over her car right now. We should have something soon."

Kevin swirled the steaming liquid around in his cup. Some of it splashed out, and he continued turning it in wider circles, making a bigger spill. Then he hurled the cup at the wall. It bounced off and fell to the clay tile floor, where it broke into pieces. He swiped at the counter with the tail of his flannel shirt but succeeded only in spreading the liquid.

"Aw, fuck it," he said and fell back against the counter again. "I'm a useless fuck."

He drank whiskey straight from the bottle, wiped it from his chin where it dribbled down.

"We've got Search and Rescue up in the area right now. If you want to join them, I can arrange to have someone take you up there. Sometimes it can help, having something to do."

"I can't go there. I can't face it. I know it looks bad," Kevin said. He shook his head. "No, no, can't do that." His voice broke. He was fighting tears.

I had never seen any emotion from the man before. I tried to tune in to what my gut was telling me, whether this was legitimate suffering or only for show.

"Kimi didn't have anything going on with Cedric. I beat the truth out of him. Sad to see a grown man cry."

"What makes you so sure Kimi was seeing someone else?" Antelope asked.

"Weird things started happening. The times she claimed not to know where she'd been, she kept turning up with stuff—jewelry, a silk blouse, other new things, a fancy gold pen. I kept track of our money. She was useless at that. She went through money like water. But she didn't charge those things. I checked the credit card receipts. And when I asked her where she was getting the cash for new stuff, she looked at me like I was crazy. Claimed she'd always had those things and I'd never noticed. She was lying, but I couldn't figure how to catch her in it. I knew if she was having an affair, it would only be a matter of time before I found the proof of it, though. I need to know who he is. He's the one responsible for whatever happened to her."

I thought about the red boots and Kimi saying she hadn't bought them for herself.

"It's best if you leave the investigation to us," Antelope said.

"You took her computer. What have you found so far? Nothing. I'll do my own investigation. I'm going through her papers. I've got nothing but time now. And I want my picture back. The one I took the day we got engaged, the one in the silver frame. When can I get it?"

Kevin pushed off the counter and leaned forward. I could smell the alcohol on his breath and the oily scent of his unwashed hair, stale clothes, and body odor. His blond beard was untrimmed.

The last thing this investigation needed, I thought, was Kevin Cahill, drunk and bent on vigilante justice, getting involved.

"Anything taken into evidence stays with us until the case is resolved," Antelope said. "If you find anything, bring it to me. It would be a mistake to try to handle it on your own. But there's something else we need to ask you about. Where were you Thursday night?"

"At the Holiday Inn with a million volunteers. You were there," Kevin said, looking at me. "You saw me, right?"

"What time did you leave?" Antelope asked.

"Who keeps track? You saw me leave." Again he fixed me in his gaze. "What time was it?"

"I'm not in the habit of keeping track of you," I said. I felt my anger flare at his arrogance.

"I didn't mean it like that. I don't know whether I'm coming or going with all this."

"Where did you go when you left the Holiday Inn?" Antelope asked.

"Nowhere. Here," Kevin said and spread his arms out.

"Alone? No late visitors?" Antelope persisted.

"So you read the papers, too. Don't bust my balls. I'm on my last nerve here." He snapped his fingers. "It had to be before twelve. I stopped at Wendy's drive-through for a burger. They close at midnight."

Kevin began to pick up the scattered shards of his cup and drop them into the wastebasket. Then he tore off a length of paper towel, dropped it, and slowly wiped the floor with his boot. "Not like she'd do it, but what the hell, she isn't here," he said, almost to himself.

"Tracy Hopkins was at the Holiday Inn. She left just before you did. Did you follow her home?"

"Give me a break. I told you I came home alone. Forget Tracy."

"The two of you were seen arguing before she left."

"Man, I can't have a private conversation now?"

"It was a public setting," I said.

"And because of my wife and this mess she left me in, I can't go about my business without sheriffs and doctors and reporters watching my every move."

"What did you argue about?" Antelope asked.

"I'm not going to tell you that. No way, I'm done. I've answered all your questions and still you haven't found my wife. You get no more help from me."

He reached down, scooped up the soggy paper towels, and stuffed them into the trash. He finished off the pint of whiskey and tossed it on top.

"She turned you down, didn't she?" Antelope pushed.

"You get no play," Kevin said. He kicked at the wastebasket.

"Quit the tantrums. Get a hold of yourself. This is a courtesy, coming to talk to you here. We can do it under safer conditions if you can't manage this. What's it going to be?" Antelope moved toward Kevin. His cell phone was vibrating in his pocket, but he ignored it and locked eyes with Kevin, who stood with his arms folded.

"I got it," Kevin said. "We stay here."

"Answer the question. What did you and Tracy argue about Thursday night?"

"She blamed me for not being able to visit her family for Christmas. No way was that my fault. I told her I didn't need any more stress. If she wasn't happy to be here supporting me, she could leave. So she did. Stormed off and left me there alone. It's what's happening to me lately. Everybody's leaving me."

"She left the bar alone, and you went out a few minutes later."

At some point Antelope had pulled out a small notebook. He appeared to be reading from it, but I could see there was nothing written on the page.

"I didn't follow her, if that's what you're implying. But what if I did?"

"Did you see Tracy again after you left the bar?"

"I looked for her, all right? But she was long gone. So I went back and grabbed my stuff from the coat check and took off. That's the moment Cedric chose to come up to me. I was already worked up. It didn't take too much for me to lose it on him. When I was done with him, I got in my truck and got out of there. I halfway thought he might call it in, and I wasn't going to wait around to deal with the law."

"You didn't go to Tracy's place?" Antelope asked.

"I was done with Tracy. Same as with Kimi. If a woman walks out on me, I don't go chasing after her. It's not my style." Kevin smiled.

"Tracy Hopkins was attacked Thursday night," Antelope said.

Kevin froze and the smile disappeared. "What do you mean attacked?"

"It was an attempted rape."

"No way. The White Mountain Rapist? The one Kimi writes about? He got Tracy?"

"She fought him off," Antelope said.

"Way to go, Trace. All that mountain survival training paid off. Is she okay? Did he hurt her?"

"She's in the hospital. Her family's flying in from Atlanta."

Kevin smacked his palm on the countertop. "Are you seeing it?" he asked and smiled again.

"What are we supposed to see, Kevin?" I asked.

"Someone's got it out for me . . . going after Kimi and Tracy. It's not them—it's me they want to bring down."

"Who would want to do that?" Antelope asked.

"You see it though, right? Someone's going after the women in my life instead of coming straight for me. This is crazy shit."

"There's another way to look at this," Antelope said. "As far as we know, you're the only connection between these two women. Maybe you hurt them."

"You know you got nothing to back that up. If you did, I'd be in a cell now. So go on, get out of my house. Now."

I looked into Kevin's eyes—the rims swollen, the whites glassy and shot with blood. He was drunk, barely holding it together.

"Don't let me find you behind the wheel," Antelope said. "Lock yourself in. You're a media magnet these days. Make sure I can find you here in town."

CHAPTER 33

Kevin knew if he didn't get some sleep he was going to pass out. He took the last beer in the refrigerator and headed to the couch. His own investigation would have to wait. He covered his head with a quilt that smelled of Kimi.

It was freaking Christmas and he was alone.

When he woke hours later, Domino was snoring and breathing nasty dog breath on him. His head hurt from too much whiskey and the fight with Cedric. He scrambled some eggs and brewed up the last of his coffee. Besides his physical pain and his sudden single status, he realized he was doing okay. So many implications to Kimi being gone—but they'd have to wait for another time. He had things to do.

The house was a pigsty. He should clean up. *Later, always later with you*, Kimi always nagged him. Damn straight. Sleep came first. He'd missed all the calls from his family and knew he wouldn't be calling them back any time soon. There wouldn't be any comfort there. His mother would find a way to make his current situation his fault.

His back ached from his long sleep on the couch. He hadn't been in the bedroom since his night with Tracy. It wasn't guilt but something darker. Some shadow of Kimi lingering, his fear of her knowing, though she couldn't know. Anyway, he was done and over with Tracy for good. She couldn't keep her mouth shut, and look what she got for it.

Kimi was a different story. You could tell her anything and she'd take it to her grave. In her Native language, her name, Kimi, meant "secret."

Kimi collected keys, but she only carried her car keys, because she never locked the house. She didn't believe in it. It drove Kevin crazy. In the early days of their marriage, he often locked up, forgetting she wouldn't have a key with her. She didn't mind, would always get in through a window. Then she would remind him not to lock the door the next time he left.

Every key she'd ever owned sat in a mason jar on the small wire shelf in the kitchen pantry. Other jars held spare change, hair ties, push pins, paper clips.

He felt drugged with too much sleep and sorry for himself: no presents, no wife to make Christmas dinner. Time to drink again. This would have been their second Christmas together. They didn't have any traditions yet. Kimi had mentioned going to her mother's for elk steaks.

He wanted his Christmas present, the backcountry GPS he'd asked for. It was on his Christmas wish list, still stuck under a magnet on the refrigerator. Funny what the cops missed. On her list, she'd written "Elk Ivory Earrings . . . Bill Coffey Goldsmith on Granite." That was where they'd bought their wedding rings. He noticed a checkmark beside the GPS. Damn, she'd gotten it for him after all.

He searched for his present. The police had pulled out everything from the hall closet, and he'd stuffed things back in, no order at all. After searching through it all, he came up empty.

He went into the bedroom. Thoughts of Tracy came, a dangerous flame that could still combust his life.

He heaved everything from the closet floor onto the bed behind him. After he emptied the closet, he realized he could have looked for shopping bags. She wouldn't have taken new things out without wrapping them. There was more stuff in there, so the search took longer but yielded nothing.

On to the closet in their office. Nothing. Back to the kitchen for a new bottle of scotch—he'd given up on his Christmas present—but then he remembered the pantry. Kimi sometimes hid gifts there.

Nothing. It sucked to be alone at Christmas. His head throbbed. The overhead light reflected off the kitchen appliances. White spots signaled a migraine approaching. *Damn it, Kimi, where are you?*

In frustration, he pushed the contents of the nearest shelf onto the floor, wanting to hear something break. The mason jars bounced then rolled across the kitchen floor, spilling coins, pins, keys. It was too much. He sat on the floor and cried—a dry, empty sound. He would never admit it, but it was Kimi's name he called out in that hollow, lonely moment.

It wasn't a prayer. He didn't believe in prayers, or in much of anything beyond the high he got from being in nature and pushing himself hard. But even so, he got an answer: when he opened his eyes, he saw the shiny new silver padlock key from their self-storage unit.

The townhouse was small. They had agreed they needed extra space for the things they valued most. He kept his sports gear there; Kimi stored her books and papers, and thumb drives.

The cops had been asking a lot of questions about the stories Kimi was working on, hinting that her coverage of the serial rapes might have put her at risk. In her spare time, she'd been working on her master's thesis, but she didn't talk about that. Something about the media and cold cases, that's all he knew. He'd told Antelope to talk to Cedric Yee.

Outside, the street was empty, no news vans waiting to bag him. With any luck, there wouldn't be many cops on the road, either. He didn't need a DUI on top of everything.

He drove north on Yellowstone Road to the self-storage facility. The road wore a sheen of black ice. His tires slid over the dangerous glaze, but he held steady. No sense killing himself.

At the storage unit he waited for the electronic gate to slide open, but it didn't move. The place was dark except for the winking light of an ancient tube television in the manager's shack.

Kevin slipped as he made his way up the slick incline toward the front entrance. He shook the flimsy storm door, but it was locked, too. Snow crystals stung his face and hurt more than they should. Tears wet his cheeks. It was beastly cold. His fist pounded the glass.

An ugly brown pit bull shot straight up from the floor, lunging and clawing at the window of the guard shack. The dog was a serious shit storm, nails and teeth inches from Kevin's face, splashing the dusty plate glass with rivulets of saliva. Kevin recoiled from the rattling door, the possibly rabid animal. He was freezing cold and had to pee. He didn't need this junkyard dog adding to his problems.

The security guard was uglier and had fewer teeth than his canine pal, who went quiet and dead still at the sight of him. Wearing a Santa hat over blond dreadlocks, the guard was slow-moving, grinning, and chilling in a sweet cloud of marijuana. With his middle finger, he pointed at a smiley face sign indicating the place was on lockdown until seven the next morning. But Kevin wasn't having it. It was goddamn Christmas. Nothing was going to keep him from his stuff today. He played the missing wife card, flashed the newspaper photo of Kimi like a police badge, and as if by magic, the gates to heaven opened. Santa offered him a sympathy toke, and he took it, then another, as they headed back to his unit.

Kevin didn't know what he was looking for, and now he was drunk *and* high, so the search proceeded haphazardly. He threw things from the shelves, and soon the storage space was a match for the townhouse. But it was worth it, because in the end, he found them: a USB flash drive and a cell phone he'd never seen before, one of those cheap prepaid ones. And she'd meant to hide them good, too.

The woman drove him nuts even when she was gone.

He stuffed the flash drive in one pocket of his down jacket, the phone in the other. His hand was on the light switch when he saw it—the REI bag and inside, the GPS from his wish list. For the first time, it hit him how gone she was.

He had what he'd come for. The flash drive and cell phone in his pockets, bulging love handles, the weight of Kimi's secret life.

■ ■ ■

Fucking Christmas; any place with a public computer was shut down. Kevin comforted himself with the thought that it wouldn't have worked anyway, sorting through this stuff at the library or Staples. The detective was right; he was a media magnet.

He could go to Tracy's place. She had given him a key in that other reality, the time before Kimi vanished. She'd asked him to water her plants while she was away for Christmas. They'd both known it meant more.

With Kimi missing, Tracy had made her move. She was smart. "Strategic," Kimi called her, meaning it as an insult, but he thought different. They were two of a kind, him and Tracy, he thought. If Kimi knew him like she thought she did, she wouldn't like him either. Tracy took an opportunity when she saw one. It should have turned him off that she used his wife's disappearance to get close to him, but it didn't; if anything, it impressed him. But she hadn't had his back with the cops. The betrayal had surprised him, and he knew he'd never get over it. Forgiveness wasn't in his nature.

That didn't keep him from wanting her, of course. Driving to her place, he indulged in the memory. He'd fallen asleep in the bath, his body spent from days of hard skiing and winter camping, his mind blown and frazzled, freaked out and Kimi-crazy. Tracy had come in through the back door he'd forgotten to lock. How had she known to go there?

He'd thought he was dreaming. The wild curls brushed his face, Tracy on her knees, smiling at him. Her hands like ice on his face when she kissed him awake.

No words passed between them—there was no need. They both knew why she'd come. He was wounded, and she'd come to minister to him. Another woman might have thought twice, but not Tracy. She was a certified emergency responder, trained to react, ready to do what the situation required. He was grateful and willing—waiting, if he was going to be honest with himself. The white angora sweater, soft on his chest, pulled up and over her head, dropped to the floor.

It had been just as he wanted: effortless and uncomplicated, the graceful, chilly workings of a fine machine. Quick but satisfying, like the burst of a falling star. Tracy hadn't seemed worried about Kimi coming home and finding them together in her bed.

After, he had been claimed by a black, dreamless sleep. By the time dawn and the news media arrived, Tracy had been long gone. Kevin had woken alone and cold, his limbs flung to the four corners of the bed. Had he dreamed the whole strange night? But no—when he pulled the sheets over his head, he found the spice and bite of Tracy in the pores of the linen. Kimi's scent was as gone as she was, overpowered by Tracy's leavings.

He couldn't deal with that now, with both his women gone. Had either one of them ever put him first?

He drove down White Mountain Road, past the turn to his place. Not going back there. Too many days cooped up, hiding from the media, hiding from everyone. Then again, what if Tracy wasn't stocked up on booze? He wouldn't make it through the night without it.

He made a U-turn, headed home to pick up his own brand— pick up Domino, too, so he wouldn't come home to a mess. And besides, they could both use the company. For three days, the dog had done nothing but mope around, looking up expectantly every time there was a knock at the door. She gave him an inferiority complex. It had always been clear: Kimi was the alpha; he was the guy who lived with them.

Domino was at the door, tail wagging. When she recognized him, she dropped to the floor. It was stupid to let this canine behavior affect his self-esteem, but under the circumstances, he gave himself a pass for being hurt when the dog crumpled at the sight of him.

He packed up the alcohol and the dog and headed out the door.

With Kimi missing and Tracy with her family in the hospital, he felt how alone he was. Remembered only by his mother, who couldn't get it together to do anything more strenuous than hit redial. He'd heard nothing from his crew since the deputies hauled him away that first day on the mountain—Tracy was the only one who'd reached out to him. It puzzled him, and the sting of the abandonment was surprisingly sharp.

Tracy rented a tiny one-bedroom in the same apartment complex as Cedric Yee. He'd seen Yee's name on the mailbox the first time he went to Tracy's place. It had felt good to teach the guy a lesson with his fists the other night. But he didn't want to see him tonight.

He hit every red light on the way over to Tracy's, sat through the useless sequence, the only car on the road, bouncing and tapping the steering wheel with the palm of his hand. This new side of town looked barren on a good day, its young trees bent eastward in the relentless wind. Tonight, deserted and rimmed with frost, it was apocalyptic, post-nuclear.

The building was dark, people tucked in and sleeping off the back end of the fading holiday. Blue light danced behind the blinds of a few windows. He thought of Tracy attacked in the parking lot, the cold and the wind that night, the shock of forceful touch. The image of her being overtaken in such a way stirred him. In the last week the two women closest to him had come to harm. His head hurt with the hard-packed fact of it, guilt like a helmet, pressing on his skull.

He parked and took Domino for her last walk of the night, making small, careful steps over frozen ridges in the icy lot. The night air sliced at his face like a razor. Once again, it came to him: the life of a loner wouldn't be such a bad thing. Let the media geeks freeze their asses off waiting in the shadows of his place; he was safe in his self-imposed witness protection program for now. The thought made him smile—the first real smile he'd managed in all the days since he was radioed off the mountain.

The thermostat inside read fifty-five degrees, but it wouldn't take long for the square little box to warm up. He dumped his boots and sour socks at the door, following Tracy's rule, even in her absence. Hers was a classic chick place. He hadn't noticed before how committed she was to the color pink.

Domino sniffed at a peach afghan draped over a mesh typing chair. The computer was on a white desk in front of the window overlooking the parking lot. He pulled the silk drapes closed, a barrier against the night and prying eyes. He craved the solitude and anonymity, a pleasant side effect of being without a wife.

At the desk, he tackled the phone first. She had a password. He didn't know it and was too impatient to guess. It would have to wait. He picked up the thumb drive, Kimi's words in his palm. The baseboard heater crackled to life and warmed his feet.

He turned on the computer, a 2003 Dell. *Trace, we have to do something about this*, he thought. While he waited for it to boot up, he watched Domino walk the room's perimeter slowly, nose down, taking in all the girl smells, hunting for Kimi in the gauze of the feminine world. That done, she settled on a throw rug at the foot of the rocking chair a room away from him. *Have it your way*, Kevin thought, and put the thumb drive in, waiting for the ding of the hardware greeting at the bottom of the screen. He clicked on the icon and began his hunt.

SUNDAY
DECEMBER 26

CHAPTER 34

Kevin pulled into the parking lot of the Hilltop Medical Building. When he cut the headlights, the surrounding night fell to pitch dark. In rare moments when death anxiety tugged at him, this was what he imagined the end would be like. Like the time he had surgery on his ACL and was taken by anesthesia. The slow countdown: one hundred, ninety-nine, ninety . . . lights out, that quick, to nothing.

Above, the sky was a moonless void. Blackout clouds eclipsed the usual riot of stars. It would snow again soon. He wished he was in the backcountry, the real world, where only physical things mattered. Winter camping separated the men from the boys and everyone else. He was not a boy. On a night like this, he'd be zipped into his Marmot Atom, good to forty degrees below, alone and liking it in the dark and cold. Like death, except for the knowing.

It was long after hours on a holiday weekend and the building was vacant. A single light was on in her corner office. In its amber glow, juniper branches jumped and twitched alive in the wind. His was the only vehicle in the lot.

After spending a long, adrenaline-buzzed night one-on-one with the computer, his eyes popping, speed-reading her notes, he'd found what he was looking for. The name he needed, bless her. Bless his lovely, naïve, cheating whore of a wife.

Kimi had written the whole story—the who, what, when, and where—all but the fucking why. Her lover's name was there.

He drew fists, ached to do damage. His hand, on the doorknob, shook. His whole body was a quivering mess.

Kimi had been looking into things that had put her in danger. That was clear now. When he got what he knew to the right authorities, they'd have a hell of a time with what he'd found on that flash drive. But reporting what he knew felt risky. He needed to talk this out with someone before he found himself in cuffs.

Earlier, at Tracy's, when he'd learned the truth, he'd fallen back on the couch. He'd felt sick, only acid in his gut, riding on empty. He'd swallowed hard and willed himself to think. He was in over his head. He couldn't blow this and end up getting himself in more trouble. It was too late to do anything about it. Exhausted from everything he'd been through the last week and everything he'd learned about Kimi, he felt himself sink into the soft sofa cushions. A part of him wanted to forget what he knew, wanted to just fall asleep and wake up to a different reality. It wouldn't hurt to get a few hours' shut-eye before he tried to figure out what to do.

He fell asleep with the lights on and slept like the dead. He woke disoriented, his muscles stiff from sleeping too long. He was surprised to find he'd slept around the clock and it was 6:00 P.M. on the day after Christmas. All the hours unconscious had given him the answer. He knew what he was going to do. He would tell Kimi's therapist. She consulted with the sheriff's department. She'd know what to do.

He'd retrieved the appointment card he'd stuffed into his wallet the last time he saw her and dialed her number from his cell, expecting voice mail, ready to leave a message demanding to see her first thing in the morning.

He'd planned to get roaring drunk—drunker than the previous night; drunk enough to forget he ever had a wife. But within minutes, her secretary called him back, telling him to go to the office and the doctor would meet him there when she finished at the hospital.

When he finished with the doctor, had dumped all the facts and images, he'd go home, open a new bottle of Maker's 46, get oblivious, and let it all play out without him.

He'd printed out the essential stuff, Kimi's own words, in case the doctor thought he was being paranoid. Then he'd dropped the dog at home and headed out to the storage unit. He wanted the thumb drive safe under lock and key. The stoner had given him less of a hassle the second time around.

Given what he knew, he worried he wouldn't make it out of this alive. And since he'd left Tracy's, he'd had the sense he was being followed. But whenever he looked back, the road was empty behind him.

He'd never wanted to talk to anyone as much as he wanted to talk to the doctor. Kimi always looked forward to going to therapy, said it helped her vent and find a new perspective. Well, now Kevin needed another living soul to know what he knew. Needed some direction about how to proceed with the new facts. Plus, he felt some pleasure in the idea of outing her to her therapist. All those psychological theories Dr. Hunt had tried to sell him about Kimi's symptoms—they were clear bullshit now. It was all to cover her betrayal. She'd never dissociated; it was a lie she'd made up so she could hook up.

Maybe now the doctor would see his side, have some sympathy for him. He wanted to know if Kimi had ever told her the man's name. Had she betrayed him twice over? The doctor would never tell him, though. So why was he there?

Because he needed the doctor's help with the sheriff's department. He didn't know who he could trust with what he knew. He had never known a night so dark or felt such soul-chilling loneliness.

CHAPTER 35

After we left Kevin, Antelope invited me to share his Christmas dinner. I declined and didn't bother giving him a reason. I'd shared too much with him. He could figure it out, remember this was a bad season for me. Or not.

I went home, watched TV, and slept. The next morning, he called and asked again. He had leftover turkey, and he wouldn't take no for an answer. I agreed to be there for dinner.

I spent the rest of that morning at home, catching up on all the household tasks I'd ignored in the previous week and arranging for the doors in the study to be repaired. It had been more than a week since Kimi had gone missing, and we still had nothing. I went into the office after lunch and spent the afternoon catching up on paperwork. I had survived Christmas for the second year in a row. I'd missed out on some vacation days because of the investigation, but the only thing I minded was missing the time to ride Soldier.

At four o'clock I got paged to the hospital and spent an hour talking with a young woman who had been experiencing panic attacks that day. The physical symptoms of heaviness in her chest and a racing heart mimicked a heart attack.

When I was finished, I drove to Antelope's old miner's cottage on D Street. The last time I'd been there was the day we went to the wild horse auction. That was the day I'd realized I needed a horse more than I needed anything with Antelope.

He came to the door in a Santa hat and a chef's apron over a T-shirt and UW sweatpants. This was a surprise, Antelope at home listening to Stan Getz on a Bose system; it beat Marla's Top 40 Christmas hits. The small cottage was tropically hot.

"Welcome, come on in out of the cold."

I gave him my coat and peeled off all the layers I wore to combat the Wyoming winter. In the kitchen, he'd been busy—the table was set, candles lit, wine poured. I'd have to skip the wine; I was on call.

"What can I get you to drink?" he asked, gesturing to the wine.

"Got a coffee for an on-call shrink?" I asked. "No alcohol for me tonight. I agreed to cover for Doctor Jorgensen, who drank too much last night, but you didn't hear that from me."

"Starbucks home brew," he said and put an Italian Roast pod into a sleek coffee maker.

"I want to talk to you about something."

The oak table was set with mismatched china plates and silverware.

"Is there something new in the investigation?" I held the heavy mug he handed to me in both hands and drank the strong coffee.

"There's something that's been bothering me, and I want to run it by you."

"Ready when you are," I said.

"It's about Diego finding Kimi's car."

"What's bothering you?"

He was at the stove with his back to me, serving the food.

"How did he find it? There's a lot of open land up there, but he went straight to it."

He carried the plates to the table and sat across from me. He shook out his napkin, folded his hands under his chin, and looked at me. "It's like he knew where to look."

"You're serious, aren't you? You're suggesting Diego had something to do with Kimi's disappearance? I thought you were just playing devil's advocate the other day with Cassandra, trying out a theory for the sake of being thorough." I took a bite of the turkey.

"Why do you look surprised? He's a registered sex offender."

I put down my fork and looked at him. "I'm well aware of his sex offender status. I did the evaluation myself. The crime he was convicted of is in a totally different category than the crimes of the White Mountain Rapist."

"Don't let it go cold," Antelope said with a smile. "I worked hard on this meal."

"I can tell—it's delicious. I'm pretty good at multitasking, though. I can alternate speaking and eating."

"I'd like to have an objective discussion. That's impossible with Cassandra in the room. She thinks with her heart. I'm going to approach this as if I didn't know him. I want your professional opinion on Diego. Pretend all I know is what I read in the police reports about his arrest and the gossip that circulated around the reservation."

"Fine," I said. "He was charged and convicted of statutory rape. He was eighteen years old when he was arrested. He'd been having sex with his fifteen-year-old girlfriend for a year. Her father waited until Diego turned eighteen to report it. If he'd been white, the old man wouldn't have cared. Don't you know all this?"

"You sound like you're excusing his actions."

"And you sound like the specifics of the offense don't make any difference."

"You rated him as having a low risk of reoffending, if I recall correctly."

"I use validated psychological assessment tools to arrive at predictive outcomes. The process remains more an art than a science, but if you want my personal opinion, yes, you don't have to worry about Diego reoffending."

"He did his time. But that wasn't the end of it, right?"

"He tried to see her again, and was picked up for stalking and voyeurism. It was the nail in the coffin, as far as the court was concerned, because he was still on parole when he pushed that envelope."

"Stalking qualifies as an aggressive act. I don't need to tell you that."

"True. But there's no history of him going after strangers."

"That we know of." Antelope leaned forward. "Let's say he's the rapist and Kimi is on to him. Remember, these two are pretty tight. He loves her, but given his history with women, he can't trust her. He needs to protect himself. He kidnaps his own sister to keep her quiet."

"That sounds pretty gruesome. I'm not sure I buy it."

"This is a dysfunctional family."

While he cleared the plates, I thought about what I knew of Kimi's family. Antelope was an intelligent man, able to conceptualize in psychological terms. But he had a blind spot when it came to Diego, and it seemed their difficult history was interfering with his judgment.

"I know Diego clinically—know his pathology, at least the part he's revealed, and the crimes he's committed. Nothing in his profile points to him being capable of the kind of intentional violence kidnapping and raping women at knifepoint requires. His relationship with Kimi would keep him from hurting her. Violence against his sister, the one person he loves and lives to protect, would be diametrically opposed to his purpose in life, which is to protect her from harm. You know him too, but in a wholly different familial way. Do you really think he's capable of hurting Kimi? Especially in the cold and calculated way you described?"

He brought a fresh mug of coffee to the table and sat down.

"I'm not one hundred percent sure of anything. And I'd honestly be much happier to be wrong about this."

"Seriously, I don't see Diego as a serial rapist capable of murdering his own sister," I said. "They're a dysfunctional family for sure, but the scenario you describe would require a degree of psychopathology I've never picked up on in Diego."

My phone vibrated. It was the hospital calling.

I rose. "Let me see what this is about."

They had three patients for me: an intoxicated, psychotic teenager, a depressed post-surgery patient, and a postpartum woman.

"I need to get over there. Dinner was delicious. Thank you. I'm human again."

I wasn't sorry to be leaving. His suspicion about Diego left me disheartened and sad. I put on my coat, and we stood at the door.

"Maybe we'll do this again when the conversation is about a happier topic. I hope you have an easy night," he said.

Outside, the cold air hit my face like a slap. I was halfway down the stairs when Antelope called my name. It would have been rude not to turn around.

He was in the doorway, silhouetted in the soft light.

"Be safe, Pepper," he said.

I smiled and felt a little less lonely, a little less sad.

■ ■ ■

I was at a computer at the nurses' station in the emergency room, typing up the report of my last consult, when Marla called on the cell phone.

"I'm sorry to bother you, but he made it sound urgent."

"I'm at the emergency room. What's urgent?"

"Kevin Cahill called. He wants an appointment with you ASAP. I offered some times next week, but he needs to see you tonight. Since you're on call, I told him I'd check with you."

"You know me well. If I'm working, I'm working."

It was past nine o'clock, a little late by conventional standards to schedule a psychology consult. But this was Wyoming. I'd left my conventional life back in Cambridge.

"Tell him to meet me at the office at nine thirty. And he should use the back door so we don't set off any of those fancy new security alarms they put in."

"Are you sure? He sounds a little agitated. Is it safe to meet with him alone at night?"

"I'm here in the psychiatric unit, Marla. I can handle Kevin Cahill. Did he say why he wanted to see me?"

"Not a word. I can meet you there and open up the office."

"No need, Marla. I'll be all right."

"Are you sure? This is the man whose wife went missing."

I thought about it for a minute. I wasn't worried about meeting Kevin. If he'd hurt Kimi, his wanting to meet with me could only mean one thing: he was ready to deal with it. Narcissist that he was, he would want special treatment; he wouldn't be inclined to walk into the sheriff's department and confess.

"Enjoy the time off," I finally said. "It hasn't been the easiest Christmas season."

"I'm worried about the sheriff," she said. "He's been having these chest pains on and off for days. The stress of this case is getting to him."

"The emergency room's pretty quiet tonight. Maybe you should take a ride over here and have him get checked out. If it turns out to be anxiety, you'll have peace of mind, and there are medications he could take."

"I'll do my best to talk him into going. I don't know what I'd do if anything happened to him."

"Try not to worry, and keep me in the loop."

"I will. Call me if you change your mind about wanting me to pop over. I'm a night owl."

While I'd been in the hospital, the weather had changed; a mean wind and whipping snow had kicked up. I drove slowly. I could barely make out Kevin's truck, parked at the far corner of the lot and buried in the fast-falling snow. I pulled up close to the building and made my way carefully across the slippery surface to the back entrance in the ambient light of the snow.

The security lights flared and lit up the entrance.

The body lying in the doorway was a black-and-white still life with two spots of color. Kevin Cahill wore his red ski hat. In the center of his chest was a large red hole. I wanted to run but didn't. I moved closer to him, took off my glove, and felt for a pulse in his neck. Kevin was warm and still. He had no breath or pulse.

Images of Zeke sprawled on his office floor. I had to stay present. I focused on breathing. My phone was in the Jeep. I ran through the snow, slipped and fell, got up and ran again. In the Jeep I locked the doors, pressed 911, and breathed.

Kevin's killer could be watching. I started the Jeep and put it in drive, ready to get out of there fast if I had to. The heat came on with a blast. I shivered and shook, teeth chattering. I thought about going into the office. I'd be safer there. My gun was in there. I was too afraid to move. Couldn't stop seeing the image of his exploded heart.

I wanted to call Antelope but decided it was better to let the patrol officers respond to the scene, make their assessment, and call in the backup required—the crime scene technicians, the coroner, and the lead detective.

I thought about calling Marla but didn't. A sympathetic voice could break me. She knew what had happened the night Zeke was killed. I would lose it with Marla offering support. I had to keep it together and get through the questions I knew would come.

Vehicles raced up College Hill, approaching from both sides of town. Flashers lit up the parking lot, the silent building, and the pines behind it. I stepped out of the Jeep as two uniformed officers approached.

"Are you Doctor Hunt?"

I nodded and pointed to the office building. Both deputies turned to look.

"He's been shot. I checked for a pulse but couldn't feel anything."

"Come with us," one of the deputies said.

They walked in long, slow strides with me between them, and I led them to the body. Falling snow formed a lacy pattern on his dark clothes and covered his face. The blood, bright red minutes before, now leaked black lines onto the white ground.

"Isn't that the guy we hauled down from Pinedale?"

"The missing woman's husband. It's him all right."

They talked and decided one of them would search the building and the other would stay with me. One of the deputies disappeared into the building. The other stood so close to me I could hear him wheezing in the cold night air. "Do you know this man?"

"His name's Kevin Cahill. He's the husband of my patient, the woman who went missing."

"What are you doing here tonight?"

"I came to meet him."

"At this hour? Kind of late for an appointment, isn't it?"

"I'm a psychologist. I was on call in the emergency room. He said it was urgent."

"I need some information from you. Your home address, please."

"I'm at 134 Hilltop."

"And a phone number where you can be reached."

"My cell, the one I called on, is the best number. I've always got it with me."

"Thank you. I'm going to ask you to wait in your vehicle until we get things sorted out here."

He left me alone and went to the cruiser. In the Jeep, I finished off a bottle of water and opened another one. I was still on call. If I got paged, I'd have to ask someone else to respond—I was in no condition to assess anyone else's sanity when my own was quickly slipping away.

Sirens blared and lights flashed as the ambulance arrived. The pulsing lights made me dizzy, threatened vertigo. I closed my eyes. A knock on the window made me jump.

"Detective Antelope gave orders to bring you in to the station, Doctor."

I was back in Cambridge on the night I found Zeke's body, being questioned as a suspect in his murder. Now someone was trying to make it look like I'd murdered Kevin. And from there it would be easy to implicate me in Kimi's disappearance.

CHAPTER 36

I was sitting on the wrong side of a table in a police interrogation room. It was all too familiar. Everything in the room seemed chosen to create despair. The air was chilly and stale, the chairs too low, with metal legs screeching on the floor tiles. Overhead, bright tube lights lit the place up like an operating room.

Someone could be watching from the other side of the gray glass. I didn't look there. I didn't want to see what I must look like at this point. If I put my head down on the table for a second, I'd be asleep. The threat of grime and the germs was the only thing that kept me upright. My hands trembled on the table. Pale and plain with prominent veins—not yet old, but getting-old hands, unadorned, no polish or jewelry. My wedding rings had gone into the ground with Zeke. At the time I'd sworn I'd never wear another one. My bare fingers were intentional reminders of what had been lost.

Why meet here instead of Antelope's office? I felt like a suspect in this room. And maybe I was . . . not that anyone had said it yet. But why else would they put me in an interrogation room?

It was the same with Zeke. I discovered his body. In the eyes of the law, I had opportunity. And when I found him, he was holding his dead lover in his arms, giving me motive *and* opportunity. I was a prime suspect.

If they found the gun in the desk drawer, what would it tell them? I also kept a gun at home. I hadn't bothered with getting a permit to carry a concealed weapon.

Antelope came in and sat down across from me. It was surreal. Neither of us spoke. His dark eyes held questions we both knew would have to wait. Then Antelope read the Miranda warning, and as I know he expected, I gave no response.

I took out my cell phone and called Aubrey Hiller, my attorney in Green River.

Aubrey never slept. He picked up on the second ring.

"You're calling me about the dead body at your office, right? Don't ask how I know—it's part of the magic."

"I'm at the sheriff's department. Detective Antelope read me my rights, so I called you."

"I've got you. Give me thirty minutes," Aubrey said and hung up.

"He's on his way," I said.

Across the table, Antelope was still as a statue. He gave me a long look, and I stared back at him. Finally, he placed both hands on the table, pushed himself up, and said, "I'll be back."

There was nothing to say until Aubrey arrived.

∎ ∎ ∎

A half hour later to the minute, Antelope came in with my lawyer right behind him. He was showered and shaved, heavy on the Calvin Klein cologne. He looked Ken-doll perfect and camera-ready in a navy pinstripe suit. At forty-three, he'd racked up three sons and three ex-wives. Aubrey wasn't popular with law enforcement types because of his history of ruining clearance rates and bringing down prosecution statistics. I felt better the minute he walked through the door.

Since I'd come close to being charged with Zeke's murder, I'd decided on two things I would never be without: a good attorney and a good weapon. I'd kept Aubrey Hiller on retainer since I'd moved to Wyoming. He knew my history, and although his specialty was criminal law, he'd been willing to do the other civil work required in sorting out Zeke's estate, and he'd represented me when the Wyoming Board of Psychology had voiced reservations about my fitness to practice because of the legal and personal events in my history.

Aubrey was a tiger. I'd heard the cocaine rumors, but the man had never lost a criminal case in Sweetwater County. With those odds, I could ignore his recreational activities. I was glad to have him on my side. Besides, I had rumors following me too; I no longer took them as seriously.

I gave my statement about finding the body, and the interview was over. Aubrey put the kibosh on any questioning, and I didn't have to say a word to the detective, which suited me fine.

"Let's get out of here before he changes his mind," Aubrey said.

I had to run to keep up with him as we made a getaway across the icy parking lot to his waiting vehicle.

"I didn't want to say anything in there, but I take it they didn't find your gun?" he asked me in his car.

"It never came up."

"I didn't leave him much room. Wait and see if they get a match."

Outside it was the darkest of nights. The snow had stopped. The stillness in the air was pure grace and all good things.

The BMW had heated leather seats, still warm from his trip from Green River.

"I skipped the part where I ask you if you can give me a ride to my car. It's still at the office."

"Not a chance. I'm taking you straight home to bed. That didn't come out right. You look like crap. That didn't come out right, either."

"I've been on call. It's been twenty-four hours since I slept last. I need my car, though."

"I'm an officer of the court. You're not fit to drive. I need some coffee myself."

He made a quick circle through the parking lot of the new Starbucks, which was closed at this early hour, then turned back into town. "I'm headed to Vegas to get a jump on New Year's," Aubrey said.

"I guess I'll talk to you next year then. You'll have your phone with you?"

He patted his jacket pocket, slipped the iPhone out. "My heart, my life. I assume you've got a watertight alibi?"

"I was at the crime scene."

"We don't know the exact time of death. Assuming it was sometime in the last twelve hours, do you have any gaps in your coverage?"

"He was still warm when I found him."

"Where had you been earlier?"

"Do you need to know?"

"We'll see what the Medical Examiner comes back with for time of death. If it's a question of alibi, you might want to give up his name."

"Who said it was a *he*?"

"*Her* name, then."

"I'm sure he would prefer to remain anonymous."

"A married fellow?"

"Drop it, Aubrey. If it's necessary and relevant, I'll tell you. Until then, leave it alone."

He went quiet, and his beautiful mouth set itself in a pout. He took advantage of the empty road and began driving faster. Was this why he hadn't been able to make any of his relationships work, this sensitivity to any resistance?

He pulled up to the convenience store and threw the car into park.

"Thanks for getting to me so fast," I said. I couldn't afford to be offending my attorney.

"Call me. Anytime," he said, and patted his pocket. His iPhone chirped in response. "Seriously, Aubrey, I appreciate how you always come through for me."

"You want something?"

I shook my head no. "I'm planning to be asleep soon."

He gave me a sly smile. I wasn't sure what had happened, but it was clear his mood had shifted back to playful. He would be a hard man to keep up with.

"Come to Vegas with me," he said. "Or do you have to check with the mysterious 'he'?"

"I don't have to check with anyone. You are the best lawyer around, and I might need you again, so I'm going to pass on Vegas this time."

"I've got a private jet waiting at Rock Springs airport."

"Don't tempt me," I said.

MONDAY
DECEMBER 27

CHAPTER 37

Antelope left the station knowing what he had to do. His thoughts about Diego killing Kimi made more sense than ever now. It was entirely plausible Diego had murdered his sister and also her husband. The drama and chaos of Diego's early life with Estella had caused him to experience primitive rage at his sister when he thought she was following in their mother's footsteps. He could easily have blamed the husband whose inability to give her the love and emotional support she needed made her seek solace in a relationship outside her marriage.

The snow had turned to sleet, and slick roads slowed his progress across town. He stopped at the light at the corner of Dewar Drive and Elk Street, the windshield wipers working hard to clear the accumulating ice. It was 3:00 A.M., and the plows and trucks would be out soon.

Not a soul stirred in the warren of narrow lanes in the Elk Street Mobile Park. He parked and made his way through a herd of rusted vehicles in the patch of yard at Estella's double-wide. He took the three short stairs in a wide jump onto the wooden porch. Plastic on the windows puffed and fluttered. A line of snow rimmed the windowsills.

He pounded on the door for a full minute before Estella cracked it open.

"What? You found her?" she asked, awake and wired.

"No. It's not about Kimi."

"Why are you here so late? Nothing else matters." A savage pull and the chain came off. Estella stepped out into the freezing rain.

"Kevin Cahill is dead."

Estella gasped and covered her mouth with her hands. "So now they're both gone. He killed her and took his own life."

"That's not what happened. Kevin was murdered. I have some questions. Let me in."

"What questions? What does this have to do with us?"

"I don't want to do this at the station."

She opened the door, waved him inside, and slammed it closed behind him, sending ice spears sliding off the roof. Space heaters glowed in every corner, and in the overwhelming heat, Antelope felt his exhaustion taking over.

"I need to talk to Diego."

There was a tricky moment when Estella put it together. He thought she was going to come at him. Wild eyes and clenched fists, swelling with anger. Then her whole body went slack, like a shot bird fallen to earth.

"You are really lost," she said. "They got you good."

"Do you want someone else here?"

He waited and minutes passed. His skin itched in the hot air. This was a bad idea. He should have cleared this with the sheriff. The sweet satisfaction he'd had when he'd decided Diego was the killer turned sour.

"What good are you to us? It was your job to find her and you failed."

"Where is Diego?"

Estella held her head up, defiance and pride in her eyes. "He's gone. You won't be able to find him either."

"When did you see him last?"

"He found Kimi's car, and now he's gone looking for her. He won't find her alive. I told him, but he never listens."

"You believe she's dead? You've given up on her?"

"You know it's true. You can't say it. But truth is better than hope. Truth won't let you down. It keeps being true. Go now. Go back to your hope. I'll stay with my truth and tears."

Antelope thought he would never share a normal moment with his aunt again. It didn't seem fair that of the two of them, he would be the one living with guilt.

He left her then. Needles of cold rain hit his face, and the sloppy mess of melting snow on the ground seeped into his shoes. Every part of him was chilled and raw.

As soon as he got in the car, his cell phone vibrated in his pocket. He didn't want to talk to anyone. Everyone he knew had murder on their minds. But when he saw it was the sheriff calling, he answered.

"We've got a problem here," Scruggs said. "I need you to do something for me, and I need you to do it fast. I'm not the only one with a past here. This isn't the first time Pepper Hunt's been a suspect in a shooting death. I made it my business to check her out before my wife went to work for her."

"She found the body and gave a statement. That's the extent of her involvement. I'm not considering her a person of interest."

"She lawyered up quick. What does that tell you?"

"She's smart."

"She's got something to hide. You know what happened in Massachusetts?"

"What does this have to do with what's happening here?"

"It was a double murder. She discovered her husband and his mistress together. Both shot in the head at close range. The position of the bodies suggested recent sexual activity. They made it easy for the shooter. The grand jury was gathering evidence to charge her. Then one of her husband's crazy patients confessed. She was in love with the doctor and had convinced herself he loved her too. When she found him with another woman, she killed them both in a jealous rage. She was proud of it, too. And here's a coincidence, the murder went down just before Christmas two years ago."

"What do you want me to do?"

"Marla's been at me all day. She's worried about her. This case is too stressful and likely to bring back memories. I have to admit, the timing of things is a little weird. Maybe we should play it safe and take her off the county payroll for now. There's too much activity around her office. If we decide a consultant is critical, there are other folks we could bring on."

"So you want her off the case?"

"Yesterday, if you can make that happen. Do you have a problem with that?"

"We're nowhere near solving this thing. We agreed she might help."

"She's too much of a complication. Pull her contract. As far as I know, I'm still in charge here."

Antelope sighed as he hung up the phone. It was too late to call Pepper.

He was stuck behind a slow caravan of city plows. Hypnotic orange dome lights flashed like disco strobes. His eyes ached and his head pounded. He recognized the signs of the migraine that would claim him soon. He wanted to make it to his own bed before it hit. At times like this he craved the oblivion of sleep.

Estella was right. He had failed to find Kimi. Her words made him doubt himself and the choices he'd made that had cut him off from the place he came from and the people who made him. Estella had cursed him and taken everything. He drove alone through the miserable night. His hope was gone, and he had no idea what the truth was anymore.

CHAPTER 38

After just five hours of sleep, Antelope was at his desk early. He still had the kind of headache that usually went with a well-earned hangover, and he resented having to suffer without the benefit of the buzz. He stopped at Starbucks on the way in and picked up two double espresso cups that he hoped would get him through the morning.

Kevin Cahill's murder brought a similar shot of energy to the ongoing investigation. He welcomed the excitement, if he was being honest. He was desperate for a break in the case.

The first thing he did was pull the previous night's call log from the hotline that had been set up to handle tips. A call had come in right after last call at the bars at 2:00 A.M. Though he had the transcript of the call before him, he replayed it to hear her voice for himself. He pictured her in the slow herd of vehicles exiting the parking lot at closing time, at the wheel with cell phone and cigarette. He imagined she slipped past the cruisers trolling for drunks who bragged they drove better high. Most male cops gave under-the-influence females a pass. The primitive reptilian brain had one priority: if she was half-pretty, he'd hold off giving her a ticket and hope to try his luck with her off-duty.

The voice was female, soft-spoken, slurred—no surprise given the hour. She didn't waste any time, maybe afraid they had the technology to place and would show up and arrest her for driving under the influence.

"I need to talk to someone about that missing reporter."

She'd left her name and telephone number and address. He was out the door and on his way to her before the recording was done playing.

■ ■ ■

Ricki Trent was surprised, like Antelope wanted her to be. He held up his badge to the security window of her apartment door. A ten-second delay, then the sound of three locks clicking and sliding open.

Platinum spikes with pale patches of scalp showing. Her left cheek was creased from sleeping, and the previous night's makeup showed in raccoon rings around her blue eyes. She was barefoot in baggy gray sweatpants and a T-shirt short enough to reveal the sapphire stud in her belly button. She'd gotten a cigarette going on the short trip from bed to door. The young woman in front of him looked totally different than the picture on her Wyoming license in the case file. It was clear she'd made an effort to change her appearance after she was raped.

"What?" she said, coughing. She fanned the smoke away to clear the air between them.

"Good morning, Miss Trent, I'm Detective Antelope. I'm following up on the call you made last night to the hotline."

A door opened down the hall, and another slammed shut on the floor above them—neighbors going to work. The woman's eyes roved sideways, and she took a small step back.

"May I come in?" He held out his badge and department ID.

"Sure, why not. Wait a minute, let me see it," she said and wiggled her finger for the badge in his hand.

She had small hands and acrylic nails done in robin's-egg blue, the same color as on her toes—the exact color of her eyes. Antelope thought of ocean and sky reflecting, one truer than the other. The apartment was small and sparsely furnished. Moving boxes were stacked like furniture against the walls. In the middle of the room, two black vinyl love seats on a red rug, a chrome and glass coffee table—Kmart deluxe interior.

She moved a laundry basket to the floor and motioned for him to sit across from her before grabbing a black sweatshirt from the basket and pulling it over her head. The room felt familiar and reminded Antelope of home, the scent of smoke and something clean, like Ivory Soap.

"Excuse the mess. I have a motivation problem, procrastination, whatever. New Year's resolution: unpack."

Antelope took out his notebook.

"Are you the one working on the case now? It was another detective, an old guy, who came when it happened."

"I'm here because of the tip you called in to the hotline. You had information about Kimi Benally, the missing reporter?"

"Right, I just figured they'd send the same guy out."

"Detective Winslow retired earlier this year. Your case may have been the last one he worked on."

"Is that why you never found the guy?"

"We're still working on it."

"Famous last words—'Don't call us, we'll call you.' I never heard anything. That reporter, she's the only one who still seemed interested in what happened to me. She came to see me last week. She was going to do another story."

"When was this?"

"The same day she went missing. Kind of creepy, gave me the chills when I found out."

"She was doing another story?"

"A retrospective, whatever that is. I told her what I remembered from the night I was raped. I thought it might help find the guy if she put it in the paper. And then she disappeared and I thought, *Now I have to do it all over again, tell my story to someone else*, and I didn't have the energy to do it. When I saw her car and the license plate, though, a little bell went off in my head. It could be nothing, but I thought I should tell someone."

Antelope felt the hair stand up on the back of his neck. His heart beat faster.

"It was more the way she reacted that made me call you. I didn't think too much about it at the time. That's how it is with me since the rape. I can't make sense of things in the moment. Only later do I see what's important."

"Reacted to what?"

"I told her what he whispered when he was done with me." She closed her eyes and shuddered. There was a faded nursery blanket printed with animals folded on the arm of the sofa. Antelope picked it up and placed it around her shoulders. She held it close and began to rock.

"'You'll always be my secret one.' Imagine that? The idea that I could be in his mind makes me sick."

Kimi's license plate flashed in Antelope's mind: SECRET1. It might not help them to bring Kimi home, but it could be useful to the unsolved rape cases.

"I saw it when they towed her car. It's her license plate. SECRET1. It freaked her out. That's what it looked like to me."

"An interesting coincidence," Antelope said, knowing it was more than that. He was certain now that there was a connection between Kimi and the rapist.

"Did you tell this to Detective Winslow?"

"I don't remember much about that night. Like I said, I wanted to forget about it."

She lit another cigarette, and he thought she might be regretting calling the hotline. He wrote the words in his notebook. *You'll always be my secret one*. He'd have to check again, but he was pretty sure he hadn't seen it in Winslow's report.

"You did the right thing making that call."

"Call it a drunk dial."

"Next time wait a while before getting in a vehicle," Antelope said.

She held out her wrists. "Want to arrest me, Officer?"

"I'd have to catch you in the act."

"How'd you know I was driving?"

"Audiotape picked up the fasten seat belt indicator."

"I keep waiting to see the story in the paper. Another reporter came to talk to me this week. A strange little man. Cedric Yee."

■ ■ ■

Back in the office, Antelope pulled the case file on Ricki Trent's rape. It didn't take him long to find the reference. It was there in his predecessor's chicken-scratch, but it was only now that he was looking for it that he found it.

Damn, how'd they miss it? It was one of Winslow's last cases before he'd retired. Antelope made his way through the handwritten notes. The guy had been technically off-duty for years. He hadn't given it a second thought. When Antelope had picked the case up with the next rape, records had gone electronic, and he'd read the transcribed notes, but he should have double-checked the original notes. If they'd had this information earlier this year, they might have gotten a lead on a rapist who called his victims his "secret."

But maybe he was wrong. When he read the files of the other victims, the word *secret* did not appear in any way. Maybe the rapist caught his own mistake, didn't make it twice. Still, Antelope cursed himself for not picking up on what was now so clear. The rapist liked small women. They already knew he had a pattern. He chose slender women with long, dark hair. No mention of their petite stature.

"Get me Winslow's number," he barked into the intercom.

He heard the edge in his voice, knew he was in the zone now, past needing to be seen as the one Native who could make it in the white world. It didn't happen often. But right now, he needed to strip away the civility and activate his primitive senses.

"You mean Detective Winslow? He'll be down in Arizona now."

"Get me the Arizona number."

The dispatcher gave the number and hung up quick before Antelope could say anything else.

He dialed the number, listened to the recorded message, Winslow's wife saying they'd gone away for the holidays. He left a message on their voice mail.

"Winslow, Antelope here. It's urgent I speak to you," he said and left his cell number.

What now? He should get the other three victims in, press their memories. He needed to know if the words the rapist used could pull in any more information.

When he got the day-shift report, he saw there had been no progress on Kimi's case. It hit him hard; he felt a soreness in his gut like he'd swallowed a rock. Over a week now and they had nothing. Was she a victim of the White Mountain Rapist? Kimi disappearing didn't fit the rapist's crime profile; as far as they knew, no other women had gone missing from Rock Springs. But he didn't want to rule it out. Sex offenders often escalated, turned more violent with each encounter.

It would be days before they had the DNA results from the semen sample at her house. With the rapist surfacing days after Kimi's disappearance, he couldn't ignore that possibility, as much as he hated the idea.

What had Kimi felt when she learned the rapist called Ricki Trent his "secret"? *Secret* was Kimi's Native name. But as far as Antelope knew, she'd left her Native name, along with the rest of her past, behind on the Wind River Reservation.

It looked like Kimi's disappearance was linked to the rapist. But where did Kevin's murder fit in? He'd been shot outside Pepper's office. What was he doing there at her office at that time of night? He wished he could talk with her without her lawyer. He recalled the crime scene. Kevin Cahill on his back, dead white and bled out, eyes open to the sky, the scent of blood and rancid evil in the biting air. The shooter was good, had landed a dead-on shot to the heart. It wasn't a random hit, out there in the dead of night, behind an office building. Someone lured Cahill there intending to kill him.

Cahill had been shot four feet from the back door of the building. Snow had been coming down hard. The techs would be lucky to pick up any traces of foot or vehicle traffic. Antelope was getting tired of the weather botching any chance of good old-fashioned police work. Without physical evidence, it was hard to solve crimes.

His head was spinning with all the directions this case was taking. He needed to talk to someone he could trust. Like Kimi, he'd kept his distance from his roots on the reservation for years. And it was complicated with Cass. She'd left a message for him on Christmas Eve, and he'd meant to call her back. But then Diego had found Kimi's car, and he'd lost track of his intention—and it was too late now. He'd missed the moment. Cass was big on moments. She'd be angry as hell that he'd let all this time go by. He didn't have room in his head for dealing with her emotions.

He'd left three messages for Cedric Yee and hadn't gotten a call back yet. On the first message, he'd left his name and requested an urgent call back. An hour later, he'd called again and told him he had important information regarding the White Mountain Rapist investigation and wanted his help releasing information to the public.

The press never liked law enforcement telling them what to print, but screw it; this was a murder case now. He didn't care if he was ruffling Cedric Yee's feathers. He was in the saddle, and he would drive this investigation the way he wanted it to go. They'd lost too much time focusing on Kevin Cahill. He wanted the new information on the White Mountain Rapist calling his victim his "secret" on the front page. And he wanted Kimi Benally's disappearance linked to the White Mountain Rapist. If there was anyone out there holding on to information that could bring down the rapist, he wanted to flush them out of hiding.

He'd had it with Yee not getting back to him. He went over his head and called the editor of the *Rocket Miner*.

"I need to get something in the paper for tomorrow. We have new information that the rapist called his victims 'his secret'. Maybe that will ring a bell with someone who knows him. I left a few messages for Yee about this."

"He took some time off. This thing with Kimi hit us all hard. No need to wait for him. I'm still a reporter. I'll write it up."

With every passing day, they lost ground and lost hope of finding Kimi alive. It was over a week now that she'd been gone. At the least, he owed it to the family to find out what had happened to one of their own. If he couldn't protect her, then he at least owed Kimi that much, too.

TUESDAY
DECEMBER 28

CHAPTER 39

It was one of those days in Rock Springs that made Antelope long for Mexico. A mean wind was up and a fluorescent glare took the place of sunlight. After a quick trip to the Get & Go to pick up a copy of the *Rocket Miner*, he spent the day at home watching the Denver Broncos blow their chances at the Super Bowl in the football game he'd taped on Sunday. He arranged with the volunteer center and dispatch to patch all calls through to his home phone. The response to the "secret" lead was underwhelming. He kept picking up the handset to see if there was an active dial tone. There wasn't one call all day, not even his mother checking on the case.

With nothing new to report, Kevin's murder was already no longer front-page news. The department was striking out. He dozed off in the boredom of the halftime show and woke in the dark of four o'clock, out of touch with his world. Domino brought him back to reality, barking and bouncing at the kitchen door, making it clear she needed to go out fast. He let her out and saw the message light flashing on the land line. There was a boozy message from his Aunt Estella reminding him that "Secret" was Kimi's name. As if he needed reminding. But what did that have to do with anything?

He had to get back to the case, even if he didn't know the next thing to do. He got dressed, got in his car, and after a quick stop at his favorite redhead's place for a fish fillet sandwich, he reported to headquarters on C Street.

As he approached the station, he saw small groups of teenagers strolling the streets. They moved with a careless grace, laughing and talking, in shirtsleeves and hatless, immune to the biting cold, the relentless wind. A memory rose—the ball in his hands, those long Sundays at the Blue Sky Community Center when basketball was his life.

The squad room was empty, on skeleton crew for the evening, saving money for the holiday overtime budgeted for New Year's Eve coverage. Kimi's dog looked up at him with eyes that wouldn't quit. He gave her another biscuit and that seemed to make her happy. With Kimi still missing and Kevin dead, she was an orphan now. Antelope had agreed to keep her when they learned the shelter was full. He had to admit, he liked the company.

He had the medical examiner's report. They had the calibration on the bullets taken from Kevin Cahill's chest. The first hit would have done the job; the second was for good measure, someone wanting to be sure he wouldn't live to talk.

Something was nagging at him. He smacked his forehead; he'd forgotten to call Pepper. He dialed her cell phone and it went straight to voice mail. He told her about the sheriff's decision to terminate her contract and said he hoped it would give her a chance for some real rest. Then he asked her to call him when she had some time to get together. When he ended the call, he noticed he had his fingers crossed.

The red light on his desk phone flashed.

"Someone to see you, Detective."

Antelope sighed. He had to get dispatch to stop sending everything to him if he was going to survive the case. "Who is it?" he asked, trying to keep the annoyance out of his voice.

"Some guy who smells like he's growing his own."

"I've got five minutes, send him in."

His dispatcher was right; the man was wrapped in the sweet smell of marijuana the way some men wear cheap drugstore aftershave. The scent was so strong Antelope thought he'd catch a contact high standing across the room from him.

The young, lanky male had a greasy blond ponytail and carried a black plastic box in both hands. The emblem on his uniform coveralls read "Yellowstone Self-Storage."

"I'm Curly Johnson. I thought you might want to take a look at what's in this box. You met my mom, Clarice Johnson, at the Get & Go last week. She's the one told me to get in here with this and ask for you."

"What is this?"

Curly tossed the box on the desk between them. It reminded Antelope of playing hot potato with his cousins; the guy looked like he couldn't wait to be rid of it.

"About that murder . . . the guy who was shot put this in his storage unit the night he was killed."

"Have you opened it?" Antelope asked.

"No sir. I don't want any part of anything related to a murder."

Antelope got out an evidence bag, pulled on purple latex gloves, and opened the small case. Inside was a USB flash drive and a prepaid cell phone. He thought about Kevin's plan to do his own research, and where he'd found these things. They hadn't been in the house when the forensics team had searched there.

"You say he put this in the storage unit the night he was killed?"

"I opened up for him. I was having my dinner break so it was past seven. Guy's got an issue showing up inconvenient, same thing the night before. It was Christmas and the place was officially closed. I was sleeping in the back, and he woke me up. Both of them acted like it was their private hidey-hole, coming in and out no matter the time. But he flashed her picture, the flyer with *MISSING* spelled out in big letters. What was I going to do? Guy looked like he might cry, so he's in, my bad, never told the boss."

"You said she was the same? When was she there?" Antelope asked.

"I'd guess last week sometime."

"It would help if you could say exactly when you saw her."

"I'm on weekends and holidays. I remember now, it was Friday night."

"Friday, December 17? The day she went missing?"

"Is that right? Damn."

"You're sure it was Friday and not Saturday?"

"I was running late getting to work. Shift runs from eight o'clock Friday night through seven Monday morning. I pulled in, and she was right behind me, didn't even wait for me to get myself situated. She followed me into the office and stood there while I clocked in. It was eight fifteen, so I got docked a quarter-hour pay. That's how I know it was Friday."

"We've been asking for any information to help us find this woman for a week. Why did you sit on this?"

"I stay up at my girl's place in Boulder during the week. Over there we're pretty much off the grid, and we like it that way. I didn't know anything about her being missing until I picked up radio service on the drive in to work on Friday. Then her husband comes in and shows me her picture . . . I still didn't put it together that it was the Friday she went missing. I might have been one of the last people to see her."

"Give me the number of the storage unit. I'll get a warrant to search the contents tomorrow morning."

Antelope took the man's information and told him he'd be in touch—gave him the usual don't-go-anywhere-in-case-we-need-to-find-you notice.

The stoner grin was gone now. "Can I get police protection?"

"Why would you need police protection?"

"There's a killer out there who might want what I gave you."

Antelope shook his head. "Do your job. Secure the unit. Don't let anyone near it. And let me know if anyone comes asking, or if you get any break-ins or attempts, for that matter."

He knew he was taking a risk. Technically, he should obtain a new warrant. But he was tired of waiting. It was one of those moments that challenged integrity. It was one of those times when integrity was the lesser value. He thought about Kimi and opened the box.

The two devices would be a few easy hours' work for his computer techies. Kevin had had these in his possession before he was killed. He'd taken the trouble to put them back where he thought they would be safe. Antelope needed to know what Kevin learned before he was killed.

He rolled the cool, oblong disc in his hand—Kimi's words reduced to an electronic seed that, if there was any luck at all in this case, would bloom into something resembling a clue. It would be a long night, alone. This was his to do now.

The only other person he might have trusted with this was Pepper Hunt. It wasn't just her professional knowledge of the people involved that he valued. He had to admit he felt comfortable talking with her about the way the case challenged him.

The phone beeped, signaling a voice mail. A missed call from Pepper. He hit redial but the phone went to voice mail.

He listened to her message. The words came out quick and determined. Her voice was low and accented. She assured him she was okay with being taken off as consultant. She wanted to retrieve her Beretta Nano from evidence.

It would have been tested for prints and evidence of recent firing in order to rule it out as the weapon used to kill Kevin. Once it was determined not to have been involved in the homicide, she would be free to collect it.

He called down to the evidence room and was told the gun was not in custody and there was no record of it having been logged in. That was strange, but it wouldn't be the first time evidence went missing. He walked down to the evidence room and did a thorough search of the secure evidence storage area, where bins marked "Cahill" contained specimens taken from the murder scene. He satisfied himself that the gun had not been overlooked or incorrectly placed with another case.

And then he remembered Kevin Cahill's scene, demanding the return of Kimi's picture, which he swore had been on the bedside table and had to have been taken by the crime scene technicians. He knew which one he meant; it was taken the day they got engaged, and Kimi had used it to announce the engagement. A copy hung in his mother's living room. The one Kevin had wanted was the original 8 x 10 photo in a silver frame. But the picture wasn't in the evidence room either. He checked the log on the off-chance Kevin had been able to persuade someone to release it to him. There was nothing there, no entries in the log related to Kimi's file. He read through the list of all the articles taken from the house. No mention of a picture of Kimi. He didn't know what to make of that, but he didn't have time to give it any more thought. Pepper's missing gun was the most pressing mystery.

Officers Garcia and Collins were the ones who'd responded to the scene. One of them would have conducted the initial search of Pepper's office on the night of the murder. It would be easy enough to check with one of them about whether the gun had been taken into evidence. He checked the rotation schedule and found both of them off-duty until tomorrow. Another frustration in a case filled with frustrations.

Pepper kept a gun in the office; she'd told him that when she opened up to him about her husband's murder. He didn't want to tell her they'd lost her gun. On the night of Kevin's murder her face was taut and haunted. It was easy to imagine the rush of feelings and memories. Finding Kevin dead in the snow must have been like reliving a nightmare. But as much as he had wanted to comfort her, he'd known not to try. Everything about her body language had told him to stay away.

His Cadillac waited in the unplowed parking lot under a crust of snow and ice. A split-second, no-brainer decision—a half hour to defrost and dig out. He warmed up the unmarked SUV, which held better on winter roads anyway. They had a twenty-four-hour reprieve, but snow was predicted to fly again. Winter was kicking the county's butt and destroying the plowing budget early in the season. The states would shut down the interstate soon. He put Domino in the backseat where she sat tall, her eyes in the rearview mirror, on him the whole drive.

He took it slow, easing the cruiser over streets slick with ice. Not a good night to be on the road, but he had two stops that couldn't wait. He signed out keys the city kept for checking office buildings on a patrol list. The Hilltop Medical Building was on the list because it housed physicians' offices and, as the sheriff had pointed out in their conversation the other day, was a likely target for medications. He would go to Pepper's office and look for the gun.

First stop was the city garage on Elk Street. Kevin's vehicle had been impounded as evidence, and now sat alongside Kimi's Honda. An eerie sight, the two vehicles sitting side by side, as if they were parked in the couple's driveway.

Security lights gave a green, radioactive glow to the deserted facility. Antelope's footsteps echoed in the cavernous building. He gloved up before opening the driver's side door of Kevin's Jeep. He turned the ignition and tapped the GPS touch screen. Three addresses in the short history: 1204 College Drive, the address of the Hilltop Medical Building; Kimberly Apartments at 1590 Sunset Drive, where Tracy Hopkins lived; and 250 C Street, the sheriff's department. Why did he use a GPS for local addresses? He removed the GPS and placed it in the evidence bag, along with a notation about the time and date of removal.

Back outside, sleet came down hard, pounding the cruiser with loud staccato shots on the slow crawl up to Hilltop Drive. He parked close to the front door and left the car running while he dashed through the attacking night. Domino had shown no interest in braving the nasty weather; he'd left her in the car. Now, as rivers of icy rain traveled down his neck and onto his chest and belly, he wished he'd stayed in there with her. It was one of those moments he seriously questioned his career choice—and while he was at it, might as well throw in his state of residence. He didn't like being back here, a recent murder scene, where Kevin's spirit might linger in the shadows.

Enough bullshit, he told himself. He was there to check real-life evidence. He turned on a light to help banish the netherworld.

The consultation room was serene and innocent. For a minute, he envied Pepper's work life in this quiet room. He moved to the table where she kept the gun. He had the evidence bag ready so he could tag it and take it. He opened the narrow drawer; the scent of fresh cedar escaped, and his fingers felt the cool, smooth surface of the empty space.

Okay, so maybe he didn't know everything. That's where she used to keep it. But it had been a year since she'd told him. Maybe she'd moved it. He searched the office—every drawer, the closet— but the Beretta Nano wasn't there.

He locked up and drove home, eager to get to Kimi's flash drive and phone. He nodded off at a red light and decided Kimi's secrets could wait; he had just enough energy to walk the dog before falling into bed.

WEDNESDAY
DECEMBER 29

CHAPTER 40

The week of short sleep had finally caught up with Antelope. If it hadn't been for Domino barking at his bedside, he might have slept through the whole day. He barely made it to the station by 4:00 P.M. for the evening shift.

He spent the next hours at his desk, making his way through routine police work, cross-checking the paper trail Kimi had left behind. The admin clerk came to deliver a FedEx envelope. It contained Kimi's phone logs for the last year. It had only taken a week for the requisition to go through—not bad timing, as those things went. He closed his door and set to the task. An hour later, things became more complicated. All along there had been the suspicion that Kimi was having an affair. The records supported that theory.

He used a yellow marker to highlight repeating numbers. He expected, and found, frequent calls from Estella's landline. But another number showed up in the month of January and again in December. On the night she'd disappeared Kimi had called that number two times: as soon as she left her therapy session and again after her fuel purchase in Reliance.

He wouldn't have to trace the number. He knew it well. It was the private cell phone number of his commanding officer, Sheriff Carlton Scruggs.

Antelope was well aware of the politics of a law enforcement career. Some things went left unsaid, some things required turning a blind eye. But some of those things required a greater sacrifice of compromising principles than others. He'd thought long and hard before applying to the police academy. He'd known the risks. And he knew his decision here could possibly keep him from moving up the ranks. But the way he saw it, there was less to lose that way. He wouldn't be able to live with himself if, in the end, he turned out to be a dirty cop. What was the point of that? A clean cop was bad enough where he came from. He'd already mortgaged his identity when he'd made his career choice and cut the cord to all things Native. The only way to play it now was straight and honest.

The frantic, beating energy of day shift activity was over and the station was quiet. Cruisers roamed the streets, ready to catch the messy business of nighttime, small-town crime: vandalism, burglary, domestic disturbances, and prostitution. If he was going to do what he knew he had to do, now was the time.

A triangle of yellow light spilled from the sheriff's open door onto the polished wooden floor. His was the only occupied office on the third floor. If Antelope needed a sign, this was it; not another soul was at work in the darkened administrative offices.

He walked slowly toward the office at the far end of the corridor, the old floorboards creaking with every footstep.

Scruggs was at his desk, a case file open before him. He'd switched off the overhead fluorescent lights. A gooseneck lamp shone a white cone of light on the desk. Later, Antelope would recall the still-life quality of this ordinary scene and rue his part in its interruption.

He stood at the doorway, and his long shadow reached the steel desk. Scruggs looked up and met his eyes. The sheriff's color was ashen, his skin slack under gray stubble. The job did this— soured the soul and aged the face, Antelope thought.

He settled in the chair in front of Scruggs's desk and placed the phone records on top of the case file.

"What have you got there?"

"Have a look," Antelope said, and tapped the stapled pages.

Scruggs paged through the thick packet silently, taking his time, then raised an eyebrow when he saw his own number highlighted in yellow.

"Anyone else see this?" Scruggs asked.

The glare from the nearby lamp gave their words the intensity of an interrogation.

"I came to you first."

"I know how this looks."

"It's not good."

"Not that I should have to, but I can explain."

Antelope felt light-headed, like he was breathing thin air at the end of a long climb. He waited. With anyone else, this conversation would be scripted, and he'd move through it sure-footed, knowing his part.

From below, a radiator released a clanging spray of steam that echoed through the empty rooms.

Scruggs turned the gooseneck lamp toward the wall and lit up the whiteboard where the investigation notes recorded the skimpy progress on the case. Kimi's picture was at the center, held in place by a pushpin. She smiled down at them as if she'd walked in and joined their strange conversation.

"Where the fuck is she, Antelope?"

"That's the question."

"It's a damn shame. She's a beautiful woman," Scruggs said, never taking his gaze from her photo.

"What can you tell me about this?"

Scruggs sighed and then looked directly at Antelope. "You mean about my number showing up here? It's got nothing to do with her going missing."

He looked tired, bloodshot eyes in gray skin.

"Would you say the same if it was anyone other than you?" Antelope said.

"I hear you. You're right. You're doing the police work the way you should. But sometimes things aren't as they seem to be. And that's the case here."

"Care to tell me the nature of these calls?"

"Not at this time. You're going to have to trust me on this," Scruggs said. He shifted papers and files on his desk, creating order out of the paper chaos.

"Your conversations with Kimi last week are not relevant to her disappearance?"

"I'm asking you to believe that, yes."

"Without any explanation from you?"

Scruggs leaned across the cleared desk and looked directly into Antelope's eyes. Despite the obvious signs of fatigue, his gaze held steady. Antelope knew his boss was a man of steel nerves. He would be hard to crack.

"Where are you going with this, Antelope? I had a professional relationship with her. End of story. Find anything else you can chew on in there?" He picked up the stack of papers in front of him and put them in the top drawer of his desk.

"Keep this between us for now. No sense confusing people and taking the focus off where it needs to be."

"And where is that?" Antelope asked, not entirely satisfied with how this conversation had gone down.

"You're working the serial rapist angle. Take it all the way."

"She called you the night she went missing."

"I don't recall getting a call from her the night she went missing. But then again, why would I remember that night in particular? I had no way of knowing she was about to disappear. Isn't that right, Detective?"

There was a strong smell of bullshit in the room.

"Notice the time. 9:05 P.M. You didn't answer."

"This conversation's over, Detective. I suggest you get busy trying to find out what happened to her and stop wasting your time looking at me."

Of all the staff working the case, only the two of them had a gut-level stake in the outcome. For Antelope, it was personal. He felt the weight of the past they shared. He owed it to Kimi to find her or find out what happened to her. For Scruggs, he had his career to consider. He couldn't take another direct hit. A case very much like this one was what had landed him in Rock Springs in the first place—a serious bounce down the slats of the career ladder of the law enforcement pecking order.

But Antelope suspected the sheriff had more at stake than job security. He had never seen the man as twitchy as he was in this moment.

In the dark room, the two men sat in silence and looked at each other, each one taking the other's measure. Outside, a moaning wind sent tatters of stray holiday debris skittering along the sidewalk and out into the far reaches of the night.

CHAPTER 41

Antelope felt cheered when he got to his house. In his rush to get to work that afternoon, he'd forgotten to turn off the lights and heat, so when he got home at 11:30 P.M., the little cottage was like something out of a fairy tale, toasty and inviting. It called up a yearning for what he'd never known: the sweetness of coming home to a waiting wife in a well-tended home.

After walking Domino, he stripped to his thermals and dropped the soaking wet clothes into the dryer. Christmas leftovers went in the microwave for a midnight snack, enough for him and the dog. Next year, he'd buy a smaller turkey. He wanted nothing more than to drink himself to sleep, escape into cop-style oblivion. But that would have to wait; whiskey would muddle his brain.

He found a universal charger for the prepaid phone. He would get busy decoding it as soon as it was fully charged. Time for the flash drive.

He clicked on the icon that popped up on his desktop, and Kimi's words filled the screen.

"Talk to me, Cousin."

He was scrolling through Kimi's writing when he sensed someone watching him. What if her fear was contagious and could enter his body as he read her words?

He looked up from the computer and saw a face in a ski mask at the front window.

He was on his feet in an instant; the chair hit the floor behind him. An automatic movement drew his gun from its ankle holster. Body held sideways, he walked crab-like to the door.

Laughter came from outside, laughter like bells, vaguely familiar. By the time Antelope got the door open, the ski mask was off.

Estella was on the porch, smiling, her gray hair streaming in the wild, snowy night.

"Auntie, what are you doing out here? It's freezing cold." He took her by the arm and pulled her into the room. Her threadbare woolen coat was covered in snow and soaked through.

"I scared you good, didn't I?" She pointed at the weapon in his hand. "You could have shot me!" she said and laughed, the deep cackle that always made him laugh with her.

He remembered that side of her, how she liked to tease and torment all the little ones. There was a time he'd thought of her as a witch, but his mother had been quick to correct him, saying there was another word their people used for the likes of Estella.

His fright when he'd seen her at the window just now had been real. What was she doing here? After their last encounter, he'd wondered if she had written him off completely.

He helped her get her wet coat and boots off. She sat down at the table, and he handed her a kitchen towel to dry her hair.

"Put on a kettle for tea," she said. "I caught a good chill walking out there. None of the cars are working. You know how that goes."

"And Diego?"

"Gone off again. He stopped by yesterday to bring me coffee and the paper from the Loaf and Jug, then he went off with Troy. You're wrong about Diego, you know. And he's wrong about you. The two of you are all mixed up about each other and more alike than either of you wants to know." She smoothed the lace tablecloth with a slow petting motion. "This is nice. It's your mother's cloth. I recognize it from the old days. So you didn't forget everything. That's good."

"I thought I was as good as dead to you after the other day."

"Don't talk that way. Too many are dead. We're family. Nothing can take that from us."

"Is that what you walked through a storm to tell me?"

"You must be popular. That phone of yours is filled with messages. No more room for me to tell you."

He set the steaming pot on the table and poured two cups. She took her time fixing the tea in the English way of the reservation with milk and sugar, stirring it to cool it.

"The way I like it," she said. "Hot and sweet."

He waited and tried to look patient while under the table he slowly clenched and unclenched his fists. He wanted to get back to Kimi's writing. He was glad Estella wasn't holding a grudge, but this wasn't the best time for a family visit.

"I'm surprised you didn't figure it out."

"What should I have figured out?"

"It was on the front page yesterday. The rapist called his victim his secret."

He felt his frustration growing. For a minute he'd thought she might have something useful to tell him. He took a deep breath before he spoke, not wanting to get crosswise with her again after she'd made this effort at reconciliation.

"I know that, Auntie, I made sure that information got in the paper. There's a chance it will ring a bell with someone and help us identify a suspect. No luck. No one has come forward."

"I came forward. I heard the bell ringing."

A crawling sensation in his neck, like the gentle movement of small insects that signaled something important was coming.

"Kimi didn't like him doing that. She told him to stop. He kept calling her 'My Secret.' Her Native name in his mouth was ruined and dirty."

"Who called her 'My Secret'?"

"That man she works with, the reporter."

"You mean Cedric Yee?"

"That's the one."

Cedric Yee never returned his calls.

"Stay right here," Antelope said, cupping his hands over hers. He was afraid she might walk off into the night now that she'd delivered her message.

He called the desk clerk who pulled up Cedric Yee's address.

He could be there in five minutes. He radioed for backup, instruct-ing the officers not to use sirens or lights. He dressed quickly and was soon at the door with his coat on and his keys in his hand. Estella was right beside him, pulling on her boots.

"You're staying here. I'll take you home when I've made the arrest."

"I'm coming with you. I'm tired of men leaving me behind."

■ ■ ■

It felt strange to have her beside him in the unmarked car. She must have felt the same because she said, "This is my first time in the front seat of a cop car."

"I'm going to be driving fast. You need to put your seat belt on."

"No way. If you crash, I'll be trapped and die in a fire."

"It's the law, Auntie, and this is an official police vehicle," he said, but he knew he was wasting his breath. He snapped the flasher on the top of the car to clear the road in front of them and accelerated fast enough to knock Estella back against her seat.

The windshield was iced over, so he rolled the window down and drove with his head out in the whipping snow.

"When we get there, Auntie, you need to follow orders."

He turned on the heater vents, creating a small windstorm of cold air.

"I'm not good at that."

He ran all three lights on the way across town. Estella sat beside him like a queen, smiling.

The lot at the Kimberly Apartments hadn't been plowed, so he made a U-turn and parked at the Holiday Inn to avoid getting stuck in snow.

He radioed the officers to park down the road and approach the back entrance of the building on foot.

Estella had the door open before he'd stopped the car.

"No, you stay here. This is official police business, no civil-ians allowed."

"Are you kidding? A woman was attacked here last week. I'm not staying here alone."

He saw that she was afraid and not manipulating him. But there was no way he was taking her with him.

"You're waiting here, at the hotel. I'm serious, Auntie. I cannot take you with me. I could lose my badge. That might not mean anything to you, but it's everything to me. Come on, let's go."

She nodded her head to let him know she would cooperate. He took her by the arm and walked her to the hotel door. He reached in his pocket for some cash and put a twenty-dollar bill in her cold hands.

"Get yourself something to eat. I'll be back to get you. Don't worry, I won't forget you."

She nodded again. He wondered if he could trust her.

"I'm warning you, stay put. I don't know how this is going to go. I can't take the chance of you getting hurt."

"You be careful," she said and touched his cheek.

When she was inside, he broke into a run. He was crossing the road as the cruiser turned in then slowed and parked. He gave the signal to proceed, and they made their way together through ankle-deep snow. When they reached the building, he went in the front door. He waited in the hallway until the two appeared with guns drawn at the back entrance.

Inside the building, all was quiet. Like a slow cat he climbed the carpeted stairs in silence. At Cedric's door, Antelope knocked hard once, twice, three times, waited. No sound came from the apartment. After a minute, he knocked again, this time adding, "Open up. Police." Still no sounds or movement from Cedric's apartment. He pushed against the locked door, and it held. He radioed for the others to come to the second floor. Antelope gave the door three heavy body thrusts. The door gave out. The three men entered the dark room with guns drawn. They stood still, poised to respond to movement or sound. In the silence, Antelope heard the others breathing.

Antelope stepped backward and put a hand out in search of a light switch. An overhead light revealed a small room furnished with only a leather recliner and a metal dining set. A galley kitchen, clean and tidy, opened to the right. Antelope sensed the swelling loneliness in the sterile space. He signaled to the others to follow, crossed the room to the closed door and the bedroom beyond. Again, he drew his weapon while one of the other men turned the knob and kicked in the door. A narrow shaft of light from the open door lit the scene on the bed in cold gray light.

Cedric Yee lay naked on his back, his hands and feet bound in rope. A pool of dark blood spread from his torso onto the floor. He had been stabbed countless times. Antelope took in the scene and was hit by images of the vicious attack. He didn't have any trouble imagining the expression on the face of the person wielding the knife.

On the nightstand was a silver-framed photo of Kimi smiling in the sunshine, a witness to it all.

THURSDAY
DECEMBER 30

CHAPTER 42

The phone rang once and Scruggs was on his feet, ready to hear whatever bad news would come. After Antelope told him Cedric Yee was dead, Scruggs sat alone for a long time in the cold kitchen. Marla had slept through the phone ringing, a well-trained lawman's wife. Now that he was awake, he couldn't go back to bed; he wouldn't sleep again. In times past, he'd already be on his way to the murder scene, like a dog on a scent, racing to danger. So Cedric Yee was the rapist; he hadn't seen that coming down the road. This case scrambled his brain. At the end of every day his thoughts were like shredded papers that he couldn't piece back together. Grief turned Antelope's voice to gravel when he said, "Yee got Kimi." Antelope was still green enough to think it was possible to tie up loose ends. Scruggs knew different.

He rubbed his chest where the dull pain pressed against his heart. The kitchen clock ticked away the minutes of his life. He wondered how long it would be before the past caught up with him. He'd had a good run, ten years next summer. Guilt sabotaged him. He couldn't get away free or go on with his life. Maybe that's why he surrendered to Kimi; let her into his life only to destroy it. He'd tried not to think about her, but she kept coming into his mind. That was the real reason he gave the case to Antelope. If he led the investigation, she would have consumed him, devoured what was left of his life.

Outside the kitchen window a pale blue dawn set his small piece of yard glowing where snow lingered in drifts. He had to get outside. It always worked for him to escape the confines of buildings. In the dark bedroom, he found his things and dressed as deft as a blind man, quietly, so as not to wake Marla. If she woke, he'd have trouble leaving. He enjoyed being secretive, stealthy, a spy in his own house.

As he shut the door behind him, the fierce morning air cut him. He felt alone and a little afraid to leave his home and the illusion of shelter. He'd seen too much and no longer believed that there was any true safe place in the world.

He climbed into the truck and turned the heater on high, blasting arctic air. He would drive and think about Kimi and the last time they were together.

He should have known something bad was coming. It was the anniversary of their first meeting. Dangerous thoughts had come to him in the incremental shortening of days, the cave of winter closing in around them. It had made him want to shutter in with her. Could he leave what had kept him trapped so long? She might be the one he couldn't stand to lose. They'd found reasons to be away: a law enforcement conference for him, a meeting with her thesis adviser in Laramie for her.

It was a rare lazy time, a deluxe stretch of afternoon before them, more hours than they'd ever shared. One of those times when he could forget about real life, the one beyond the locked hotel door and all the choke-collar tightness of it. He smiled remembering. Her head rested under his arm like a warm globe, the silk tassel of her hair grazed his chest. They breathed in tandem in a grateful lull he'd known couldn't last. Then she spoke words that never introduced a good conversation.

"I need to tell you something."

He'd sat up and turned on the bedside lamp, wanting all his senses ready for whatever was coming. Looking surprised by his moving away from her, she'd sat up, too, and folded her legs under her, hands on her knees. The brief, sweet moment defaulted to memory. Still, he'd carry it with him for all his days as one of the finest he'd ever known. He'd taken a minute to notice the blue tones of the shadowed room, her rippling jet hair freed from the braid and splayed across the swell of her breasts. The hotel walls had pulsed and breathed around them.

When she'd spoken, she'd told him about her research in unsolved missing persons' cases. Her voice had a quality he remembered from when they first met in the hallway of the hospital, uninflected and sterile. When they'd gotten to know each other, she'd begun to use her other voice with him—the voice that let him know he was a familiar, he could come closer and didn't have to keep his distance like the other Anglos. He liked her private voice, her smoky voice, the one that obscured their differences.

"You must remember Lisa Bennett."

The Native woman who went missing and was never found, the woman it had been his job to find.

He had never talked to her about his past. But now it was there, alive between them, in this most private intersection. She would never know what a mistake she'd made choosing that way to tell him. The thought entered his mind like a bullet, fast and hard, an unbidden, mean thing striking: *That's all she ever wanted.*

He was off the bed without having to will it, a spring uncoiled and vibrating. Insanity to be near her, lying flat and naked like a belly-up mutt. Pulling on jeans and a sweatshirt before the mirror, he saw a ghost staring out with a haunted face and wild hair.

Behind him, she was quick to cover her body. With a sheet pulled tight up to her throat, she looked like a corpse, sexless. He understood why she was afraid. Recently aroused, his veins still throbbed with desire, hormones enhanced his anger. He could go off easy with just one wrong word.

She knew it, knew him, and stayed silent.

He had two options. Open the door and walk away or sit down and hear her out. Doing anything with his anger, going anywhere near her, was out of the question. It occurred to him that he was overreacting.

He moved to a small seat, his back to the window, watched her from that distance. Her eyes bored into him, she moved slightly, and he held up his hand, halting her with a familiar, traffic-stop-ping gesture. He felt the afternoon's chill on his neck. Outside, a tentative rain spat at the window with small, sad tapping sounds.

She must have felt the same chill travel the space between them. She pulled a blanket over her shoulders and in an instant transformed herself from dead girl to Indian princess, the red wool coloring her face.

"You're writing about my case?"

He heard the ownership in his phrasing. Damn right it was his case, and she could mind her own business. She had no right to dig this up, not after all these years, all the layers of days crafting a film over the truth of it.

"Yes," spoken in yet another voice, one that sounded certain and separate.

Who is this woman? he thought. He knew how to keep women in their places, but this one had come too close. He would stop her.

"It's for my thesis, an important story about the problems we have in the state coordinating missing persons' cases."

"What's your interest here?"

"There's no single database for the counties to check. I'm writing about the role of the media in these cases, raising aware-ness across county lines. I know what it's like to be lost. It's given me a fascination with people who go missing."

Her arrogance and detachment got to him. How could she write about the ragged tragedy of Lisa Bennett's life from her chilly intellectual distance?

"Fascination? About a murdered woman. That's cold, even for someone who does the work you do, exploiting other peoples' tragedies."

"Doesn't it bother you that so many go missing and are never seen again? I want to see how the press has helped, how we could do more. In most cases, the police lose the trail and the investigations stagnate."

"So that's your angle? Exposing bad police work. Guess that's where I come in."

With her eyes closed, she began to nod, and then she looked

straight at him. "I get it now. You think I'm holding you responsible because Lisa Bennett was never found. That's why you're so
mad and sitting over there. But you're wrong. I was touched by
Lisa's story. I identify with her."

He didn't like hearing Lisa's name coming from her mouth.

"Because she's Arapaho? You're reducing her to that?"

"That's a bond, for sure. But there's more to it."

"What else?"

"She was unhappy, lost. Searching for something."

Off the bed, trailing blankets and heading toward him with
open arms. He was on his feet and moving past her, avoiding
her touch. That would be bad. From the top of the bureau, he
snatched his sheriff's star, wallet, and ring of keys. Minutes later
he was in his truck driving away. The phone in his pocket knocked
against his heart.

She wouldn't call after what he'd pulled. But he didn't trust
himself to resist the sound of her. So he took the prepaid phone
apart and then dropped the separate pieces into dumpsters outside
several gritty convenience stores on either side of Grand Avenue as
it cut through Laramie.

He wasn't a lawman for nothing. Whatever evidence the phone
held, it was now as broken and scattered as the thing they'd briefly
had. No one would ever find the private thoughts they'd shared. The
phone had been his idea when he'd noticed her number was coming
up too often on his phone. Sooner or later, Marla would know.

A strong arm of wind had pushed the truck to the right. He'd
tensed his muscles to hold the wheel straight and keep the vehicle
on the road. The tautness and the effort had made him want her.

She'd stayed away until last week. She'd asked to see him,
had something important to tell him. It felt dangerous to meet up
with her. There was the chance she would want to talk about his
past, about Lisa and Lander. Their last conversation had stirred
up stuff he'd just as soon keep buried. Since their angry ending,
he'd felt sick at heart, and he blamed her for probing where she
had no business going. Memories of Lisa, their last days together,
and everything that happened in the investigation made him see

things he couldn't see at the time. But something important might mean some kind of trouble. He didn't need any trouble or secrets dug up from the past. In the end, though, he'd sent her a text: "Meet me at Dry Well Ranch Friday night."

And that was all it took. She was back in his head again. His brain sparked with firecrackers and magic and the world was restored to a place he wanted to walk in. It was Christmas. He wanted to buy her something to let her know she'd been on his mind. The mall was open early to catch the last minute shoppers. He spotted the boots, fine red leather covered in hundreds of silver studs, in the window of the Maverick Western Wear store. That combination of flash and elegance was Kimi. He'd deal with explaining the $700 charge later.

CHAPTER 43

He'd planned to skip the appointment Marla made for him with their general practitioner, but the pain in his chest was growing into the size of something dangerous. A half hour later he was leaving the doctor's office with a prescription for an anti-anxiety medication. He tossed it in a trash can on the way out of the office. No way was he taking anything to steady his nerves. His heart was beating too fast, that was the problem and the reason he made the appointment. When this case was over, he'd schedule a stress test and meet with the cardiologist. For now, it was back in the saddle.

At the office, he banished all thoughts of taking care of his health and got down to work. After Cedric Yee's murder the night before, he'd ordered Antelope to take a forty-eight-hour leave. The job was done and the man needed time to grieve. He had the detective's report in front of him. It would fill in all the gaps in their telephone conversation the night before. They'd found Kimi's silver-framed engagement picture in Cedric's apartment, along with the driver's license pictures of the other victims, lined up in a gallery on his bedside table, like toys a boy might hide from his mother for private play after lights-out.

In five days, they'd have the results of the comparison tests of Cedric Yee's DNA to the ejaculate sample found on the tissue taken from Kimi's bedroom. The lab had already matched his prints to the ones taken from the banister, doorknobs, and furniture in her home.

Yee had raped his first victim, Ricki Trent, on New Year's Day. One year was a short career life for a serial rapist, and that was the grim truth. The White Mountain Rapist case was the case that had brought Kimi into his life. Now it was over and she was gone. He felt no celebration at the conclusion, only resignation about the sad events of the year. If everything had gone right, no booze-brain retiree running off to Arizona, they would have stopped Yee sooner.

Detective Winslow had contacted Antelope and confirmed that Cedric Yee knew the rapist called the victim "secret one."

The room swirled, a speeding carousel, vertigo and nausea. What the hell was happening to him? He closed his office door and rested his head on his desk. An ache like a horse on his chest, and the sound of his breath like something out of a horror movie, raspy and dangerous. He should have stopped to fill the prescription. Like every other important thing in his life, he left it too late.

A black thought came to him: Kimi's body might never be found. Like the other woman in his past, forever a black hole in his existence. Both of them dead stars pulling at him until he disappeared, lost in the void with the others.

In the months after Lisa Bennett went missing, he'd run the interminable, worthless investigation. No one could ever know about his affair with her. No point when she was gone. There was her memory to consider, all the things her family and husband thought they knew about her. She'd died as she lived, a girl who met everyone's expectations but her own. He'd never gotten why she'd chosen him. Maybe he was just the worst thing she'd found to do in her need to rebel.

Lisa was going to leave her husband. That would have been a problem for Scruggs. But she hadn't lived that long. She'd disappeared, just like Kimi.

He'd felt guilty when Marla stood by him through all the shame and crap that had come to him when he didn't solve the case. She seemed to believe in him and love him completely. A stronger man might have told her the truth. Would it have turned out differently if he had? After everything she'd done to keep them together, he could never leave her.

His chest ached in a crushing way that took his breath away. His stomach ached and burned with acid. From his desktop refrigerator, he grabbed a bottled water and swallowed the whole thing fast. Instantly, a volcanic nausea swelled in his gut. The urge to rest was followed by a lightness as he dropped down into welcoming darkness, taking the heavy phone console with him in a tangle of wires and buzzing tones.

CHAPTER 44

I woke early. An orange sun burned through frothy, celestial clouds, and the desert below was awash in reflected light.

I made coffee and listened to a voice mail from Antelope. Cedric Yee was dead, stabbed to death in his apartment the night before. Evidence pointed to Cedric Yee as the serial rapist. DNA tests would tell them if he'd been at Kimi's house.

I'd known all along Cedric was strange and his relationship with Kimi was obsessive. With Cedric dead, we would never know what happened to Kimi. And who killed Cedric?

An hour later I was in the office. Marla had scheduled eight sessions back to back. It felt good to be doing clinical work again, treating other patients. When I stopped for a break before my two o'clock session I had a message from Marla. The sheriff had collapsed in his office, and then drove himself to Sweetwater Hospital, where he was scheduled to have cardiac surgery later that afternoon. I heard the tension in her voice and called her back.

"How are you holding up? It sounds pretty scary," I said.

"I'm out of my mind with worry. The damn fool didn't have the sense to call for an ambulance and could have died on the drive over there."

"He's a proud man. It's part of why you love him."

"He's been a bear to live with lately. It's this case. It's taking a toll on him, and he's taking it out on me. We've been at each other's throats. It'll do us both good to have him in the hospital for a while. He could be there up to a week after surgery. There goes New Year's and our plans to go to the ranch."

"That's a shame. I know you were looking forward to having that time away."

"Why don't you go up and make up for what you lost at Christmas?" she said.

It was a generous offer. I should have felt guilty, but she was right. I'd been counting on that time away.

"That's very generous. I'd love that."

"I've got a local boy doing the feeding. I'll tell him you're coming up and can take over. It'll help me out a bit with the cost if you don't mind doing some of the chores, the same plan we had at Christmas. When would you be going up?"

"I can head up there tomorrow."

The thought of quiet days on the ranch, hours on horseback, made me feel happy for the first time since the sheriff came into my office and told me Kimi was missing.

When my last appointment canceled at four o'clock, I was more than ready to go home.

I was at the door with my hand on the light switch when the phone rang.

"I'm coming over. I need to run something by you," Antelope said.

"You caught me as I was walking out the door, literally."

"I need a minute."

"What is it?"

"I'm on my way."

"Can't you just tell me?" I asked.

"I need to see you," he said and hung up.

I opened the blinds to let in the last of the daylight. There was no wind and the desert was a still life of violet and dark blue. In the bleak uncertain light, clouds shifted and rearranged themselves and cast moving shadows on the ground. I switched on the Tiffany lamps for light and the warmth they brought.

Antelope knocked loudly, and I crossed through Marla's office to let him in. The temperature outside felt like ten degrees. Antelope wore a long leather coat and dress shoes. No sign of a hat or gloves. I didn't know how he managed to stay warm. He took off his coat, folded it, and placed it on the chair beside him. His precise actions signaled he was getting down to business. We sat across from each other in the leather chairs arranged for patients. Antelope leaned toward me. It felt strangely intimate to be alone in the room, sitting so close to him. I was glad to have him here. I had felt lonely in the office when my work was over and only realized it when Antelope showed up.

"So it was Cedric and he was right in front of us. We should have been more suspicious of him. He was so obsessed with her. I know what that can lead to," I said.

"He kept pictures of all the victims, the women he raped. There was a picture of Kimi in his apartment. It was taken from her home, most likely on the night she disappeared. Forensics is testing a sample from her bedroom, a tissue with semen. If Cedric is a match, it would make a pretty strong case."

"But you have doubts?"

"All the other victims came home. They're alive. Kimi is still missing. If she's dead, it would be a departure from his pattern," Antelope said.

His eyes held a deep sadness that came from giving up on finding his cousin alive.

"What did you want to run by me?"

"Cedric's motive for murdering Kevin."

"Kevin did his own research. Maybe he found something that pointed to Cedric. If he confronted Cedric, that would be a reason for Cedric to kill him."

"There's one thing I can't figure out though."

"What's that?"

"How did he know Kevin would be at your office?"

"He might have followed him there. We know he has a history of stalking. When he parked and the place was deserted, he took his chance."

"I went through Kimi's credit card receipts, followed the

paper trail for the months before she went missing. She definitely got around. There are fuel and other charges to the east in Riverton and Casper, north to Pinedale, west to Green River, Little America, and Evanston."

"She's a reporter for the southwest region. Why is that a surprise?"

"She wasn't reporting on any stories in those places. I checked."

"Her dissociative episodes often began while she was driving. She'd come to, not knowing where she was or why. That's the nature of it. It could have been happening more than she was telling me."

"I cross-referenced her expenses with the sheriff's. All those trips out of town, he was there, too. All the dates line up, every single one. There are four out-of-town trips this calendar year, the last one in November to Laramie. She's telling you and her husband that she's dissociating, can't remember a thing. But her credit cards are telling a different story."

Antelope looked up from his notes. He'd been arranging and sorting them into small stacks, and then resorting. His dark eyes clouded with worry. I knew how much he admired the sheriff who had taken him under his wing and served as a mentor.

I'd turned off the heat just minutes before, and already the air was frigid and goose bumps rose on my arms. I switched on the heat, and the baseboard heaters sprang to life with a welcome pinging sound. When I turned back, I saw the dejection in Antelope's posture and knew why he had come here. Faced with evidence of a relationship between his mentor and his cousin, he was struggling with the implications. The suspicions lay heavy on his heart.

"Her cell phone records show a lot of contact between the two of them. The night she went missing, the last phone call she ever made, she called the sheriff."

"You know him well. Is he capable of hurting Kimi?"

"He's never lost it on the job. The man's a rock."

In one of my internships I'd treated victims of physical and emotional abuse, so I recognized the signs of abuse. A while back, I worried about Marla's marriage. I was careful when I raised the

subject with her. She was evasive and skillfully changed the subject. I didn't want to take a chance of losing her as a friend or an
employee. I didn't confront her. Instead I stocked the office with
brochures about local resources. I knew it could take a long time
for a woman to find the courage to leave an abusive partner.

"Twice I saw bruises on Marla's arms."

"I work for the man. I can't imagine him doing that."

"I tried talking to her about it. She got defensive. That's typical, and not surprising. Maybe I jumped to conclusions. In psychology it's understood the best predictor of violence is a history
of violence. I'm worried about Marla. She could be in danger."

"Right now he isn't a danger to anyone. He'll be in the hospital for a while."

"What are you going to do?"

"I don't know. Any other time, I'd be asking him. I don't have
that option now."

"I wasn't much help. I confirmed what you don't want to
be true."

"Someone told me recently the truth is better than hope. I'm
working on it," Antelope said.

We left the office together, and when I said good-bye to Antelope, I told him I would be up at Dry Well Ranch for the weekend.

As I drove home, I thought about Antelope's question that
led to so many others. As far as I knew, only one other person
knew Kevin Cahill would be at my office the night he was killed.
Marla had scheduled the appointment. Did she tell the sheriff?
Did he overhear their conversation? Did Kevin arrange for someone else to meet us? What had he discovered? What did he plan to
tell me? Who would be threatened by what Kevin knew?

FRIDAY
DECEMBER 31

CHAPTER 45

The rising sun revealed a bright world on the last morning of the year. From the county's highest vantage point, Antelope looked down on the place he had sworn to serve. It was rough country, torn by glaciers, strip-mined, and slashed by the interstate—a timeless, stricken, enduring land. In the night another blizzard had dropped more snow on the crooked streets of the old mining town. Rock Springs sparkled and was briefly beautiful.

Inside Sweetwater Hospital, the assaultive scent of cleaning products masked the true business of the place. The modern, bright rooms dared the patients to be sick.

The sheriff was sitting up in bed when Antelope entered his room.

"So I'm not crazy after all. Marla had me convinced it was all in my head. She thinks she's a shrink because she works for one. But I'm all right now. They put a stent in here," he said and tapped lightly at his chest.

Antelope had never heard anyone so relieved to have a heart problem. The sheriff's color was good, and he smiled at the nurse who was changing out the IV drip. Her laugh was like glass bells chiming. It matched the sound of the beads in her dark braids when she turned to look at him.

Antelope had never seen his boss look better. The combination of heart surgery and the news of Cedric Yee's death had restored the sheriff's health.

"Say hi to Krystal, Antelope. She's the best nurse here, and the prettiest. She's been taking care of me." The sheriff was beaming.

Krystal blushed, smiled, and nodded. Her silence was part of her charm.

"Krystal, meet Detective Antelope. He's my second-in-command," Scruggs said.

Again she smiled and nodded in his direction but stayed silent. It was a captivating approach, Antelope had to admit. Where was the woman who would look at him that way?

"Krystal says I'm good to go," Scruggs said.

He pounded his chest like some jungle book hero. It was a little too much gusto because he ended up wincing, which brought the nurse to his bedside in an instant, where she fussed at his wires. "But my doc's on the slopes at Snowbird, so I'll be spending New Year's Eve here in this bed with my nurse."

That got a response from Krystal: a deeper blush.

"The way you said that, it didn't come out right."

Her voice matched her laugh, soft and lilting, familiar to Antelope. It was a Native voice, the known and comforting speech of his childhood. It was the perfect voice for a nurse, he thought. It was like Kimi's voice.

The sheriff laughed along with Krystal. Antelope thought it had been a long time since he'd heard that sound, and wondered if it was because the business with Kimi Benally had taken a toll on him. That was what he'd come to find out.

"You know what I mean," Scruggs said. "I'm not going anywhere. Be a good nurse and smuggle in some champagne to replace that happy juice you're giving me."

"Where's your wife?" Antelope asked.

"She's going up to the cabin for a few days. No sense in her hanging around here. I'll be laid up for a week at least. She'll be all right without me. She invited Pepper Hunt up to ride with her."

Krystal left them, taking the party atmosphere with her. Scruggs put on his wire-framed glasses and looked at Antelope.

"What's on your mind, Detective?"

"Kimi's phone records."

"Is that a question, Detective?"

"Why did she call you the night she went missing?"

"We did this already. It's none of your business. You need to drop this."

"You went to her house that night," Antelope said.

There was no way he could prove it. Cedric Yee had claimed he saw the sheriff at Kimi's. Now Cedric was dead, and there was no way of knowing if he had been telling the truth or lying to keep the focus off himself. But Scruggs didn't know that.

The sheriff took in his words with a grave look on his face. For a brief moment, it looked to Antelope like he might say something. When he didn't speak, Antelope placed a cell phone on the metal bedside table.

"Do you recognize this?"

"Should I?

"It belonged to Kimi. It's a prepaid phone she used between February and November of this year. There's one number saved in the Contacts section. The name on it is 'Carlton.'"

Scruggs went to grab the phone, but his IV line caught. "What are you planning to do with that?" he said, his voice a growl.

"Enter it into evidence on the case you assigned me. Kimi's still missing. I'm not stopping until I find her."

"You solved that case. Cedric Yee did it and he's dead. It's over. Case closed. Congratulations, Antelope, no one's going to run you out of town for not doing your job." He removed his glasses, rubbed his eyes, and looked into the distance.

"We're waiting on the DNA results to establish a link between Cedric and Kimi," Antelope said.

"You'll find it, and when you do, I want you to drop this business about me and her. If my name gets into this, I'll be out of a job. Think about that."

"Kimi's probably dead and you're worried about your job?"

"It's not the first time. I told you what happened in Lander. I won't let it happen again. So now I'm a cold bastard. I can see it in your eyes. It's not only myself I'm concerned about. It won't do any damn good for Kimi or her memory if people find out about us."

Scruggs sank back onto the pillow and closed his eyes. It was clear to Antelope he was done talking. He tapped on his chest with a light, rhythmic touch, his breathing slowed.

Antelope watched as the man who had been his mentor surrendered to sleep. He looked frail and old in the hospital bed. But Antelope wasn't bothered by the physical weakness; what saddened him, what troubled his soul, were the cracks he was seeing in the sheriff's character.

CHAPTER 46

It was four o'clock when I pulled onto the dirt road to Dry Well Ranch. Overhead the sky had darkened to a deep purple hue. I unpacked the Jeep and changed into riding clothes, then headed to the barn through shimmering twilight. Black birds rose from the rail fence and settled in the bare branches of a cottonwood tree.

The sight of Soldier made my heart lighter. The gray and white horse signaled his own happiness by neighing and stomping and flicking his mane.

He was most content when I rode bareback. I got the reins and blankets from the tack closet. Marla kept the barn as neat as she kept her desk at the office.

"I'm glad I caught up with you."

I jumped and turned to see Marla behind me.

Soldier stomped and kicked at the wall behind him.

"What's wrong with your horse?"

I moved to Soldier and stroked his neck, spoke his name. He shook his head as if tossing off worry, then quieted and stood at attention.

"I'm sorry, I didn't mean to speak so sharply," Marla said. She patted Soldier's flank, and he began to stomp again. She stepped back and he got quiet.

"It must be my nerves he's picking up on. But the surgery's over, maybe I can relax now."

"I expected you tomorrow."

"I planned on celebrating with the sheriff, sneaking in a bottle of champagne for a little toast. But he wasn't up for it. It wouldn't have been much of a party. He threw me out. So I'll do our rituals without him. We always have ribs and cornbread on New Year's Eve. Sound good to you?" She spoke quickly, the stress of the last two weeks showing in her face.

"I was just getting ready to ride."

"I'll make dinner and we can ride at midnight, like the sheriff and I always do. We can see the fireworks they set off over in Lander."

I wanted to ride, but I recognized Marla's need to keep things as normal as possible. The whole Christmas season had been lost to grief and murder, with the sheriff overworked to the point of needing cardiac surgery. I could wait a few more hours and give Marla what she needed.

She insisted on preparing the dinner alone. I made a fire in the stone fireplace that covered one whole wall of the main room. We opened the champagne early, and I fell asleep in the warmth, watching the weaving flames.

When Marla woke me for dinner, the table was beautifully set with antique china dishes, sterling silver flatware, and crystal. Dinner was a full rack of ribs, pan-fried potatoes, a salad, home-made squash soup, and corn bread with honey.

"It looks amazing Marla, thank you."

She gave a tight nod, then sat down and gestured for me to do the same. "It's been hard this week with everything that's happened to see the goodness in the world," she said. "I'm glad it's over. Cedric Yee always gave me the creeps. But a rapist and murderer? You never know, I guess. People are devious. But why did he kill her and let all the others live?"

"There's so much we don't know. Like why Kevin was shot outside the office. The killer had to know he was going to be there."

"We're the only ones who knew," she said. "I didn't tell a soul. Of course, *he* could have told someone. He was hell-bent on talking to you, must have had something pretty important to tell you. Something that got him killed."

"Kevin was convinced Kimi was seeing another man. He was determined to find out who he was."

Outside, the moon was rising over the snow field.

"But why come to you? Why not go straight to the sheriff and have the guy hauled in for questioning? Why not handle it himself? I know I would."

"It sounds like he's afraid to go to the sheriff. What if Kevin found out Kimi was having an affair with someone in the department?"

"If he couldn't handle it himself, the law would have taken care of it," Marla said.

"Not everyone has the confidence you have in the legal system."

"Now you sound like everyone else. That's the thinking that got us tossed out of Lander ten years ago when Lisa Bennett went missing."

"What really happened there?"

"She disappeared on a summer morning, went running on the mountain loop road. They found her car but no trace of her. Somebody had to pay. The family was out for blood. At first they thought her husband killed her, but the department never found evidence linking him to the crime. My husband was the lead investigator, and he took the brunt of the suspicion they planted. He was never going to make sheriff if he stayed in Lander. Sweetwater County was the only place to make him an offer."

"You stood by him all the time. It must have been so hard for both of you."

"It hit him hard when this one went missing. The memory of that time, everything came back to him. He said it was like a ghost rising from a grave."

CHAPTER 47

When Antelope left the station at 5:00 P.M., the squad room was quiet. The shift was heavily staffed out on the street. Only a lucky few would spend the holiday with loved ones. The cruisers drove the main drag and parked outside bars and known party spots. Everyone prepped for a wild ride on the worst night of the year—"amateur night," they called it, a term borrowed from the AA folks. If it was like any other New Year's Eve, they'd be dealing with some combination of traffic accidents, assault and battery, and domestic violence incidents.

At the end of his shift, there was no one left to talk to and nothing left to analyze. Outside, the evening was still and light, no wind at all. Bracing cold air made him want to walk the planet forever under the stars. All around, the night's potential hummed and vibrated like high-tension wires. He wished there was somewhere he wanted to go.

Back in the Cadillac, he cruised the city and considered his options. It was too late in the game to call a beautiful woman, especially one he'd slept with a week before and hadn't talked to since. He called Cass, but of course, she didn't answer. The phone went straight to voice mail, and he hung up without leaving a message. He was a fool to call her.

He stopped at the Shooting Star for a quick drink on the way home. The bar was deserted, and Diego was nowhere in sight.

Antelope sat alone and nursed a beer and thought about Cass. The woman was too much for him, a cauldron of needs he couldn't meet. How many times did he have to prove it to them both?

He should have known better than to hook up with her the other night. She was his first love, and he was the wild mustang she'd broken. There was no such thing as casual sex where Cass was concerned. The problem was she always wrecked his head. It was time to let it go. Again.

But when Kimi disappeared, he'd needed to touch something real, something of home, in order to be grounded and confident. He didn't regret the night he went to her. It was a good night. The memory of love, as good as love itself. He ordered another beer, a shot of whiskey, the whole time knowing he couldn't stay away from her.

He left the bar and didn't bother to pretend he was going straight home. He was prepared for the scene he would face, her hot anger. He knew he deserved the rant; it wasn't right the way he treated her. Especially now, with Kimi gone. He knew he was a total asshole where Cass was concerned. He'd hear her out, and then she'd take him in again, slam the door on the cold and the heartache.

When he pulled into her street, the house was dark and her car was gone. He'd convinced himself that she'd be there waiting for him when he was ready. Now he had to talk to her. He called her cell again and debated leaving a voice mail, decided he had to if he wanted any chance of seeing her. He phoned in a takeout order then circled her neighborhood, waiting for her call back. Fifteen minutes later, he picked up the pizza and drove home.

■ ■ ■

As he walked in his house, his phone vibrated in his pocket. He let it go to voice mail.

Cassandra's frosty tone told him everything. She was at the Wind River Casino. In the background, the pounding bass of disco music, slot machines ringing, loud laughter. He got the message. She was with another guy. He felt a small tug of jealousy that he knew he'd live with. He'd let her go a long time ago. Being alone on New Year's Eve was the least of his troubles.

Next year would be better; he'd avoid getting tangled up in a murder. It wasn't so bad being off the streets and lounging on the couch with the dog. He'd ordered a Domino's Supreme Meat Pizza, in the dog's honor. He fed her pieces of sausage, bacon, and meatballs, and between the two of them they polished off the whole thing. He drew the line at sharing his beer, though.

He'd had two beers at the Shooting Star and would limit himself to just one more. Technically, with the sheriff in the hospital, he was number one in charge of the department and always on call.

He lost his will and drank down another beer. He felt more of a buzz than he should at his weight.

The beer gone, he turned in early, weary from carrying the weight of this heartbreaking, stalled case. Domino joined him on the bed and lay curled in a circle at his back. It couldn't hurt to get a good night's sleep.

An hour later his phone rang.

"Antelope," he answered, already sitting up, his feet on the floor.

"Hello Detective, this is Krystal from the Cardiac Unit," she said. The nurse with the voice like tinkling bells.

"What is it, Krystal?" he asked, shaking his head to clear the sleep and booze from his brain.

"The sheriff's gone. I went in to check his vitals, and he's not in his bed. We've checked the whole unit, and security made a check of all the other floors. He's not in the hospital."

"Have security keep looking. He won't make it easy to find him. I'll send some deputies to help search inside the hospital and the surrounding area for an adult male on foot."

"He drove himself to the hospital the night he was admitted. He has access to a vehicle."

"On my way."

He took Domino for a quick walk and got the Cadillac warming up. Back in the house the dog curled up in the middle of the warm bed. All the way to the hospital, on Dewar Drive and up

Hilltop, traffic was light. It was still early, the bars packed to over-flowing, house parties in full swing. He radioed dispatch and sent cruisers to Sweetwater Hospital to be on the lookout for an AWOL patient, adult male. Then he added the make, model, and license plate number of the sheriff's truck.

At the door to the cardiac unit, Krystal came running toward him, her beaded hair swaying and jingling, white clogs squeaking on the polished floor. She handed him a pink paper from a tele-phone message pad.

"I found this on the floor of his room. The unit clerk took the message about an hour ago, see right there, 7:55 P.M. The woman wouldn't give her name. She said he'd know who she was. "

Antelope read the note: "Meet me at Dry Well Ranch." He recognized the number from the phone records: Kimi's Verizon phone number. He searched the sheriff's room and he left the unit without saying good-bye to Krystal.

On the straightaway up to Lander, he turned off the head-lights. He didn't want Scruggs to know he was following him. The moon above was so bright, it lit the road up like an urban superhigh-way. He had to get to Pepper. She was his first concern. Whatever domestic craziness went on between Scruggs and Marla because of Kimi, Pepper didn't need to witness it.

He was worried about Scruggs's state of mind. The sher-iff's earlier giddiness took on a new meaning in Antelope's mind: euphoria approaching a manic state. Sometimes pain medications could set off psychotic symptoms in vulnerable individuals. And Scruggs was definitely vulnerable. He had a heart condition, newly diagnosed. That would be enough to rock most men's stability. His mistress was missing, and they'd thought she was dead. But now she'd called and left him a message.

And the sheriff had responded by unhooking his IV lines and leaving his hospital bed. He was on his way to his wife *and* his lover. Antelope feared what Scruggs planned to do. There had been no sign of his service weapon, but that didn't surprise Antelope.

CHAPTER 48

The sheriff had been sleeping. He woke as Krystal was leaving, her petite form a silhouette in the harsh light of the hospital corridor. She closed the door behind her, and he was alone in the dark room. He pulled the chain on the headboard and squinted in the sudden white glare. He picked up the note she'd left on the metal tray beside his bed.

He read the phone number and felt his heart beat dangerously.

With effort, he reached over and pulled the heavy black hospital phone onto the bed.

He dialed nine for an outside line. When he had a dial tone, he called the number he knew so well, reading it from the note to be sure.

He listened to her recorded message. "Kimi here. Leave a message."

At the sound of her voice, his breath came hard and fast.

He felt exhausted. He hung up the phone and closed his eyes. It was a few minutes before his breathing and his heart rate returned to normal.

He read the note.

Meet me at Dry Well Ranch.

The last words he'd communicated to Kimi.

He found his clothes in the closet and quickly changed. Visiting hours had ended and the hallway was empty. One person at the nurses' station, her head turned away and facing a computer screen. The strong overhead lights had been turned off and replaced with the soft glow of track lights. His was the last room, farthest from the station. He slipped silently out of the double door and closed it behind him. Once he was off the unit, he made his way to the hospital lobby, past the information desk and gift shop, both shut down for the night. He passed no one as he exited the hospital. In the parking lot, he found his truck and was pulling out onto Hilltop Drive in no time. It had taken him less than ten minutes from the time he read the note to get himself on the road.

Behind the wheel, he felt light-headed. He was risking his life with this drive. But it didn't matter. He had to go to her.

That day in his office, when his heart exploded in pain, he'd thought his life was over. But he'd managed to get himself to the hospital, and when he woke up after the surgery, he wasn't sure how he felt about still being alive. They'd fixed his heart. He felt it working, felt the strong, steady beats in his chest. He would handle whatever waited for him in Lander. It was the last night of the year. He would deal with whatever future was left for him when it was over.

He pushed the Chevy 4x4 to its limit and flew over dry roads. New-fallen snow was bright in the desert. He turned off his headlights and drove in the light of the rising moon. It was a purely beautiful evening, the first in a long while. He took it as an omen of good things to come.

■ ■ ■

Two hours later, he parked under the cottonwood at the entrance to the ranch. He wanted the advantage of surprise. As he approached, the lighted house beckoned deceptively. It was an idyllic scene: the cabin's small-paned windows glowing with amber light and smoke curling from the rock chimney. The house was surrounded on three sides by a grove of thick evergreens. From the front farmer's porch, the land spread out for miles before it ended in another border of dark pines. Marla's car was parked in front of the barn beside a Jeep he recognized as Pepper Hunt's. How much did she know about his involvement with Kimi? He'd have to deal with her, too. But first, he had to find Kimi.

Dry Well Ranch was Marla's inheritance. She'd spent much of her childhood there. She shared it with him as she shared everything. Whereas he kept so much secret from her, so much for himself. Over the years there were signs that Marla suspected he had something going on with Lisa Bennett. But there was no way she could have found out about Kimi. He'd made sure of that. It had occurred to him his life was like the Wyoming wind, alternately calm and chaotic. He hadn't thought of himself as a stupid man, but he'd proved it was possible to fall into the same hole twice. He hadn't seen it coming. She was beautiful. Could it be that simple? Could he be that stupid? After the other one, after Lisa, he'd thought he was immune to anything resembling passion.

He steeled himself before going in the house. Whatever was waiting for him would not be good.

But inside, he found no signs of the women. Of course. Pepper had come to the ranch to ride; the women had gone out on horseback.

He felt a swooning lightness in his head and the desire for sleep. Dehydrated, he figured. He swallowed a mug of cold tap water and splashed his face at the sink before making his way slowly through the heavy new snow down the slope to the barn.

The stalls were empty. Pepper's horse, Soldier, Marla's brindle mare, Agate, and Black Star, his stallion, were gone. Imagining Kimi on the back of Black Star stirred him.

The new brown mustang Marla had picked up at auction stood alone and abandoned in the last stall, staring with questioning eyes.

He stood and thought about what he should do. After the mad race up here, the thought of returning to wait in the house filled him with a kind of stir-crazy agitation. It would be so easy to follow the horses' tracks in the snow. He had no idea how much of a head start they had, but he had to find them.

It would take strength he didn't have to saddle and manage the mustang on the cold, slippery ground. The horse didn't know him and would be spooked by his weakened state. It would be suicide.

They stored the snowmobiles at the other side of the barn. After a few false starts, he got the machine going and guided it out and onto the field. He rode slowly, protecting his heart from unnecessary movement. The pain medication had worn off and the place where the surgeon's knife had gone in burned and radiated. He tracked the three horses on their path across the snowy terrain.

CHAPTER 49

An hour before midnight we set out on horseback across the field toward the deep woods beyond. The rising moon spread a gentle light over the glittering snow. Tomorrow the New Year would come, with another chance to see things in a new light and make the world a better place. In spite of everything, I was happy to be alive.

When Zeke was murdered, I lost more than a husband. That life was over, and all the things I'd taken for granted, gone. But here in this wild place, riding Soldier slowly over new snow as silver stars emerged in the violet sky, I felt life grab hold again.

I rode behind Marla, who had the sheriff's stallion, Black Star, on a long lead. She hadn't had the heart to leave the stallion back at the barn alone. The horse had celebrated every New Year's Eve with them. She would keep everything the same.

The moon turned the snow field a cool, cobalt blue. For a long while, we rode in silence. Steam from the horses' breath floated past our faces like a warm caress. I hadn't felt more alive on any day of the long last year.

Ahead of me, Marla stopped. "Ride alongside me," she said. "It's so peaceful. A night like this, riding horseback, it's possible to believe nothing bad can happen." Her voice came out clear and true as a handbell, ringing with sweet precision in the still night air.

"I envy you, being born to this," I said. "I came to it so late, and now I can't imagine being without a horse in my life. Riding saved my life when everything else failed. All the talk therapy, it didn't do a thing for me when I lost Zeke. I was numb. But when I got on a horse, everything came back. Riding Soldier, I was alive for the first time in a year."

"I know what you mean. It's like nothing else matters, nothing else is real. It's not true, though. Just another illusion we use to get through a day."

I felt a chill despite my many layers of clothing, and my heartbeat slowed, a primitive survival mechanism signaling danger. I didn't know where the danger was, but the signals were coming loud and clear.

We had come to a narrow path that wove through a dense stand of trees. Up ahead was a wide clearing surrounded by black woods.

"Follow me," Marla said. "I've got something to show you." She galloped ahead into the darkness, and I rode behind along the narrow way. The horses brushed clumps of snow from laden branches as they passed.

Marla stopped at an old stone well in a circle of moonlight. "Right here," she said.

We tied the horses to a hitching post between two trees. Moonlight poured into an open space enclosed by a ring of trees. The night was still around us. I sensed the presence of animals asleep in the woods. For a moment, in the moon's white light, Marla was a warrior statue carved from marble, glowing incandescent. She took the pack from Agate's back and dropped it on the ground beside her. It landed with a metallic clink on the stones that circled the well.

CHAPTER 50

Scruggs guided the snowmobile slowly to keep his approach as quiet as possible. His stamina was reduced and his breathing was labored. For the first time he considered that he might not make it and would take his last breath out here on what felt like the coldest night he'd ever lived.

Shaking with cold, he willed himself to keep moving and not give up before he did what needed to be done. He slogged through the snow, feeling old with his wounded heart beating too fast in his chest. Up ahead, firelight flickered beyond the pines—a hot orange light, straight out of hell.

At the tree line, he veered off to the left so he could observe the women without being seen by them. When he reached them, the truth would come out. He'd have to face Marla and her response to his betrayal.

And what about Kimi? What would she expect of him? He would have to make a choice between the two of them. Had she gone missing intentionally to have him experience what it would be like to live without her? It worked. Now he knew he didn't want to live without her. He had tried to avoid the confrontation that waited for him at the ranch. But now, with his wife and his lover waiting here, it was inevitable. There would be no turning back. Some things, once spoken, rearranged the known world, making it impossible to go back.

He'd loved Marla for a long time. He was just a boy with a pure heart and fire in his soul when they got together. But along the way his heart had turned into something darker. Maybe it was the work, how it showed him things he didn't want to know, the desperation and evil in some people—or maybe it was just the years piling up. But the fire still burned, and he'd found other women to quench it. He longed to love again and have it turn out right. He suspected it was his own lost innocence he was after. A wiser man would have concluded once was enough, given the way the first one ended.

CHAPTER 51

Antelope saw the sheriff's vehicle parked on the side of the road. He pulled over and checked that his boss wasn't slumped over the wheel, dead of a heart attack. There were no signs of life inside the cabin. Then he spotted the tracks in the snow.

He didn't know what was in the sheriff's mind or if he was playing with a full deck this wintry night. All he could hope was that Scruggs remembered who he was and what he stood for, and managed to stay within the law.

In the barn, a brown mustang waited alone in a stall. He approached the horse and spent some minutes taking the measure of it. It was a young horse with a strong spirit. A ready horse, not yet claimed, waiting for a rider. Antelope carefully placed the bridle. The horse accepted it. He ignored the saddles on the wall. He preferred to ride bareback, and it would be easier for the horse.

He opened the stall and led the horse out of the barn. They stood side by side under the stars and took in the night. After a few minutes, he mounted the mustang, and the animal stiffened beneath him, held his ground. It took a minute to establish control, but soon Antelope had the mustang in a trot, and then a gallop, following close the arc made by the women on horseback and the man on the snowmobile.

He felt one with the horse as he rode toward the mystery ahead. He had not yet been able to work out what he would find when he caught up with the others. Questions came to him that he hadn't thought to ask before because he'd been so hopeful at that message from Kimi: Why had Kimi summoned the sheriff to the ranch? How had she known to call him at the hospital? Maybe it wasn't Kimi but Marla who had called. But how would Marla be in possession of Kimi's phone? The same thoughts must be going through the sheriff's mind, and Antelope didn't know what the man was capable of in his vulnerable state.

Through the thick forest, about a mile ahead, he was able to make out the flickering light of a fire. It was a small thing, a primitive thing, but it brought him no small comfort as he crossed the lonely, unknown land. A wind came up and rogue clouds obscured the stars and moon above. Snow swirled before his eyes like released butterflies. He rode toward the distant fire that burned in the depths of the woods.

CHAPTER 52

On the opposite side of the clearing, across from the well, Marla was on her knees at a stone fireplace, stacking wood into a pyramid.

"A New Year's Eve bonfire . . . another one of our traditions."

She quickly had a fire going. I felt the warm air on my face as the heat made a room around us. She spread blankets on either side of the fire and sat down. "Sit with me. Time for a ghost story that's been waiting a long time to be told."

In the light of the bonfire, I noticed Marla's boots. Red boots with silver studs and spurs. Just like the red boots Kimi wore on the night of her last session.

"They're beautiful, aren't they?" Marla said.

"They're gorgeous. Distinctive." Panic rising, remembering opening the door to Zeke's death scene. *Did the sheriff take those boots from Kimi after he killed her?*

The moon disappeared behind a cloud. The woods grew darker. Between us, the fire danced and crackled. The world was reduced to the bonfire and the black night.

Marla confirmed my gruesome thought. "My Christmas present from the sheriff." She rubbed her hands over the red leather, traced the lines of the intricate designs, and tapped her nails on the silver studs.

"Kimi was wearing boots like that the night she disappeared," I said.

"I know what you're thinking," Marla said.

It was now or never. This wasn't going to be an easy conversation.

"Kimi was involved with the sheriff. And now you have those boots . . . I'm sorry, Marla."

"I found them in his closet. I thought he'd gotten them for me for Christmas. I stuffed them back in the tissue paper and hoped he wouldn't notice. I told you, he always buys the best presents. The next day, I couldn't find them. I figured he moved them. It wasn't a good hiding place, and he loves surprising me. The next time I saw them, Kimi was wearing them. That's when I knew for sure she was the one. I'd suspected for a long time. After he cheated the first time, I learned to read the signs."

I had been clueless about Zeke's affair, never imagined he'd be unfaithful, let alone betray me with a friend and colleague.

"Was it Lisa Bennett?" I asked.

"These last few weeks, he can't shake her ghost. Only one person knows what happened to her. Kimi wanted that story. She had to get close to him so she could pick his brain. The two of us spent years putting that behind us, and she dragged it all up again."

In the firelight, Marla's face looked feverish and harsh.

"Why are you telling me this?"

"That's what you do for a living. You listen. You ask questions. Pretty soon, you'll put the pieces together. I need you to hear what it was like for me. After what happened with your husband, you might be the one person who could understand. His patient shot him, but I wouldn't have blamed you if you'd done it. You must have wanted to kill him when you found out he was cheating on you with your friend, didn't you? Be honest."

"He was already dead," I said. "I didn't have that option. But even so, a fantasy about killing is one thing—carrying it out, taking a life in a violent way, is something else entirely. I'm not capable."

Marla leaned over and unzipped her backpack. When she sat up, she had a gun in her hand. I recognized my Beretta. She pointed it at me.

There was no mistaking her intention—and finally, I saw

what I should have seen before. It wasn't the sheriff who'd killed Kimi.

"Why couldn't you let it go? You're just like Kimi, pushing and asking questions, not leaving us alone to live in peace. That's all I wanted—to live in peace with my husband. You would have put it together soon enough. And I can't let the sheriff come under suspicion. He would lose everything. I can't let that happen."

"Tell me what happened the night Kimi went missing."

I had to keep Marla talking. I knew she planned to kill me, too.

"I've always wondered what it would be like to be one of your patients. To have a whole hour to talk and spill my deep, dark secrets. So now it's my turn. I followed Kimi from the office, realized before long that she was on her way up here to meet the sheriff. Just before Ocean Lake a storm hit hard. It was a whiteout. I could hardly see to drive. All of a sudden she was right there in front of me. I slammed the brakes. Her car was stuck. I got out of the car. She thought I was there to help her. The snow fell like petals around her. It was beautiful there in the snow and the quiet."

"What did you do?"

"I pointed the gun at her, your gun. You should have seen the look on her face when she saw it was me. She was on her way to meet my husband. We both knew what she was going to tell him. She'd figured out that I was the one who killed Lisa. She understood what I had to do. I saw it in her eyes."

"You killed Kimi?"

"Right there on the road. It wasn't how I'd planned to do it."

CHAPTER 53

Antelope stayed well behind the sheriff as he approached the clearing. When he saw him move along the tree line to the right, he went the other way, careful to stay hidden in the shadows. He positioned himself ten feet away from the clearing where Pepper and Marla sat facing each other. In the light from the fire, he could make out the sheriff's crouched figure and see the glint off his Glock as he held it steady, pointing into the clearing. Antelope had to figure out how to intercept the sheriff before he could get a shot off.

Marla held the Beretta Nano steady and pointed at Pepper.

"Does the sheriff know?" Pepper asked.

He inched closer to the scene he still hadn't quite worked out. Why would Marla have a gun pointed at Pepper? It didn't make any sense.

"He's figuring it out now."

He watched as Scruggs stepped into the clearing.

"Drop the gun," the sheriff said. He held the Glock in both hands, pointed at Marla.

She turned toward him but kept the Beretta Nano aimed at Pepper, who sat motionless, watching the scene play out in front of her.

"I could say the same to you," Marla said. "I knew you'd come."

"It was you who left the message? How'd you get her phone?"

It wasn't until that moment that Antelope understood. He and the sheriff had both been hoping to find Kimi alive up here.

"You thought she was alive all this time?" Marla said.

He watched grief descend on the sheriff, who held the Glock steady in his right hand while he placed his left hand on his heart. The sheriff swayed and it looked like he was going to go down. It was a miracle the man was still standing.

"You brought my horse along to trick me into thinking it was three of you riding." He winced and bent forward, his left arm at his chest, the gun in his right hand, still pointed at his wife.

"Are you in pain?" Marla asked. "You can put that weapon down any time. We both know you're not going to use it."

Pepper sat still as a stone. She seemed to be shutting down, trying to escape this replay of her own story. The scene had all the elements of what had happened to her in Massachusetts: betrayal, infidelity, jealous rage, and murder.

The horses shook their manes, snorted and stomped, distressed by the raw emotions and evil energy alive in the clearing.

"I'm here as an officer of the law," Scruggs said. "I won't lay down arms in the line of duty."

"*Now* you want to follow the rules?"

"Rules are important. That's why I became a lawman."

"What about our marriage vows?" Marla asked. "You haven't shown any respect for them."

"We're still married, aren't we? I didn't leave you. That's all you cared about."

"You brought her here to this special place, my place." She gestured with the gun then pointed it back at Pepper. "How could you do that?"

"You killed a woman because I brought her here?"

"She was going to ruin everything."

Antelope kept his eyes on Pepper, who sat in the snow, still and silent. That was good. Any sudden movement could spook Marla.

"It was you who killed Lisa."

"You figured it out? When it first happened, I worried you would know and leave me because of it."

"I only wanted to forget. When Kimi asked me about it and it all came back, I was able to see what I had been blind to when it happened. They were right to run me out of town. I couldn't solve that case even though the killer was right in my own house." Scruggs had both hands on the Glock again. "The night Kimi went missing she was on her way here. She must have figured out you killed Lisa. She never got to tell me because she met up with you first."

The sheriff's face was bright red. Whether it was from the heat of the bonfire or the rage he must be feeling, Antelope couldn't tell for sure, but he saw pure hatred in his eyes, and he knew he wanted to kill his wife.

"Don't look at me like that, like I'm a criminal. I did what I had to do."

Antelope watched as the sheriff moved closer to Marla, the weapon steady in his hands and pointed straight at her heart. If it looked like he was ready to take a shot, Antelope would try to stop him.

"You're my wife and you're a cold-blooded killer. It hasn't been easy living with that knowledge these last few weeks."

His voice was weary, and he looked weak and sick, as if the new knowledge had turned on something toxic in his cells and he was dying from the inside out. Did he have the energy to pull the trigger, let alone hit his target? Antelope wasn't sure.

Scruggs took another step forward, and Marla turned the Beretta on him.

"Put the gun down, Marla. I'm taking you into custody."

"Not if I shoot you first," Marla said and smiled.

The smile made her look crazy to Antelope. And he supposed she was; she'd murdered two women to keep her life going the way she wanted it, after all.

In what seemed like one swift motion, Marla jumped to her feet, the Beretta trained on the sheriff all the while. She seemed to have forgotten about Pepper. Antelope willed Pepper to move while she could, to get the hell out of the line of fire, but she was still frozen in her spot in the snow, her face expressionless, her long hair, the color of chili peppers, glowing bright in the firelight. Soldier whinnied, as if giving his own sign for her to move to safety.

"So you want to kill me?" the sheriff asked.

After hearing her whole story, to Antelope it seemed clear that was what Marla wanted.

"All I ever wanted was for you to love me. But it's too late for that. It will all be over soon."

"What did you do with the bodies, Marla?"

Marla turned her head toward the well and smiled. "I saved them for you," she said.

The woman's insane, Antelope thought.

"The world's not safe with you in it. I'll see that you spend the rest of your life in prison," the sheriff said.

Then the night exploded with sound; bombs went off and flares colored the night as fireworks lit up the sky over Lander. The noise and the light broke the spell and set everyone moving.

Pepper ran to Soldier, who was up on his hind legs, kicking wildly.

Marla took aim at the sheriff and put a bullet in his chest. He went down like a felled tree, landed face-first in the snow.

The stallion, Black Star, broke free of his ties and ran in circles around the clearing.

Antelope rushed at Marla and grabbed her around the waist, lifted her off the ground, swung her around, and tried to force the Beretta out of her hands. She twisted and kicked, tried to get out of his grasp. He lost his balance, and the two of them toppled in slow motion onto the frozen ground. Antelope turned and twisted and came out on top of her. He pushed up onto his knees and planted his hands on her shoulders to hold her down—and realized that even though Marla was looking up at him, she couldn't see him. In the struggle she'd gotten off a shot and ended her own life. The bullet must have entered her heart, because she'd died instantly.

Marla had gotten what she wanted. She wouldn't have to live without the sheriff.

SATURDAY
JANUARY 15

CHAPTER 54

Two weeks later, the sheriff was still recovering from the gunshot wound to his chest. The bullet had entered his chest on the right side, missing his heart by two inches. He was a lucky man, but he was facing more surgery and at least twelve weeks of recovery time given the damage to his internal organs.

The bodies of both murdered women, Lisa and Kimi, were pulled from the well and transported to the medical examiners' offices in Fremont County. It would be weeks before they were released to their families for proper burial.

Antelope wanted to see the place where Kimi had left the world, and he asked me to go with him. It was a Saturday afternoon in the middle of January. It had been two weeks since he saved my life at Dry Well Ranch on New Year's Eve. Of course, I said yes. I'd thought a lot in the days after she went missing about where Kimi had ended up. I'd never been to Ocean Lake. The news coverage of the place where her car was found showed an eerie, empty landscape around the unfrozen saltwater chop, an angry heave of dark water. I'd been hit with a shivering wave of cold desolation that chilled me for hours after.

Antelope was in a somber mood and quiet as we headed out of town. He stopped for fuel at the Get & Go in Reliance. After he pumped the gas, he opened the door and said, "Come in with me. I want you to meet someone. I interviewed her early in the case, and she ended up helping us out. It was her son who gave us the lead to Kimi's writing."

A big woman behind the counter smiled when she saw Antelope.

"Hello, Detective. I thought I'd never see you again. Now I hear you solved the case. You found that girl's killer."

"I'm on my way north," Antelope said. "Figured I'd stop in and thank you for sending your boy to see me. The information he gave me was a big help."

"He was afraid coming forward with what he found in the storage unit might put him in some danger. He just needed a little nudge to do the right thing."

"It's much appreciated. I'd like to introduce Dr. Hunt. She worked on the case with us."

"Pleased to meet you, I'm sure," Clarice said and held out her hand for me to shake. Her hand was warm and strong, and her smile genuine. "You're the psychologist doctor, right? I bet folks around here keep you real busy."

"I didn't see Troy Kinney's truck out back. Does he still work for you?" Antelope asked, pointing to a Help Wanted sign taped on the counter.

"He left. Packed up and moved out a few weeks ago. Snuck out in the middle of the night. One day he was on the job and the next day he was gone."

"Do you remember when?"

"It was right before New Year's. We had to close up New Year's Eve because we didn't have anyone to run the shop with Troy gone. Daryl and I always go out on New Year's Eve. It's our one big night to party all year, and we weren't willing to give it up." She tapped her nails on the counter. "I can tell you the exact day. It's fixed in my mind because it was on the news at noon about that reporter getting himself killed. I was planning on telling Troy about it when he came in for his shift. I'd do that, fill him in on what went on in the world while he was sleeping."

"Thursday, then," Antelope said. "Cedric was murdered on the Wednesday of that week." He grabbed two bottles of water from the refrigerator, a bag of popcorn, and a box of dog treats for Domino, whom he'd adopted, unofficially. "It sounds like Troy will be missed around here."

Clarice rang up the items. "I'm still looking for his replacement," she said and tapped the sign. "It would have been Thursday noon I saw the news. Troy had to have left the night before. I never noticed his Dodge was gone all day. When I come in to work, I work, and never leave my spot right here all day long. But as I've been saying, he didn't show up for work that night. I never knew the two were kin until I read the obituary and saw Troy's name listed with the rest of the family. Must have hit him hard, especially learning his uncle was a rapist."

"Did he leave a forwarding address for his paycheck?"

"He didn't leave an address. Grief does strange things." She shrugged. "He left without saying good-bye. I don't suppose I'll ever see the man again. It's too bad. He was a good worker, responsible and loyal. He'd do whatever needed doing without having to be told. If there was a problem, Troy would handle it."

We said good-bye to Clarice and left the overheated store. Back in the car, Antelope said, "Cedric was murdered before he was charged and brought to trial for multiple rapes. But his story and the stigma of the crime will stay with the family forever. Troy's been living with the consequences of his own sex crimes for a long time. It's not unusual for sex offenders to relocate after getting off probation."

He handed me a bottle of water and offered the bag of popcorn, then tossed a few treats in the backseat. Domino turned in a circle, trying to decide which one to go for first.

"You sound doubtful. Why else would he leave?" I said.

"We don't know who killed Cedric."

"Are you suggesting it was Troy?"

"The crime scene had the markings of a crime of passion. Isn't that the definition of family love? A web of passionate entanglements so intense they implode?"

"I've known that to happen," I said.

Then Antelope slipped away, back into his somber mood, and we rode in silence. Two hours later, as we approached Ocean Lake, a storm came up. The wind came up fast and snow started flying, obscuring the road. It must have been like this on the awful last night when Kimi met Marla, all the world lost in a swarm of snow. At Milepost 17 we took the cutoff to Ocean Lake. I knew from reading the news coverage that the saltwater lake was thirty-one feet deep and didn't freeze even in the frigid winter temperatures of Wyoming winters. It was less than a mile on the access road through the campground to Long Point's beach and boat ramp. At this time of the year, the campground was closed.

Antelope took it slow down the slick gravel road to the narrow beach and came to a stop in the relative shelter of Long Point Harbor under the snow-laden branches of ancient cottonwood trees. The water was a basin of murderous gray, a witch's brew of froth and choppy swells cresting on the undulating surface.

He opened the window and let in the sound of clapping wings; dozens of whooping cranes rising and clustering, seeking shelter in their nesting structures. Domino leaned forward from the backseat, wanting the window, nostrils twitching at the scents of the wilderness.

"Cranes are an endangered species. But they're safe here, hidden away in this place like beautiful secrets." He rolled up his window. "Come on, let's walk."

The snow was soft and wet, big flakes falling slowly and straight down, as if poured from a hole in the sky. We walked slowly, Domino following with dainty steps over the uneven ground.

"I have to accept she's gone," he said. "When she went missing, I had to believe she'd come back to us. When I saw her picture with the others at Cedric's place, I still wanted to believe she was alive. It's always been hard for me to give up. How's it been for you?"

"I know what you mean. I'm still trying to wrap my mind around some things. Kimi was my patient. I thought I knew her, knew her secrets more than anyone else. It's like I didn't know her at all."

The three of us walked through the snow in a solemn funeral procession. I felt the isolation of the place where Kimi died stake a claim in my memory. Grief descended and my heart felt like lead, the sadness too heavy to hold. And the quiet all around became unbearable, the quiet became death and the end of all things human and alive. It might not be the time for it, but I had to break the spell and push away from the feelings.

"There's something I've been wondering: Marla was convinced Kimi knew she murdered Lisa Bennett. You've read all of Kimi's writing. How did she figure out it was Marla?"

Beside me, Antelope shook his head. "Marla's guilt must have caught up with her and made her paranoid. There wasn't anything in Kimi's writing to suggest she thought Marla had anything to do with Lisa's disappearance."

"But Kimi asked to see the sheriff that night because she had something important to tell him."

"I don't know if I ever told you this, but the techs found a positive pregnancy test in the trash in Kimi's bedroom. Kevin didn't know she was pregnant. The way he responded when I told him, it seemed he was having trouble believing it. He admitted there wasn't much action in their sex life at the end."

"So that's what it was? Kimi wanted to tell the sheriff she was pregnant?"

"It's the kind of thing a woman would want to say in person, especially if she wasn't sure how he'd react. Doing it face-to-face would give her the answer."

"Does the sheriff know Kimi hadn't figured out it was Marla?"

"I figured I'd wait until he's back on the job. I'm sorry for the guy. Two women he loved murdered by his wife, and one of them pregnant with his child. How much can a person handle?"

"You lost faith in him for a while. Looks like he's back in your good graces."

"I have no right to judge. He didn't rape or murder anyone. He took big risks with love, and he paid a high price. That's how it is in my experience. Love takes a payment."

We stood on the ridge above the reservoir. The wind howled and there was nothing to see but the manic snow. After a while, we turned and headed back to the parking lot. A few miles out, the snow quit. The storm had been a tease, nothing sticking to the snow fences or the stiff vegetation beyond. The clouds broke up, and we were cheered by brief glimpses of pale blue sky above the thin, wrinkled clouds. On either side of the highway, pronghorns grazed in the winter grass.

The drive back was as quiet as the one going up. This was a day for remembering Kimi, each with our own memories. At Rock Springs city limits, Antelope pulled into the parking lot where Wild Horse Loop Road led up White Mountain. Domino had been sleeping in the back, but she was up on her feet as soon as the motion stopped.

"I want to show you something. Come with me," he said.

We walked up the winding gravel road over stones danger-ously slick with new snow. It was early evening and the air was turning colder. A silver disc of moon hung above White Moun-tain, like a welcoming porch light. A short distance up, we came to a rise where the road turned and continued up a steeper incline. The desert glowed in the moonlight, and in the distance the city lights of Rock Springs showed the way home.

Antelope said, "January's moon is called 'The Moon When the Snow Flies Like Spirits in the Wind.' That's what Kimi was, a spirit in the wind."

This same beautiful scene that took my breath away had been the backdrop for violence. We would never forget the crimes this mountain had witnessed. Still, the ground and the rocks and the horses that ran free there remained pure and wild. I wondered if it was some consolation to Kimi that she closed her eyes for the last time outside under a watching sky on the land she knew and loved.

ACKNOWLEDGMENTS

I will forever be grateful to the talented teams assembled by Brooke Warner and Crystal Patriarche at She Writes Press, Sparkpoint Studios, and BookSparks PR, for their excellence at every juncture of publishing my debut novel. I am grateful for the supportive and skillful contributions of the production team headed by Lauren Wise, and to Krissa Lagos and Pamela Long for their fine editing and proofreading. Their careful polishing made the writing shine.

This book has been many years in the making, and early on Stuart Horowitz and Sydney Bailey, novelists and developmental editors, helped me build a reliable structure for the story.

Thanks as well to my patient beta readers—Louise Doucette, Margo Edney, Julia Goldensohn, Judith Jamieson, Janice Larivee, Deirdre Lottridge, Stephanie Lottridge, Stephen Lottridge, Patricia Martin, Penny Mohan, and Ellen Wolfe—who made their way through early drafts. Each offered thoughts that helped craft the rough pages into a finished work.

ABOUT THE AUTHOR

J.L. Doucette returned to Rhode Island after living many years in Wyoming. She earned a doctorate in counseling psychology from Boston University and has a private practice in Providence. She is at work on her second novel, *On a Quiet Street*, also featuring Dr. Pepper Hunt.

SELECTED TITLES FROM
SHE WRITES PRESS

She Writes Press is an independent publishing company founded to serve women writers everywhere. Visit us at www.shewritespress.com.

Again and Again by Ellen Bravo. $16.95, 978-1-63152-939-9. When the man who raped her roommate in college becomes a Senate candidate, women's rights leader Deborah Borenstein must make a choice—one that could determine control of the Senate, the course of a friendship, and the fate of a marriage.

In the Shadow of Lies: A Mystery Novel by M. A. Adler. $16.95, 978-1-938314-82-7. As World War II comes to a close, homicide detective Oliver Wright returns home—only to find himself caught up in the investigation of a complicated murder case rife with racial tensions.

Just the Facts by Ellen Sherman. $16.95, 978-1-63152-993-1. The seventies come alive in this poignant and humorous story of a fearful rookie reporter at a small-town newspaper who uncovers a big-time scandal.

Murder Under The Bridge: A Palestine Mystery by Kate Raphael. $16.95, 978-1-63152-960-3. Rania, a Palestinian police detective with a young son, meets cheeky Jewish-American feminist Chloe at an Israeli checkpoint—and soon becomes embroiled in a murder case that implicates the highest echelons of the Israeli military.

The Wiregrass by Pam Webber. $16.95, 978-1-63152-943-6. A story about a summer of discontent, change, and dangerous mysteries in a small Southern Wiregrass town.

A Girl Like You: A Henrietta and Inspector Howard Novel by Michelle Cox. $16.95, 978-1-63152-016-7. When the floor matron at the dance hall where Henrietta works as a taxi dancer turns up dead, aloof Inspector Clive Howard appears on the scene—and convinces Henrietta to go undercover for him, plunging her into Chicago's gritty underworld.